UNKNOWN VENGEANCE

PAT O'BRIEN

WHISTLER
Cayélle

UNKNOWN VENGEANCE

by Pat O'Brien

For permission requests, contact the publisher below:

Cayélle Publishing/Whistler Imprint
Lancaster, California USA
www.CayellePublishing.com

Orders by U.S. trade bookstores and wholesalers, please contact Freadom Distribution:
Tel: (833) 229-3553 ext 813 or email: Freadom@Cayelle.com

Categories: 1. Crime 2. Thriller 3. Action
Printed in the United States of America

Cover Art by Robin Ludwig Design, Inc.
Interior Design & Typesetting by Ampersand Book Interiors
Edited by Ashley Conner Editing

ISBN: 978-1-952404-37-5 [paperback]
ISBN: 978-1-952404-36-8 [ebook]

Library of Congress Control Number 2020944878

First Edition

CHAPTER 1

A BEAD OF SWEAT FORMED BETWEEN THE SHOULDER blades of a naked killer. As he remained hunched and panting over his prey, the greasy droplet stayed suspended by the ripples of his trapezius muscles. It slid an inch along the thoracic spine until it remained nestled between the T2 and T3 vertebrae. With another deep breath, the killer straightened ever so slightly. The new angle allowed the slithering drop to ramp up and over the T3 hump. Meandering along the rest of the spine, it continued south. Any moisture lost along the glistening, slimy trail was more than recovered as other pores continued to spew their oily excrement onto his skin. The droplet continued picking up size and speed as it dribbled over his tailbone. For just a moment, it remained dangling with a death grip on a hair in the crack of a killer's ass, before falling into the navel of the recently deceased with a *plop*.

"Sorry, Doctor Coleman." The killer sighed. "As I said, this is nothing personal. I hope you understand now. I wish it didn't have to be like this, but it just had to be."

The vacant blue eyes did not answer or acknowledge him. The only movement was the blood that continued to trickle to the floor. Without a beating heart to hasten its flow through the open slices, only gravity could pull the warm fluid to the cold tile.

The naked man separated his sweaty thighs from where Coleman's arms had been pinned to the dead doctor's ribcage. The killer lifted his knees and squatted over the dead man's stomach. After losing his balance, he landed back on the doctor's stomach and was surprised at the burst of blood that sprang from the slashed throat. With a look of amusement, he bounced one more time and watched as the blood spurted from the doctor. He stood and twisted his neck back and forth as he rolled his shoulders to get the kinks out. He hadn't planned on being this sore and tired. Killing someone like this was more physically demanding than he thought it would be.

There has to be a better way to do this, without all the fighting and struggling.

This was just the second time he had ever killed someone. His first had only been an hour earlier. The first one had been tiring, too. But doing this twice in a row was more exhausting than he imagined.

Careful not to step in the blood, he tiptoed over to an exam table and opened a black backpack. After pulling out a canister of bleach wipes, he began to wash the doctor's arms and stomach. He twisted the end of a fresh wipe and inserted it into the dead man's belly button.

"Again, my apologies, Doc. No disrespect." He gave a hollow laugh as he swished his hand around. "Just gotta make sure I get all of me off all of you."

He grabbed a towel next to the large wash basin and turned on the hot water to begin washing himself. Placed one muscular calf into the sink and washed his leg, then switched to clean the other. Continued scrubbing his upper body until he was satisfied he had cleaned off any remnants the doctor may have left on him. After drying the floor in front of the sink, he stepped over to the backpack, slipped into a dark sweatsuit, laced up his shoes, checked a piece of paper sitting on the exam table, pulled the hoodie further down over his head, and slid out the door.

CHAPTER 2

"IT'S BULLSHIT!"

Detective Rhody Richardson slid to the side and rose from the diner booth as he shook his head and rolled his eyes. The holster from his 9mm Glock knocked a dangling fork to the floor. He bent over to retrieve the wayward piece of silverware.

"How the hell am I supposed to notice every little thing. I swear…"

"Wouldn't be morning breakfast without you swearing, Rhody," said fellow detective Jon Wayne. "You know I've always had your back—through college, through the academy, through all these years on the force. But sorry, partner, I gotta go with her on this one."

Richardson took his empty dishes over to the counter and nodded at the waitress. He gave Jon a helpless look as he sat back down in the booth. He slid over another few inches so the rip in the rust-colored vinyl wouldn't irritate him any more than he already was.

"Really, Duke? She thinks I should notice even the tiniest things all the time. And when I don't, she takes it personal—like it's some big failure on my part. What the hell?"

"C'mon, Rhod. Look at it from her side. You are Detective First Class Rhody Richardson. Best closing rate in the history of the Buffalo Police Department. You close cases because you notice everything. Wasn't it you who busted open the Delaware Park Stalker case? We all saw the same video of the perp tripping over the curbing by the zoo and limping away. But a week later, when we interviewed Conley, it was you that noticed one sock was slightly puffier than the other one. You figured out he had wrapped his ankle. That's what turned our focus to the right guy, and we were able to put it all together from there."

"Well, that was fairly obvious."

"Then how come in a room full of DAs, cops, and other detectives, you were the only one who picked up on it?"

"I don't know. Just lucky, I guess."

"Lucky, my ass. Tell you what. Don't turn around. When we came in, Julie was serving that customer two booths behind you. What's he wearing?"

Richardson shook his head with a look of annoyance. "Unreal. A pair of dirty cargo shorts, with work boots covered in black. Probably lays down blacktop for a living. He has on a red tank top and is wearing a Bills hat, also smudged with tar. And before you ask, it looked like Julie was handing him the number three special—two fried eggs, sausage, bacon, and home fries. Who friggin' cares?"

"You're the type of guy who can see a bolt from across the room and tell if it's a nine-sixteenth or a half-inch."

"I know, but this is different. So her hair is a quarter-inch shorter and a thousandth of a shade lighter. How or why am I supposed to notice that?"

Wayne smirked. "Because, buddy, she's your wife, and she tries to look beautiful for you. The least you can do is use those ultra-high powers of perception to let her know you notice!"

"I know. She's worth it. But I'm telling you, there are some days this job just drains my brain. I can hardly remember my own name by the time I get home." Richardson sighed. "About the only thing I want to recognize is an ice-cold PBR sitting on the fridge door."

The beeps from their cell phones cut through the diner. Both detectives grabbed their phones and grimaced at the text message from their lieutenant.

Get to the med campus NOW! Nia Buff Plastic Surgery. CSI and coroner are already there.

As Wayne texted back to let him know they were on the way, Richardson stood and threw a twenty-dollar bill on the table.

"Keep the change, Julie." He waved. "We gotta run."

"So much for a nice, easy morning." Wayne sighed as he pushed open the door and slipped his sunglasses on. "You ready, Butch?"

"You bet, Sundance. Leave your car. I'll drive."

"As usual."

CHAPTER 3

As Richardson turned his F-150 up Ellicott Street and hit the gas, Wayne looked around.

"Hard to believe this is even the same city we spent those college summers delivering mail," he said. "Looks a hell of a lot better than some of those shitty areas we used to walk through."

"Yeah, I know. It's nice to see. I guess a few gazillion dollars can do that to a neighborhood."

The Buffalo Niagara Medical Campus had become a crowning jewel for a city that had pulled itself from the brink of extinction. After the steel mills pulled out, the blue-collar town declined and drifted aimlessly for decades, with a reputation that dropped as fast as its population. Politicians from the east side of the state ignored Western New York and spent the bulk of their time over-serving the needs of New York City and Long Island. Eventually, state officials acknowledged that there was a whole other part of the state west of Albany. Once they realized there were votes to be had, they decided to throw money to the left side of the state in an effort to keep the votes coming.

While the politicians were busy elbowing each other to get in front of a camera and claim credit, the city had picked itself up, brushed off the rust-belt persona, and moved forward into the twenty-first century, riding a wave of technology and a new infrastructure. The medical campus had become a source of pride, earning a national reputation for excellence, and attracting some of the best talent.

The campus, between Main Street and Michigan Avenue ran from Goodell Street up to East North Street. Many of the vacant and dilapidated houses had been razed and replaced by gleaming structures of stainless steel and mirrored glass. In addition to the shiny new buildings, the area had been randomly populated with sculptures, murals, and other public art. It was one part of a newly regenerated pride sweeping across the area.

The rejuvenated campus had created enough buzz to lead to the revitalization and renaissance of the surrounding neighborhoods. Murals painted on buildings throughout the city had become must-see items for out-of-town visitors. Millennials had moved back in, repopulating the area, from the artsy Allentown crowd to the Fruit Belt section. Even the vacant warehouses at the northern end of downtown Buffalo had been converted into desirable lofts.

The area had transformed from a destitute, high-crime area into a bustling center of renovation. These days, there was little need for police, let alone two homicide detectives, to respond with lights flashing. The biggest issues coming out of the neighborhoods these days were the complaints about self-absorbed patients too cheap to pay for parking, and who would park illegally throughout the side streets in the residential neighborhoods.

But this morning was different. From blocks away, Richardson and Wayne could see the lights rotating like an early morning dance party. A couple squad cars, several unmarked sedans, and the coroner's van were parked at odd angles in front of the building. As they pulled up, the mirrored glass reflected the police presence, projecting an image of twice as much chaos.

"Hey, Bill," Richardson said. "What the hell is going on? It's not even seven-thirty yet. Shift hasn't even started. Not exactly what I'd call a great way to start the day."

"Sure isn't. But it's even worse for them." Lieutenant Bill Finch nodded to the frosted glass of the front door to the Nia-Buff Plastic Surgery Center.

Ironically, the slogan read, *A new start to life—a new you.*

"Them?"

"Yeah, Jon," Finch nodded. "A custodian came in this morning and found Doctor Charles on the fourth floor. Coroner says he was probably the first one killed. Then we got another call just a few minutes later while we already on our way. A nurse walked in and found Doctor Coleman in the back exam room. She didn't even know about the other one yet. She's pretty shook up."

"I'll bet," Richardson said. "Two doctors. You thinking it might be a junkie looking for some kind of fix?"

"No. Quite sure it's not." Finch grimaced.

"Why's that," Richardson said.

"Let me tell ya...I've been a cop for damn near thirty years—the last eleven as a lieutenant." Finch ran his hand through his thinning gray hair. "You'll see when you get in there. This kinda crap doesn't happen in real life. I'm telling ya...this is the sorta shit someone in Hollywood dreams up. I want both of you to drop everything you're are working on and focus on this. We need to stop him."

"Stop him?" Richardson said. "You really think there's gonna be more?"

"Yes, there will. Unless we stop him. Come on, let's go to the fourth floor first. He was the first to go. Jeff and the guys from CSI are up there working the scene now."

Richardson and Wayne followed their lieutenant through the lobby, to the elevator at the far side. They both glanced to the right at the nurse sobbing in a dark leather chair. An attractive woman sat next to her, whispering as she held the nurse's hand. A female officer rubbed her back to console her. The nurse lifted her head from her hands as streaks of mascara cascaded from bloodshot eyes.

"Oh, my God, I just can't believe this." She sniffled as the tears flowed, and her eyes pleaded to them. "Please find whoever did this."

"We will do our best, ma'am," Richardson said, as the elevator doors began to close. "I'm very sorry for your loss."

The fourth floor looked simply, but tastefully, decorated. Cream walls held inspirational pictures and quotes. The well-lit hallways were broken up by solid brown doors with nameplates attached. At the end of the hallway, the door holding the nameplate of Dr. Joseph Charles was open as several people processed and photographed the scene.

Richardson and Wayne nodded to the others as they walked in. The office was large, but seemed cramped with all the equipment and people working within the confines. Richardson knew all the people from the forensics department except for one new younger man who was bustling around and taking pictures. Before he could introduce himself, he saw the coroner, Dr. Daniel Matthews, standing near a potted plant.

"Good morning, Dan. What can you tell us?"

"Well, Rhod…" the doctor drew a deep breath, "…I don't know if I can understand the twisted depths of some people. Simply unbelievable. This one, and the one downstairs, have personal written all over them. It is just gruesome. The burgundy carpet hides it in here, but he lost a lot of blood before he was finally killed with the throat slash. Facial cuts tend to bleed a lot. The number appears to have been done postmortem. I'd estimate he was probably tortured with the cuts for about an hour, before he finally died."

"Ugh. Tortured?" Richardson said, with a look of disgust. "And what do you mean the number was done post?"

"C'mon, you'll see. Take a look on the other side of the desk—but walk around the other side, though. Most of the carpet on this side is soaked in his blood."

The two detectives stepped around the executive-sized dark walnut desk and stopped cold at the feet of what remained of Dr. Joseph Charles. Around both his eyes were several deep symmetrical gashes, with trails of dried blood looking like red tears that had halted their descent prior to reaching the carpet. From each side of his mouth, four angular slashes created a demented whisker effect. Less than an inch above the half-Windsor knot of his silk tie, the doctor's throat had been slashed all the way through to his spine.

The doctor was still wearing a lab coat, which at one time had been all white. As the newly reddened fabric stuck to his shoulders, the white end fell at his hips. Except for the top button, his light blue—and now maroon—dress shirt had been unbuttoned and folded back to reveal his pale chest. In large, precise cuts was the number 67. The bold face font was a half-inch thick to make up the five-inch high, three-inch wide numbers. The skin had been peeled off and laid on the floor next to the doctor.

"Damn." Richardson shook his head. "Looks like our killer is probably a southpaw. Or at least used his left to do the deed."

"Ah, very observant, Detective," said Dr. Matthews. "I will confirm when we get him back to the lab, but I was thinking the same thing."

Wayne tipped his head with a puzzled look. "Care to share? What makes you think that, Rhod?"

"Well, take a look at the depths of the cut. It starts a little higher on the left side of his throat, and then goes much deeper as it continues to the right as he was able to put his weight into the knife a little easier."

"But couldn't he have started deep on the one side and then pulled the knife higher as he straightened up?"

"Yeah, but if you look at the tissue, the cuts tend to follow the direction of the knife—and they all point to it going to his right. So the killer pulled it across that way. It would be too awkward to do it with the right hand."

"I agree," Dr. Matthews said. "I will get you the final report as soon as I'm done."

"What the hell is up with these cuts on his face, though? The whole thing is messed up. And the number cut out of him—sixty-seven? Any idea what that means? How about the one downstairs? Does he have that, too?"

"Almost, but not quite," said Jeff McDonald, the lead forensic investigator. "The one downstairs went the same way, but he has number sixty carved into him."

"Damn, Jeff," Wayne said. "Sixty-seven and sixty? Do your guys have any thoughts on that?"

"None at all." McDonald shook his head. "We'll keep working on it. And the note, too. Same one at both scenes—signed by Arthur Seth. We'll be pouring over that."

"What note?" Richardson said. "And who is Arthur Seth."

"Our killer fancies himself to be a poet," McDonald said. "Doubt it's his real name, but we're looking into it. It's hanging on the bathroom mirror." He waved his latex-covered hand toward an office door in the back corner. "My new intern was the one who discovered it up here, and also the one downstairs."

Using the elbow of his suit jacket to push open the door, Richardson stepped onto the tiled floor, with Wayne right behind him. Hanging from the center of the mirror was a sheet of copy paper with neatly written lettering.

Ten years lived and loved.
Ten years I thought I had won.
For each of those years I've lost,
One of these monsters will be done.

—Arthur Seth

CHAPTER 4

ONE AND A HALF BLOCKS UP FROM THE FLASHING lights, Paul Schon drove his Fusion into a parking lot. After pulling his ticket from the machine, the gate lifted and he drove in. He backed into a convenient spot directly across from the exit gate. He smiled and thought maybe it would be decent day. With all the sadness in his life, the thought of any goodness brought about a respite of hope.

Paul liked having an early doctor's appointment, even though he was tired from another restless night. It was much easier to find a good spot before all the Buffalo General visitors hogged up every spot within a five-block radius. As he walked toward the building, he tapped the key fob before he dropped it in his front left pocket. The Ford chirped back to confirm it was secure.

A glint caught his eye. He went over and lowered his sunglasses to see Lincoln's copper profile smiling back at him.

Yes, maybe it really will be a decent day. Paul slipped the penny in with the key fob.

"Good morning, Mister Schon." The receptionist, Kathy, smiled. "You're our first guest this morning. Just sign in, and I'll take you right back so Phil can get all your vitals."

Phil, the nurse, was a big, tall man with a smile that was as kind as his eyes. Paul enjoyed coming on the days when he was there. Phil had a way of putting him at ease and making even his bad days seem less troublesome. After another restless night filled with more nightmares, it was nice to see a friendly face.

"Well, good morning, Paul." Phil beamed, and his brilliantly white teeth contrasted with his dark skin. "I missed you on your last visit. Come on back, and we'll get you all set for the doc. It's so good to see you again."

"Good to see you, too, Phil." Paul said, before asking his usual question of the six-foot-eight nurse. "How's the weather up there?"

Phil smiled down with twinkling eyes, and gave his usual reply.

"Clear and bright, sir. Clear and bright!"

Paul sat in a chair next to the scale in the hallway. Phil pulled a sphygmomanometer from the wall mount and wrapped it around Paul's bicep. Then he pumped up the pressure cuff.

"I gotta tell ya…you're looking kinda buff these days, Paul. Looks good. You been working out?"

"No, not really. People at work have been asking the same thing when they see me." Paul kicked off his shoes in front of the scale in the hallway. "Not sure why. I've been eating like a horse lately. But after I take those new pills, I am out like a light."

He stepped off the scale as Phil continued typing the results into his computer.

"Wow, you've already dropped thirty pounds in the last few months. Your blood pressure is great, temp is normal, your color is good, and you look strong as a horse. Maybe those new meds agree with you. Have a seat in room one, and Doctor Chandler will be right in after I speak with her."

"Thank you, Phil."

Exam room one looked like every exam room he had ever been in—sterile, and lacking personality. Random posters showed drawings of the internal organ systems. Another posting advised diabetic patients to remove their socks for the doctor. Emojis ranging from a big smile to a scream allowed patients to point to their current pain level. Next to the sink with the high, goose-neck faucet was a soap dispenser and instructions for anyone who may not have learned the proper technique for using soap and water to wash their hands.

Paul adjusted the blinds to let in a little sunlight and to take a peek outside. High Street was filling in with people hustling to wherever they were already late for. He cringed as he saw a BMW X5 driver bend down after he dropped his phone, and slammed the brakes to avoid a crossing pedestrian. The driver's face flushed beet red as he glanced around with a *holy crap* look. Paul wasn't sure if it was out of concern for the woman, or if it was because he was so close to damaging his precious beamer.

Paul thought back to something he read once. In some areas, BMW cars were called *bimmers*, and the motorcycles were called *beamers*. It made no difference to him. Around Western New York, he had only heard them called *beamers*.

Either way, the woman in the tweed skirt and matching jacket was oblivious to the upscale SUV. She continued her march across North Oak, her left hand erratically swinging a briefcase as she pressed her phone to her right ear. Paul couldn't hear what she was saying, but he was glad he wasn't the one on the other end of her ass-kicking diatribe.

He chuckled and tried to imagine how much more aggravated she was going to be when she saw that the thin heel on her left shoe had pierced a potato chip bag. It reflected the morning sun at odd angles while it continued to hitch a ride on the brown leather Prada.

A double knock announced the arrival of Dr. Jessica Chandler. As usual, she entered the room smiling. She reached out to shake Paul's hand, and greeted him warmly. She held Paul's folder, but sat in front of the computer monitor to look at the same information that was on the paper.

"So how have things been going since our last visit, Paul?"

"Going as well as can be expected, I guess. Not a whole lot has changed in the last few weeks. My legs still feel tired and sore, but not as bad. My hands still get shaky at times."

"Are you still seeing Doctor Taylor regularly. Is it helping at all?"

Paul nodded. "I guess so. But there's only so much a shrink can do. Kaileen may be a great psychiatrist, but sometimes I think I might just be a little too messed up for even the best and the brightest."

"Hardly. You know, there are plenty of support groups out there, too. It could help to talk about it. I understand how hard this has been for you. Losing a spouse is difficult for anyone. It's been almost a year. There are people you can speak with. People who have gone through similar losses."

"Yeah, I know. I'm just not ready for the whole group talk thing yet. Besides, lately I just don't have the energy for it. I come home, eat some dinner, take my meds, and I am out until the morning alarm screams at me. Even then, I sometimes wake up and feel like I've been run through a gauntlet."

"Phil is a little concerned about your weight loss since you've been taking the new med. Frankly, I am, too. You've been dropping about ten pounds a month for the last few months. Unexplained weight loss is always troubling. But he's right, though—you look great and have really good muscle tone. Your vitals all look perfect. If you hadn't told me otherwise, I would believe that you're working out and dieting correctly. You seem like you're ten years younger."

"Thanks, Doc. It'd be nice to be twenty again." Paul smiled. "I do feel stronger lately. A little tired, but stronger. It has been nice to buy some smaller clothes. After Sheila started getting sick, I got a little pudgy, and then it got worse…after she passed…" He gazed down at the floor.

"I know. But that's what concerns me, too. Doctor Taylor still has you on Pentozipratol, right?"

Paul nodded. He had been taking one pill after dinner every night, for almost four months now. In some ways, it was a welcome release. His brain would shut down as he slipped into sleep. Aside from the occasional nightmares, including the one from last night, he was glad for the relief of deep, mind-numbing lack of cognizance. It took his thoughts away from the memory of watching the love of his life waste away to a fragile shell in constant agony.

"It's still a relatively new drug," Dr. Chandler said. "It has shown a lot of promise in the trials. But to me, there are still a lot of unknowns. I hope it helps with your anxiety and depression. We all want what's best for you, but I don't think we know all the effects just yet. For one, meds like this are known for being weight gainers. But you have been losing weight each month. I'm glad she wanted me to check on you monthly. It's always better to catch changes early. Think I'll give her a call and discuss some of my concerns."

"I still see her every Wednesday. I'll let her know this afternoon that you're going to call."

"Sounds good. Let her know that I'll probably call her tomorrow or Friday. I want to check out a few things first. Make sure you stop at the desk on your way out. Kathy will set you up for next month."

CHAPTER 5

McDonald was right. The scene on the first floor was nearly identical except for the large number 60 cut across the doctor's chest. But this scene had Dr. David Coleman splayed out on cold tile. There was no carpeting to soak up his blood, and no grandiose desk to hide behind in the small room.

The blood had followed the path of least resistance along the textured tiles, creating a macabre mosaic around the recently deceased surgeon. Coleman's face had also been mutilated with identical cuts around the eyes and mouth. The deep gashes created a ghastly look of dark red against the pale, drained skin.

The appearance would have rivaled the hideous and harsh clown faces of serial killer John Gacy. But this wasn't the face of a warped killer. This was the victim— a man who had met his demise in a sanguinary pool of his own fluids.

The lead forensic investigator had brought them down and reviewed the limited information they had. McDonald had relayed that he and Dr. Matthews believed there was only one killer. Both surgeons had been killed in an identical manner—faces cut up and throats slashed. Because the cuts went from the right side to the left, they believed the killer held the knife in his left hand as he sliced across the neck. After measuring liver temps, they estimated Dr. Charles had died first, around midnight, and believed Dr. Coleman was maybe an hour or two after that.

"Jeff, doesn't that seem pretty late for a doctor to be here," Richardson said. "It's a plastic surgery center, not a twenty-four-hour urgent care or something."

"I thought so, too," McDonald said. "But we were talking to the nurse, and she said that neither of those doctors work on Wednesdays, so they regularly work late on Tuesday nights. Apparently, they even take patients right up until nine or ten at night. I guess it makes it convenient to get a late-night facelift or tummy tuck. Then they would stick around for a couple hours, finishing up paperwork, reports, or whatever else. She also said they sometimes take part in live streaming med conferences from halfway around the world, but she doesn't believe they had one scheduled for last night."

Richardson continued looking at the victim. "Hmm. Maybe the killer knew their schedule and targeted them. Dan said he thought this had personal written all over it. But according to the note he left upstairs, we could have another eight more coming. Didn't you say there was also another note down here, too?"

"Yeah. Same poem, with the same block letters, and same name at the bottom. My new guy located it under the exam table, but he doesn't think the killer put it there. I believe he's right. I want you two to meet him. I think you'll like him. He's young, but he's good, Rhody. I'm going to push the chief to hire him. His internship is almost done, and he's one of those kids who just seems to get it." McDonald stuck his head out the door and yelled into the lobby. "Hey, Connor. Come on in here. I want to introduce you to the detectives."

Connor Patrick glided across the lobby with an ease that showed of quiet confidence, not arrogance. His six-foot-three body looked calm, athletic, wiry, and muscular all at the same time. The twenty-three-year-old had already graduated with degrees in mathematics, biochemistry, and computer technologies. He was nearly finished with a master's in forensic sciences, and hoped the scholarship money would keep coming in long enough to earn his doctorate in pathology.

"Hey, boss. What do you need." The intern smiled.

"Connor Patrick, I'd like you to meet detectives Rhody Richardson and Jon Wayne."

Patrick reached his hand out to Wayne. "Like the actor?"

"Yeah." Wayne sighed as he rolled his eyes. "But spelled differently."

"They're going to be the leads on this case," McDonald said. "All information will be going to them."

Richardson extended his arm to the young man, and they shook hands.

"I've heard some good things about you. You're the boy genius people are talking about."

"Hardly a genius." Patrick blushed as he pushed his glasses back up his nose. "I'm just pretty good with numbers, and I like researching stuff. Sometimes I get lucky with finding things."

"Yeah, kinda funny how the people who keep working are the ones who get lucky like that. Well, right now I could use some good luck on the numbers sixty-seven and sixty. Jeff says you found the note here under the table, but he said you didn't think the killer put it there. Why?"

"Well, bear with me. I'm still a little new to all this, but I still notice some things. The note was spun around, and looked like it was pushed under the exam table, all the way to the wall. The only reason I even noticed it was because I was down on a knee taking some closeups of the eye cuts. I'm sure one of the other techs would have found it when they all came down here."

"Okay," Richardson said. "But maybe he hid it under there just to mess with us? He hid the other one in the bathroom, but there are no other rooms in here."

"I kinda thought that, too. But let me explain." Patrick stepped further into the room and swept his hand over the body. "Look how precise he is. Just like upstairs, the shirt is folded back as a perfect mirror image on each side. Each cut on the left side of the doctor's face is in exact symmetry with the right. And the note that was upstairs…I'll bet if we had measured before we took it down, it would have been exactly dead center. Wouldn't have been more than a millimeter off from top to bottom or left to right. This guy is meticulous. So I started thinking how odd it was that it was down there. Then it hit me—arterial cuts like the one on his neck not only create a spray, but they also make a mist. Probably has this entire room coated in the doctor's blood."

Two detectives, a coroner, and a lead forensic investigator stopped leaning against the walls or resting their hands on a counter. Wayne made a face at Richardson as he wiped his hands down his jacket.

"Remind me to wash up as soon as we're done here." Wayne shook his head.

"Yeah, that'd be a good idea," Patrick said. "Anyway, I decided to grab the UV light and take a look around. Let me show you what we found."

"And by *we*, it really means *he* found it," McDonald said.

As Patrick sprayed the area with luminol, he nodded over to McDonald, who reached over and shut the lights off in the interior room. Patrick flipped the switch on the handheld light, and the room was bathed in a deep purple. The telltale light grew brighter and glowed as it passed over the liquid remains of Dr. Coleman. The luminol reacted with the microscopic bits of iron in Dr. Coleman's hemoglobin to create an iridescent glow. As Patrick continued raising the light over the vinyl exam table, they all saw it. Dead center of the table was a blank spot measuring 8.5-by-eleven inches. The paper had created a void pattern precisely in the middle of the table.

"This guy seems a little too OCD to have just thrown it down," Patrick said.

Richardson peered closer as McDonald flipped the lights back on.

"Good catch, kid," Richardson said. "So now we have to wonder, did someone mess with our crime scene?"

"Maybe. But probably not," Patrick said. "At least, not intentionally. Let me show you what I think happened. Doors create a vacuum when they close. The quicker it's closed, the more pronounced the vacuum becomes. Did you ever notice the dust bunnies that go swirling around in a dirty room?"

The detectives nodded.

"Watch this." Patrick placed another sheet of paper on the exam table.

He then slammed the office door. The ensuing vacuum created a rush of air to fill in the void left by the closing door. The paper skittered across the table and then floated to the floor.

"I think the nurse came in, opened the door nice and calmly, then saw all the blood and freaked out. I know I would have. She probably yanked the door closed, and the paper came off."

Jeff McDonald had a pleased look on his face. "I told you he was good, didn't I?"

He then furrowed his brow and turned back to the intern.

"But let's get one thing straight, Patrick. Don't you ever let me catch you dragging anything through an active crime scene again. There are plenty of other doors in this building if you want to play show and tell."

Patrick swallowed hard, and his face turned scarlet. "Sorry, sir. Won't happen again."

Richardson and Wayne exchanged smirks and left the forensic team to finish up, and the coroner filled and zipped up the body bag he had brought in. They walked back across the lobby to speak with the nurse they'd seen earlier.

Kim Thatcher had been a nurse for twelve years. She had often joked with her friends about how she had seen it all. She liked to brag that she was immune to the gory things that made her girlfriends queasy. But seeing a mutilated Dr. Coleman first thing in the morning had relieved her of that belief. The sight had also relieved her of a sausage and egg bagel, along with the cup of hazelnut coffee she had grabbed on the way in.

In addition to the police officer who was still with her, a tall, thin man with wire-framed glasses stood over her. He held a hand on her shoulder and was whispering.

He stood straight and offered his hand to the detectives.

"I'm Doctor Mike Mitchell. Joe and Dave were my partners here. This is just devastating. I don't understand why any of this happened." He tilted his head in an effort to lead them to an area a few yards away from the tear-filled nurse. "Kim is absolutely beside herself," he whispered. "I feel so bad for her. Dave brought her with him when we started the practice. They have known each other for years. As soon as you guys are done, I'll have someone drive her home. I don't want her behind the wheel when she's like this."

"That's very understanding of you, Doctor Mitchell," said Richardson.

"Please, call me Mike."

"Okay, Mike. Is there anything you can tell us about your partners? Did any of you have any problems with anyone in particular? Have there been any threats?"

"None that I'm aware of. Our practice has done remarkably well with both our reputation and our finances. We built this up by making sure our customers were given the best results. About the only upset people we've had are the ones we turned away because they don't have realistic expectations. There are plenty of other places in town that will do that sort of stuff. We don't need to."

Nia-Buff Plastic Surgery had come together over eight years ago, when the three colleagues were sharing a platter of chicken wings and a pitcher of beer at the Anchor Bar. They were all sharing their concerns about the corporate mentality and legal mumbo-jumbo being forced down their throats from the hospital's board of directors. By the time they'd finished another pitcher of fermented hops and barley, the three men had decided to pool their resources and strike out on their own.

There had been no buyer's remorse with the decision. They hit the ground running, finding a convenient location in the suburbs, and brought in a good support staff, including Dr. Coleman's nurse, Kim. From the beginning, the three partners set realistic expectations. And for the most part, they built their practice based on word of mouth over the first two years.

Shortly after they held their second anniversary staff party, things really took off. Two wives of Buffalo Bills players posted several pictures on their social media pages. Their new curvaceous figures outdid anything previously seen on the now-defunct professional cheerleaders who had strutted and jumped around to work the Buffalo crowds to a frenzy in-between plays. In addition to the provocative pictures, the wives made sure to mention where, and who, had created the new look that had their husbands going wild.

After that, it became a whirlwind of growth. While the partners were living more than well-off, they were also willing to invest their profits back into the business. They moved out of the cozy one-story building with a ten-car parking lot, in Orchard Park. Now, adjacent to a multi-floor parking ramp, they were surrounded by four-stories of gleaming technology and pristine equipment that was all their own. More support staff was brought in to handle the increased workload, facilities, and paperwork. Several young, talented doctors jumped at the opportunity to come on board.

Things had been going well for the partners. But after one horrible night, nothing would ever be the same.

"I will send out a group email to everyone who works here," Dr. Mitchell said. "I'll ask them to relay anything they can think of. If there is anything you need at all, please let me know."

"Thank you, Mike," said Richardson . "You can send your nurse home. She already gave her statement to the officer. We'll probably speak with her again later, after some of the shock wears off."

Dr. Mitchell turned to head back to the distraught nurse.

Just before he reached her, Wayne said, "Hey, Doc. This is a beautiful building. Any chance you have security cameras?"

"Um, yeah, we do. But just on the outside. We considered putting them in here, but we decided that the patients' desire for privacy was too important. I'll contact IT and ask them to send you the video. I think the hard drive holds stuff for about a week or so."

"Thanks," Richardson said. "A week would be great. But right now, I'm more interested in the last twelve hours."

CHAPTER 6

"COME ON IN, PAUL. I LIKE YOUR TIE. IT GOES very nicely with your shirt."

As usual, Dr. Kaileen Taylor's voice was soft and even, dripping with compassion. She always made Paul feel comfortable right from the start.

"How was your drive in this afternoon?" She smiled and a gave a reassuring tilt of the head.

"It wasn't bad. Certainly better than when I left Doctor Chandler's office this morning. By the way, before I forget…she said she wants to call you this week to go over some things."

"Okay, great.

"Did you hear what happened right down the street from her place?" Paul asked.

She nodded.

"I can't believe it," he said. "I saw all the police around when I got there, but I had no idea."

"Yes, I heard about it, too. It's been all over the news. I can hardly believe it, myself. Doctor Coleman was a year ahead of me at med school. I didn't really know him, but I met him a couple times at various conferences and functions. It is just so shocking."

Dr. Kaileen Taylor had become a leading psychiatrist in the Buffalo area, but it was a career path that almost didn't happen. As a young idealist, she had known she could change the world and make it a better place for everyone. In an attempt to better understand the people she so desperately wanted to help, she received her bachelor's degree in psychology and sociology. With starry eyes, she set out with a grand plan to become a lawyer and then a politician. She was sure that once other leaders saw the errors in their thinking, they would come around to the right way. Even if she couldn't make everything right all at once, she knew she had the patience and tenacity to keep tackling issues one at a time. Unfortunately, there are few things harsher than reality which can tarnish even the brightest dreams of a young dreamer.

Over and over again, she witnessed scandal after scandal bringing down the mighty. Innuendo and accusations flew across both sides of the political spectrum. While she openly cheered when those she despised stumbled, she also watched in horror as some of her inspirations and political idols crumbled before her. Those she supported turned out to be just as flawed as those she opposed.

It wasn't long before she viewed politics as a depressing quagmire of self-serving media whores who only loved to see and hear themselves on the evening news. This would have been all right with her if any of them had anything meaningful to say. This was not the case. Everything released these days was so overanalyzed, processed, and edited that it all became bland, banal bits of nothing. Not that she would ever eat meat, but it was about the same as comparing the beef in a fast food hamburger to a filet mignon. Overprocessing sucked out all the true flavor of any real ideas and motivations.

There was nothing of real change in the air—just one side accusing the other of impeding progress. Anyone who had the audacity to speak outside the norms was chastised, ridiculed, and shunned. Once shunned, it was impossible to do anything on your own or make any kind of real impact.

Despite the rhetoric spewed during the fall campaigns every couple years, nothing ever changed. Kaileen began to realize there was too little movement of any real ideals. Politics was not going to be the way to make the world a better place in her lifetime. As a lawyer, she hoped she could make a difference by working as a defense attorney, helping the oppressed, wrongly accused, and under-represented. Or perhaps she could serve the greater good by becoming a district attorney and prosecuting the evildoers who plagued the city.

Although those ideas seemed attractive in theory, neither one of them appealed to her sense of purpose and benevolence. She had already seen too many defense attorneys being forced to defend the scum of the earth. She didn't see how or why she could provide a rigorous and robust defense while fully knowing they were lying through their teeth. The idea of advocating for murderers, molesters, and other criminals repulsed her to the core.

Conversely, being a prosecuting attorney did not hold any allure for her either. She never cared for the idea of using her knowledge to punish people. Although she realized she would be making the world a better place for any future victims, she wanted to use her abilities to lift people to a higher place. On occasion, though, in her current field, she was more than willing to work with the police to provide them with psychological profiles and insight into the minds of local predators and their victims.

Undeterred by the futility of grand-scale changes, Kaileen decided that another way to make the world a better place was to have better people in it. As a psychiatrist, she felt she had the power to help those who needed it. She enjoyed guiding individuals back on a path to fulfillment and happiness. As someone in private practice, she had the ability to be selective with the patients she accepted, and the income allowed her to not only live comfortably, but to continue to donate to the causes close to her heart.

One of the new patients she had accepted was Paul Schon. A little over a year ago, he was referred to her by one of her former patients. Paul was interesting and complex. When Kaileen first met him, he was dealing with his wife's illness. From what she had gathered, Paul and Sheila Schon had led an idyllic, but simple, life right from the start.

Paul was always happy to retell the story of how they met. There had been a school mixer with a live band at the campus center to kick off their junior year. Paul was hanging out with friends and standing near the dance floor entryway. Sheila and her friends were trying to walk past. When she stepped around a table, her foot became tangled in another girl's purse strap lying on the floor. As she stumbled forward, she doused Paul with a full beer. While she was apologizing profusely, Paul interrupted her, smiled sweetly, and said if she were truly sorry, she would make him a dinner that didn't involve ramen noodles. To his surprise, she agreed. Paul's eyes still sparkled every time he told the story, and he said he knew right away she was the one for him.

After dating through their junior and senior years in college, they married shortly after graduation. They remained deeply and passionately in love until her untimely death. Sweet notes, gifts, gentle touches, and making love were part of their daily routine until she became too sick.

Sheila had contracted an infection that would not go away and continued to get worse, sapping her strength and creating excruciating pain throughout her frail frame. Countless doctors and specialists had been brought in to combat the spreading illness, to no avail. Antibiotics had no impact, and as the illness progressed, Paul and Sheila could see the end was inevitable. Paul tried to remain supportive and strong for his wife, but the stress and anger ate away at his mind as quickly as the infection ate away at her fragile body.

Til death do us part had no meaning for Paul. His feelings for his bride were destined to live well beyond the grave. The helplessness and hopelessness he felt were magnified by his survivor's guilt. During those last few months, as she fought the pain that gripped her every waking moment, there wasn't a day that he didn't pray to swap places with his love. Watching her suffer was harder than anything he could ever imagine.

His beautiful bride begged him to talk with someone. Even as the infection ravaged her systems, her biggest concern was for his welfare. She pleaded with him to seek a counselor to help him move on. She made him promise that he would keep living. Although he didn't want to be away from her at all, he couldn't say no to her. He would never break a promise to his love.

Following Sheila's death, Paul sunk further into himself. He maintained his weekly appointments, mainly out of loyalty to his wife's wishes. Although he seemed quiet and reserved, Kaileen could sense an underlying rage and resentment that continued to build. It was certainly understandable. Over the last couple months, however, the anger had seemed to be dissipating. His sessions were more beneficial and progressing. He appeared to have a sense of acceptance and a willingness to speak more openly and honestly. Kaileen could still detect the anger and survivor's guilt, but he appeared to be handling his raw emotions in a more productive way.

Paul spoke softly as he sat on the comfortable brown sectional. "Sheila worked just on the other side of the parking garage from those doctors. They were nice and let her park in their parking ramp when the weather was bad. It was great when she didn't have to brush off the snow all winter. I just can't believe this. You never know what can happen to you, I guess."

"It really is sad, Paul. But how are you doing? How are you feeling today?"

"Well, Kaileen, I feel about the same. I do think I'm sleeping a little better, though. At least the leg pain has eased up over the last couple weeks."

Along with the anger and guilt after Sheila died, Paul became increasingly depressed and anxious as the months passed by. Traditional medications to treat the depression seemed to have little effect. Dr. Taylor and Paul decided to turn to a newly approved drug which had shown a great deal of promise. Shortly after she had prescribed the Pentozipratol, Paul became more focused and felt a greater sense of purpose. His only complaint had been about muscle stiffness in his legs and feeling dehydrated. Getting out of bed in the morning became a chore as he stood on sore legs. His quadriceps and calves would scream at him as he went into the shower and then down the stairs. He was concerned that he may have been running a fever every night after taking the new med. Especially in the first few weeks, he would wake up covered in the salty residue of dried sweat. His thirst also seemed never-ending.

He would go through several glasses of water each morning as his depleted body strained to strike an equilibrium again.

Dr. Chandler had found no indications of an allergic reaction, and Paul was glad when the symptoms started to ease. He wasn't as sore anymore, but would still wake up parched and craving a drink. He added the new habit of chugging a sport drink each morning before brushing his teeth.

"That's good, Paul. You had mentioned last week that it was easing up a little. Have you had any other issues?"

"Not really. Except maybe..."His face turned red.

"What is it?"

"Probably nothing. But sometimes I have some pretty bad nightmares. I can't remember what they're about, but I just know they're scary. I don't know what I dreamed last night, but this morning I woke up frightened, like something terrible had happened. Maybe that's why my hands get so shaky sometimes. And not to sound paranoid, but there are times I think someone has been in my house."

"Hmm...that does sound troubling. With everything you've been dealing with—and sometimes *not* dealing with—the brain will find outlets for the anger, hostility, and bad thoughts that have plagued you for so long now. If it's of any comfort, medications like the Pentozipratol have been known to cause nightmares in a small percentage of patients. I know it doesn't make it any less scary, but it's something that has been known to happen. So you're not the only one. Maybe we should look at that. I think we should monitor these dreams and see if it gets any worse for you. Try to recall things as best as you can, even the smallest tidbits. I think it could help you and me in finding out what your brain is trying to tell us. Maybe you should keep a pen and paper by your bed. Sometimes we can remember things about a dream for a few moments after we first wake up. Try to write down anything you can think of before the memory escapes."

"Sure thing, Doc. I don't want to give up on the med just yet, though. I really do feel like some of my issues are letting go. Or at least doing a little better. Even this morning, I woke up terrified, but surprisingly focused and refreshed, like things were finally moving forward for me."

"I am glad to hear that. But I also want to ask you about something else you said. You mentioned that you thought someone has been in your house. Is that part of your nightmares, or do you really think someone had been there?"

"No, it's not part of the dreams. It's hard to say without sounding like some sort of paranoid nut. It's more of a gut feeling than anything I could put my finger on. For some reason, things just seem a little different, like something has been moved, or like a door is in a slightly different position than what I thought it was when I went to bed. Sometimes the things in the closet and drawers seem different to me. I don't know. A glass seems like it might be on the other side of the end table, or the towels seemed like they've been moved around in the bathroom. Sometimes when I open up my laptop, it will be on a page I don't think I ever looked at—nothing majorly wrong, but it seems a little different and kinda weird."

"And you don't recall getting up to use the bathroom or to get a drink or anything during the night?"

"No, not at all. Once my head hits the pillow, I am out like a light. Like I said, I don't want to sound like some paranoid weirdo, but it just seems odd to me. I know my door is locked every night, but if I didn't know any better, I'd swear someone was in there watching me. Gives me the willies."

CHAPTER 7

Late Friday afternoon, Dr. Kenneth Harrison slipped off his Oakley sunglasses as he pulled his Lincoln into the driveway of his beautiful house on Nottingham Terrace. He loved his home, and was glad his ex-wife had no more interest in Buffalo winters. She was more than happy to let him keep the house up here. She was doing well with his monthly bank transfers and his former home down in the Keys. It was all fine with him. The further away she was, the better. He made sure he set up the auto-payments with his bank. She always received her money on time, so she would have no reason to even speak with him.

Nottingham Terrace was known for the massive, if not ostentatious, homes of some of Buffalo's affluent citizens. This didn't matter to Dr. Harrison. It wasn't about status. This place was his reprieve, his sanctuary. He enjoyed the peace and quiet of living in a well-to-do neighborhood. With homes on only the one side of the road, he could sit on his second-floor balcony and overlook the greenery on the other side, all the way to the serenity of Hoyt Lake.

After changing into a pair of jeans and sweatshirt, Ken opened the doors that led from the master bedroom to the balcony. This was his favorite time of the evening. There was still enough sunshine to see everything clearly, but the light was fading just enough to bring an aura of stillness and calm. In the distance he could see a young couple pushing a stroller near the Albright-Knox Art Gallery. The whole view always reminded him of a scene from a Thomas Kinkade painting.

The light breeze carried the familiar smells of the lake as they mixed with the pungent smell of the marigolds from the landscaping beneath him. Statues of cherubim endlessly poured water into the large coy pond. Watching the white and orange fish glide around in sync through the lily pads brought about a hypnotic peace of mind. Everything about this house put him in a better place.

On the road below, Ken could see Jim, a local bank president, walking hand in hand with his wife. They lived at the other end of Nottingham, near Delaware Avenue, but would walk past Ken's house every evening when the weather would cooperate.

"Good evening, Doctor." Jim looked up and waved. "It's another nice night for walking."

"Sure is, Jim." Ken took a deep breath of the fragrant air. "I think I'm going to be walker tonight, too."

Jim and his wife smiled.

"I'm sure you will, Ken." Jim laughed. "Have one for me, too!"

Ken nodded and went back into the bedroom. He strolled past the king-size bed, to the small bar on the far side of his room.

After flipping a rocks glass right-side up, he pulled open the door on the small freezer and dropped in a few half-moon ice cubes.

"Yes, sir. Time to be a walker." He smiled as he searched the bottles lined up at the back of the bar. "Ah…there we go. Nothing like a little green label Johnnie Walker. Just what the doctor ordered." With a nod and wink to the man in the mirror, he took his first sip of the fifteen-year old scotch.

After a full day of dealing with patients, it was nice to just kick back and binge on several episodes of his favorite mind-numbing crime shows. After a couple episodes and a few more trips back to the bar, he was drifting in and out of consciousness.

He jerked awake as if he had heard, or sensed, something out of the ordinary. Rubbing his eyes, he looked around the dimly lit room as it basked in the glow from the television. On screen, a stylishly dressed detective was sliding across the hood of a Mercedes-Benz while emptying the magazine from his impractically large handgun.

"Well, alrighty then." Ken laughed as he pointed the remote and clicked the television off. "It's midnight, Cinderella. Time for this pumpkin to get his ass to bed."

He entered his bedroom and turned on the bedside light. Kicked off his slippers and reached up and then back as he stretched and yawned. His elbows were yanked behind him as his chest was stretched far beyond what a fifty-four-year-old man should be. Someone behind him drove him face first into the bed. As Ken struggled with his arms pinned behind him, an arm snaked around his throat and began to tighten. He couldn't swallow and was making gurgling noises as he struggled to breathe.

Ken looked around in wide-eyed bewilderment. As his carotid artery began to collapse under the pressure, stifling the flow of oxygen to his brain, he felt himself, once again, slipping in and out of consciousness.

"Hello, Doctor," a gravelly voice hissed, behind his left ear. "It's time for us to get to know each other a little. Do you know how much pain people like you have caused me? I think it's only fair that you know some pain, too."

The dazed doctor mumbled, "Why are y…"

Everything went dark.

Dr. Harrison started to wake. He had no sense of the time or how long he had been unconscious. Things were blurry, and he couldn't move his arms or legs. Something was in his mouth, and tape was over his lips holding them in place. Over the tape and directly under his nose was a damp rag. The acrid smell was a mixture of something that reeked of a sweet gasoline. It reminded him of a young girl's scented nail polish remover, but was much stronger. Whatever it was, it was making him dizzy and nauseated.

As his eyes began to regain their focus, he could see blue cinch straps binding his legs and squeezing his arms against his body. Other straps held him to the bed, at the end of which stood a man wearing a black and gray sweatsuit. The black hood flared out at the sides like a striking cobra. It draped low across his brow, hiding his eyes and casting a dark shadow across his face.

"Well, that didn't take long at all. I barely finished getting you ready for our night," the man said, in an eerily calm and measured tone as he approached the bed. "Sorry about this smelly thing here, Doc." He removed the rag. "Just a little homemade ether I derived from a bottle of starter fluid. Fascinating what you can learn to do on the Internet. I didn't want to use too much, though. I needed you to stay out just long enough to get you ready for our discussion." He turned and moved to the end of the bed. "Looks like a busy, busy night. I believe I will be able to make my other appointment later on. I'm so glad you're awake already."

From a black backpack on the dresser, the man pulled out two large, clear plastic storage bags and calmly placed them on the bed. From the front pocket, he removed a thin, eight-inch black canvas bag that was rolled up. He placed it alongside the plastic bags. He then bent over, untied each of his running shoes and stepped out of them. With his eyes still on the doctor, he then tugged at the black ankle socks and placed the left sock into the left shoe, and then did the same for the right side. Slowly, he picked up one of the storage bags and placed both shoes inside before grasping the blue slide and sealing the bag shut. While looking across the bedroom, he grasped the zipper on his sweatshirt and methodically pulled down on the tab to reveal his bare chest. He slid the hood from his head and let the jacket fall down his toned arms. He placed the hoodie on the bed and folded it, pausing for just a moment to smooth out a wrinkle.

With his back to the supine doctor, the intruder hooked his thumbs on either side of his waist to push his sweatpants down, and stepped out naked. Dr. Harrison started moaning and thrashing in a futile effort to free himself. His eyes were wild as a single tear rolled down the right side of his face. The gag muted the anguished cries of, "No! No! No!"

The naked man came around and sat inches away from the panicked captive. The doctor could smell the musky scent of sweat on the man. With a vacant and hollow look in his eyes, the intruder smiled and patted Ken's chest. Fear and revulsion began coursing through Ken's body as he threw up a small amount of bile and scotch into his gagged mouth. It wasn't enough for him to asphyxiate, but enough that he could feel the acid eat at his esophagus when he choked it back down.

"Now, now, now, Doctor. There's no need to worry. Well, actually, I guess it would be normal to worry. But not about that, anyway. This is not, nor will it be, sexual in any way, shape, or form. This is simply a necessity an educated man, such as your-self, could appreciate."

The restrained doctor could only respond with unintelligible grunts and muffled cries of distress.

"You see, Doctor, like you, I am a fan of crime shows. We both know how that pesky DNA always seems to catch the bad guy. As I said, this isn't sexual at all. You won't have to worry about me leaving any DNA samples in or on you." The man's once calm voice became venomous, and as cold as the edge of a knife. "You, on the other hand, are going to be leaving plenty of DNA evidence all around us." The naked intruder stood, his manhood only inches from the doctor's tear-streamed face, and the calm, methodical voice returned. "I just find that cleanup is so much easier this way. You see it all the time on TV—you can never completely wash the blood evidence out of your clothes. No clothes, no evidence. That's all it is, Doc. Just making sure I don't take you home with me. And let's face it, if I run all the way home in the nude, someone just might notice. Yeah, that sort of thing tends to get reported. So anyway, here we are. Clothes are sealed in plastic, the cinch straps have already been wiped clean of any fingerprints, and I will be able to wash any traces of you from my bare skin. Simple as that."

He walked to the end of the bed. After untying the canvas bag, he unrolled it to reveal two small scalpel-like knives and a large, glimmering steel hunting knife.

"I'm sure you think you're just some great guy, don't you Doctor Harrison? Think you're something else with your ultra-busy dermatology business. Well, you're about to learn that there is a blemish on that record—every pun intended. I think you're about to find out the damage you *great guys* can do to us regular Joe's. Please listen and learn. I have to get busy. In just another couple hours, I'd like to get to another appointment."

Nearly forty-five minutes later, the naked killer was straddling a deceased doctor. He admired the perfectly carved *10* for a moment. Then he placed a neatly written note on the middle of the unused pillow next to the doctor. He got up and began to clean before heading downstairs to get dressed and slip out the door.

Swiftly and silently, the darkly clad hunter began the three-mile run to a hotel on North Street. He wanted to meet with a guest there.

He glanced at his watch. Plenty of time. The run should take less than twenty-five minutes, and morning was still a few hours away.

Nonetheless, he decided to pick up his pace. It was a busy night, and rushing a job caused mistakes. Sloppiness and inattention to detail could not be tolerated.

CHAPTER 8

"Damn it." Richardson groaned as he reached for his phone.

Being woken early on a Saturday morning was bad enough, but when it was the morning after another karaoke night with Wayne, it was significantly more painful.

It had been a rough week, with no breakthroughs on the case. The two detectives took their wives out to blow off some steam. The four had stayed out a little later than usual, swapping stories, telling bad jokes, and taking their turns on the microphone to belt out some of their favorite songs.

Richardson had always been a hardworking man, but having a little fun was just as important to him. He needed it to balance the intensity of his career. The ability to enjoy life was one of his driving forces. Life, liberty, and the pursuit of happiness were concepts he jumped at. He pursued happiness with friends and family as often as he could, and he wanted to make sure others didn't interfere with someone else's pursuit.

The criminals he went after had clearly violated that principle. Richardson firmly believed you could be whoever you wanted to be, do whatever you wanted to do—as long as it didn't interfere with someone else's right to be happy and enjoy their life.

But this morning, a ringing phone, along with a few too many PBRs and shots of Jameson the night before, were definitely interfering with his happiness. The thought of doing anything first thing in the morning was not appealing at all.

"Are you kidding me?" His wife, Kerry, moaned. "If that's Jon, tell him I'm going to kick his ass." She rolled over and pulled the covers over her face, leaving only a tangled mess of blond visible across the pillow.

Richardson picked up the phone, glanced at the caller ID, and swung his feet around to the floor as he cleared his throat. With a grimace and a sigh, he slid his finger across the screen.

"Hey, Lieutenant. What's going on?"

He stood, running his hand through his hair, and walked to the dresser as the lieutenant filled him in. He pulled out a pair of pants and moved toward the bathroom. Shrugged and shook his head at Kerry, who had pulled the blanket down enough to reveal her sleepy brown eyes.

When he emerged from the bathroom, he tossed the phone down on the bed, near her feet. As he buttoned his shirt, he leaned down and kissed his wife's exposed forehead.

"Sorry, babe. I gotta go. It's another doctor, and a new poem. Meeting Jon there, too. Looks like the same guy again."

"Oh, my God. Are you kidding me? That's awful." She sat up and reached out to hug him. "Please be careful."

"I will, babe."

He stepped back and gave her an approving glance and raise of an eyebrow. She never seemed to get it, but this was when Rhody thought she was the most beautiful—her hair a tousled mess, her lips pouting, and no makeup. All he saw was her. Beautiful. Natural. His.

He desperately wanted to crawl back in bed with her and love the morning away.

Instead of the welcoming feel of his warm, soft wife, he wrapped his hands around the cold, hard leather of his holster, and jammed it on his belt while he climbed into his truck. Twenty minutes later, he pulled off the Scajaquada Expressway, onto Elmwood Avenue, and made the jaunt around to Nottingham Terrace. For the second time in a week, he could see a normally quiet neighborhood ablaze with rotating police lights.

"Hey, Bill. Hell of a start to the day again." Richardson approached his lieutenant.

"Sure is. Not exactly where I want to be. Here comes Jon now." Finch nodded back toward the road. "I'll take you two upstairs."

Wayne walked up carrying two cups of coffee. As they entered the mansion, he handed one to his partner.

"Hey, bud. I figured if you feel anything like me this morning, you're gonna need this."

"Sure do. Thanks."

As they approached the wide, winding staircase, Wayne said, "Hmm...I'm thinking a butchered doctor is going to significantly lower the property value for this place."

"Yeah, but still way beyond our pay grade, Duke." Richardson chuckled.

As the two detectives walked into the stately bedroom, Lieutenant Finch gave them some of the victim's background.

"Doctor Harrison owns—or rather, owned—Ken-Ton Dermatology. He has a cleaning woman that comes in at seven every Saturday morning. She was the one who found him like this. As you can see, this is very similar to the scene at Nia-Buff."

"Yeah, but a couple big differences." Richardson moved toward the king-size bed. "This is his personal house, not work. And he's bound up. Other than being a night owl and handy with a knife, it seems our serial killer doesn't stick to a script."

"You're right," Finch said, "but don't use that term just yet. The mayor is really concerned about this, and all the bad press. Doctors being targeted is never good for a city's image. Hell, anybody being targeted is bad. He's gonna have a shit-fit when he hears about this one. He sure as hell doesn't want this being called a serial killing."

"Just callin' it like I see it," Richardson said. "This is our third vic this week. Cut up face, slashed throat, carved number decorating his chest, and a poem for a calling card. What the hell else are you going to call it?"

"I know. Let's just hope we can solve this quickly." Finch handed him a sheet of paper. "And speaking of not sticking to a script, take a look at the new poem he left for us. It's not the same as Nia-Buff."

All those years loved and lost.
Now three have paid the cost.
Seven more will know my pain.
And just like me, they will cry in vain.

—Herbert Noak

"Just great," Richardson said. "Is he taunting us, or telling us? We still have nothing on an Arthur Seth, and now we have Herbert Noak. Who the hell are they."

"I've got a few people working on that." Finch turned toward Wayne. "Alyssa said the guys from IT were looking for you yesterday. Please tell me you were able to get something from the surveillance cameras at the other scene."

"Sorry, boss. About all I can tell you is that mayflies and nocturnal orb weavers are a pain in the ass." Wayne shrugged.

"Yeah, I hate mayflies," Richardson said. "So what if they don't bite. You can barely breathe near the water without sucking a few in. They're all over. That reminds me...I gotta wash the bike. Kerry and I went for a ride along the inner harbor, and the windshield is plastered with the damn things."

"Whatever," Finch said. "My wife hates them, too. She calls them sandflies." He scrunched his face. "But what the hell does that have to do with any of this? And what the hell is a nocturnal orb weaver?"

Wayne laughed. "I asked them the same damn thing. Let me save you the textbook version the science geeks gave me. Nocturnal orb weavers are those big-ass ugly spiders that make those huge webs up by the eaves. Let's just say that having a couple dozen annoying mayflies stuck to a big web right in front of a camera lens does not lend itself to useful imagery. We could barely see a few women coming in and out, a couple cars stopping right out front, a jogger in a black hoodie who may have walked in, but nothing is all that visible or usable. It's all clouded over. Can't get a clear image of anybody."

"Un-friggin-believable." Finch shook his head as he walked off. "Spiders and mayflies."

Dr. Matthews stood off to the side as Jeff McDonald and his forensics team continued gathering evidence. He nodded to Richardson and Wayne before heading out to the balcony. The two detectives followed him out into the cool morning air.

"Good morning," the coroner said. "Looks like your man was back at it again."

"Sure does, Doc." Richardson placed his hand on the railing and sipped his coffee while looking out over Hoyt Lake. "Anything new turn up during the autopsies of the other two?"

"Yes. I sent up a report late yesterday. I'm sure you'll see it as soon as you get back to the office. As we suspected, death was caused by exsanguination—they both bled to death. But we did discover something else yesterday which I think may explain the use of those cinch straps on Doctor Harrison."

Richardson turned around with a raised brow. "Really? What did you find?"

"Some postmortem bruising finally made its way to the surface. Because his heart stopped beating so close to the time of the injuries, and of course, with so little blood left in him, it took a couple days for the bruising to show up."

"What kind of bruising?" Wayne said.

"Faint, but still noticeable on both sides of their rib cages. Turns out, both doctors suffered cracked ribs shortly before their passing."

"Interesting," Richardson said. "Maybe they put up a fight. What do you think caused it?"

"Well, it's why I think he used the straps here. As I said on Tuesday, I believe he kept them alive and tortured them with the cuts before the final neck slash. You can be sure that they had to have put up a struggle at some point. I believe our killer drugged them, or maybe choked them into submission, or perhaps used something else to incapacitate them. It's hard to determine any bruising on their throats because of the slashing, and the tox report hasn't come back yet. He probably had to sit on top of them to hold them down while he did his work. He could have sat on their chests and used his knees to hold their head in place while he cut them. If they struggled, he probably jammed his full weight down, damaging their ribs. It had to be horrible as they struggled to breathe, knowing what was going to happen."

"So with this one," Wayne said, "he drops them and then straps them in place just to make it easier for himself. Just great. A lazy serial killer who wants an easy job."

"I wouldn't say lazy," McDonald replied. "Just efficient." The forensic investigator joined the trio on the balcony. "I think you're right, Dan. We found knee impressions in the bed on either side of the victim. He knelt over him while he did this, but he certainly isn't lazy. He has everything wiped clean, and he was thorough. There isn't a bit of evidence that we've been able to find yet. He even wiped the straps with a bleach solution, so we can't even find any usable epithelial cells or fingerprints. This guy is educated."

"Yeah, well, so are we." Richardson turned back to look over the balcony.

"I'll let you know if come across anything," McDonald said.

Richardson looked down at the railing, furled his brow, and walked over to the side of the second-floor deck.

"Hey, Jeff. Come take a look at this. Have your guys see if they can get anything here."

"What's going on?"

"I noticed there are a few marks on the top of this railing. It rained a few days ago, and there's a little dried silt on top. I doubt the maid cleans this very often. Take a look. Looks like eight marks—maybe fingers from grabbing the rail."

"I'll have them take a look, but I'm sure the doctor has had his hands on the rail countless times."

"Yeah, I'm sure he has, but probably not from the outside. Notice they start in the middle, and the smudge goes to the outside. It's a pretty good drop to the ground, and I don't see any ladder indentations, so it might be nothing. Just let me know if you get anything."

"Of course."

"Richardson and Wayne! Let's go." Lieutenant Finch walked out, holding his phone against his ear. "I've got uniforms out canvassing the neighborhood to see if anyone heard or saw anything here. I can't believe this crap. We just got a call from the Lenox on North Street. Looks like we got another one."

"What the hell?" Richardson said. "Is it another doctor?"

"I don't know. Maid just found him this morning when she went in to clean the room. I spoke to the responding officers. This one is wearing a *4* across his chest, and has a new poem. I'll meet you both there in a while. Jeff, I need you to get your forensic guys there, too. Dan, I'll see you there after you get this one zipped up."

"Sure thing," said Dr. Matthews. "I will literally be zipping this one up as soon as Jeff's team in done.

Richardson and Wayne followed Finch down the stairs, dropping two steps at a time. The lieutenant still had his phone pressed to the side of his head as he waved to them and jumped in his cruiser.

"Okay, Rhod," Wayne started jogging toward his car, "I'll follow you down Delaware."

CHAPTER 9

THE TWO DETECTIVES STEPPED OFF THE ELEVATOR, onto the third floor of the historic hotel. Two uniformed officers were standing in front of the taped-off room. The detectives nodded to them as they stepped aside and let them in.

Laying on the bed was the remains of Sean Hill. He was wearing light blue boxers and a blood-soaked T-shirt that had been sliced open to the collar and folded back on each side. A large, reddish-brown *4* was cut into the middle of his chest. His lily-white belly spilled over the elastic edges of his boxers. The shoulders of his tee were still white, and made it even more obvious that his left arm was darker than his right. Two inches above the t-shirt collar, Hill's throat had been slashed. Across from him, in the dead center of the television, was the tell-tale poem.

Feeling pain from a life ripped apart.
Tears flow free from a lost man's heart.

Revenge has taken four, with six to go.
There is a cost they all should know.

—Odel Ives

Richardson pointed to the note. "I'd say that's a pretty good indication it's the same guy."

Wayne nodded. "Yup. That, and the newly carved tattoo on his chest."

"Now we have to figure out who the hell Odel Ives is."

The two detectives slipped on latex gloves and began looking over the scene. The body was laid out in a similar manner as Dr. Harrison's. The covers had been pulled back and dumped in a crumpled heap between the bed and the dresser. One corner of the light blue paisley comforter still clung between the corner of the mattress and the box spring. Hill's legs were still bound together, and his arms cinched against his ribs at the elbows. The stiff hotel sheets were crimson on both sides of his carved face. Impressions were visible in the soft mattress where the weight of a killer's knees had pressed down close to Hill's head. His open eyes were fixed and dilated, staring at a ceiling fan he could no longer see.

"Damn it." Richardson sighed. "None of this is making sense to me. Something's off here."

"What's goin' on, partner?"

"Again, some of the things are the same. But they're different, too. The first two were at work. Harrison was at home, and this one is at a hotel. First two were obviously awake—they were at work. Harrison was in his night clothes, but he hadn't gone to bed yet—his bed was still made, and we found him on top of the covers. This one looks like he had been sleeping, but was then killed. So did he let the killer in? Nothing makes sense. Those other three were obviously doing really well, but look around at his stuff. This guy's traveling light. Just a few basic things in that suitcase. A couple average suit coats hanging in the closet. Couple pair of well-worn pants. All normal, regular stuff. Look at the shoes there by the dresser. They look like shoes you can get at any department store for less than thirty bucks. And look at this room. This looks like the kind of place you or I would stay at if we had to travel somewhere without the girls. But that's only because we're pretty damn cheap. I mean, it's clean and decent, but it's just a place to sleep, that's all. I know they also have some fancier rooms here, too. This is not the type of room I would expect a doctor to be staying in."

"And that would probably be because he isn't a doctor," a uniformed officer said, as he entered, holding a notepad. "Don't know if you remember me. I'm Dave Pawlowski. We met a couple years ago when that girl was attacked over in Lovejoy."

"Sure, Dave, I remember you," Richardson said. "You did some good work canvassing for us. Helped a lot. Gave us some good info, and we caught him. What do you have on this one?"

"I went down to the front desk to see what they know. Seems Mister Hill here was in town for just a couple nights. He was supposed to check out this morning." Pawlowski looked over at the bed. "I guess you could say he really did check out."

"That's for sure," Wayne said. "How'd you know he isn't a doctor?"

"The maid said she spoke with him yesterday morning. Said he was pleasant and nice to her. Told her he was a salesman in town for a few days, making some sales calls. She couldn't remember if he said what company he worked for. He works out of Syracuse and does sales all across the state and through the Northeast. She said he has a wife and a kid back home. Captain Reynolds is reaching out to have someone out there go notify them. I asked the desk folks about his ride, and they pulled his room registration card. He has a car out in the parking lot. I gave it a quick walk around. Nothing out of the ordinary, but I didn't touch it or move anything. It's a maroon Chevy. Parked all the way around in the back. I figure you're probably going to want to check that out when you're done up here."

"Thanks, Dave," Richardson said. "That's good work. Well, Jon, there's another big difference. I guess it's not just doctors. What the hell? There's something here I'm not seeing yet. Different poems at each location, and different names. There's a connection. I know it. I can feel it. He's selecting them for a reason. My gut is telling me this isn't random."

"Well, so far, listening to your gut has done us pretty well," Wayne said. "What do you want to do now?"

They both looked up as two CSI techs entered with their cases and equipment. Following closely, Connor Patrick came in holding his camera.

"Hi, Detective Richardson. Detective Wayne. Jeff called me this morning. He said things are stretched a little thin. Asked me to take the photos and help where I can. I can't believe we had another one, let alone two.

"I can't believe it either," Richardson said. "What happened to the days when a serial killer would wait weeks, months, or years between murders? By the way, kid, please just call us Rhody and Jon. Looking at you makes me feel old enough as it is. That formal stuff just makes it worse."

"Yes, sir. Um, I mean, sure, Rhody."

"That's a little better." Richardson smiled. "First things first. Can you get pics of those keys there on the dresser? And let's get them dusted for any prints. Probably only be the vic's on there, but we want to make sure. Jon and I will need to go through his car—gives us something to do while you guys are processing. I'm sure Jeff and the rest of the guys will be here any minute."

After spending some time speaking with the staff at the front desk and the distraught maid, Richardson and Wayne headed out the front door. They both slipped on sunglasses as they turned left. The parking lot ran along Irving place and wrapped around the back. Officer Pawlowski had said Hill's car was parked in the lot behind the building.

As they came to the back lot, Richardson held up the key fob and clicked the lock button a couple times. A horn beeped back in an electronic game of Marco Polo. He pointed to a burgundy sedan parked along the hedge line facing the drive thru lane for the Walgreen's. He hit the fob one more time as they approached, and the Malibu lights flashed and the door locks popped.

The two detectives put on latex gloves and opened the front doors, then bent down to look inside. An overwhelming odor of grease, sweat, stale coffee, and other pungent aromas assaulted their noses before they even looked in. The passenger side bucket seat and floor were littered with a half-dozen hamburger wrappers and French fry containers. An empty donut box on the seat held a few crusty remnants of its previous occupants. The backseat was decorated in a like manner.

"Damn, Rhody. I'm thinking our killer just did a quicker job at what the cholesterol was already in the process of doing to him. You think this guy ever ate anything that wasn't deep fried?"

"I doubt it. But I can understand why his left arm was so much darker." Richardson leaned in over the steering wheel.

"Why's that?"

"This car freaking stinks. I mean, come on. At least throw this crap out when you make a stop. Every drive-thru I've seen has a trash can. There's dipping sauce in the backseat that is growing some friggin' hair! What the hell. Makes me wanna puke my guts out." Richardson stood and looked at Wayne across the Chevy's roof. "If I had to drive in this mobile sewer, I'd probably have all the windows open just so I could breathe. The maid says he does sales all over the Northeast. He's a traveling salesman. So he probably drives up and down the thruway wearing a comfy T-shirt, with his arm hanging on the door. Left side gets a toasty suntan. Right side stays pasty white."

"Good observation there, Sherlock. What now?"

"Not sure my nose can take much more, but let's pop the trunk and see what it looks and smells like."

After using the fob to unlock the trunk, Richardson used two gloved fingers to lift the trunk lid.

"Holy crap!" Wayne said. "Look at all those drugs."

Overflowing bags spilled out of packaged pharmaceuticals. Small packets of foil blister packs tossed back the late-morning sun invading the dark interior. Bright-colored boxes were sealed shut and scattered from the front to the back of the Malibu's trunk.

"What do you think, Rhod? We're right across from Walgreen's, and none of this stuff seems opened. You think this guy was helping himself to a little five-finger discount?"

"Doubt it. Way too much of it. This all looks like something that would be locked up behind the pharmacy window, anyway. Couldn't have just walked off with all this, and we haven't heard anything about a robbery."

"You're right. But even though he looks like he had an unhealthy lifestyle, that's still way too many drugs to haul around for personal use."

"Yeah, I don't think these are all for him. Looks like some lady-type drugs are in here, too. I highly doubt those are for him. Let's see what we have back here." Richardson reached in and pulled a long, thin box of business cards from the back of the trunk. "*Pharmer-Grown Med Sales.* Hey, that's pretty good. Cute name. Says here, *Sean Hill—Pharmaceutical Sales, Regional Account Manager.*"

"Well, that explains all the stuff," Wayne said. "Probably gives samples to each of the doctors he visits. Maybe our killer saw him at a doctor's office and just assumed he was a doc, followed him here, and killed him. Wrong place, wrong time."

"Maybe, Duke. Makes sense. But I just don't see it going down that way." Richardson stared back at the hotel. "Our guy seems too meticulous to make a mistake like that. I'm telling ya—I can feel it in my gut. There is a reason he's picking them. He knows who he's going after. There's a pattern here. I can't see it yet, but it's there."

"Okay. What's next, then?"

"Let's head back in. CSI should have something more by now. But I also want to stop back at the desk. They've done a great job renovating this old hotel. Glad to see it back to some of its former glory. Kept the original feel, but added some updated tech. I noticed a camera above the archway when we came in. Let's see if we can look at any security video."

"Sounds like a plan. I don't think there are any mayflies or nocturnal orb weavers hanging out in the lobby area."

After checking in with Jeff's team on the third floor, the two detectives headed back down to the front desk to see the manager on-duty. She escorted them to a small back room next to her office. After logging on to the computer, she gave them a quick tutorial on how to navigate through the security camera's DVR. The detectives leaned back in worn-out office chairs, staring at the screen as they tried to fast-forward quickly to get through over eight hours of images, but slow enough that they wouldn't miss anything. They paused several times, jotted down details, studied each person, and made notes for follow-up.

"There! That's gotta be him." Richardson knocked over a couple empty coffee cups before pointing at the screen, and clicked the mouse to freeze the image. "Son of a bitch. That's him. I know it."

"Are you sure? You can't see his face at all. Might just be a guest. Looks like a jogger who just finished his run."

"Yeah, I know. But it's the middle of summer, and he doesn't look like he needs to lose weight. Why wear a black sweatsuit to go running in the middle if the night? Not very safety conscious. Why have his hood on at all? Let alone pulled down so low. See how he slipped in after that woman used her keycard to open the door? He was waiting, biding his time for the right moment to come in unnoticed. This guy is smart. He knows there are cameras around, and he's intentionally hiding his face. Remember what the guys at I.T. told us about Nia-Buff? They couldn't get good images, but they could make out a few things."

"Holy shit! That's right. They said there was a jogger in a black hoodie! Damn, Butch. You've got vision, and the rest of the world needs bifocals."

Richardson laughed. "My favorite line from the whole damn movie, Sundance. What do you think the chances are that two different joggers are out running in the middle of the night, wearing a dark sweatsuit with a hood?" He leaned in closer to the monitor. "Okay, you twisted bastard. What are you thinking? What makes you tick? You can keep trying to hide your face—I'm gonna find you."

CHAPTER 10

"OUT OF THE WAY, POINDEXTER! GO PLAY WITH your computer," an officer growled, as he shoved Connor in the hallway.

The cop and his partner both laughed as they continued along.

"Hey, Brian. Don't be such a dick," Jeff McDonald said.

The two cops scoffed as they pushed open the door and walked out into the morning sun.

McDonald turned back to his intern. "Good morning, Connor. You can't let them push you around. Most of the people in here are good guys. But I gotta admit, we have more than a few macho pricks who think they're all that. Don't let it get to you."

"Doesn't get to me at all." Patrick smiled. "Maybe if their opinion mattered in my life, it would. But it doesn't. They can say whatever they want."

"I like your attitude. Glad you could make it this morning. The whole task force, a lot of other cops, and some top officials are going to be at the briefing this morning. We want everyone on the same page. I made sure to tell the captain how observant and helpful you've been. He said you could be part of these meetings, too. That's a good sign. Here's your chance to start making an impression on someone whose opinion does matter in your life."

"Thanks, Jeff. I really appreciate it."

McDonald pushed the door open as they walked into the large meeting room. About two dozen officers, detectives, other CSI techs, and administrators were standing around in small groups, sipping coffee. Near the front of the room, Richardson and Wayne were talking with Lieutenant Finch and the coroner. On the other side of them, Alyssa Joseph was reaching as high as she could and writing with a blue dry-erase marker across the top of a large white board.

"Come on, Alyssa. Can't you reach just a little bit higher?" a voice called, from one of the desks.

Without looking back, Joseph said, "Not sure, Randy. You could come up here, and I can knock your ass down and stand on your nuts. But that would only put me up maybe another millimeter."

The room erupted with laughter.

Joseph had been the public information officer for the department for two years. She was petite, but fierce, with a playful side. Any officer who'd underestimated her had learned a painful lesson about her intensity. She had earned her reputation and current position based on her actions, not her looks. At first glance, she seemed a natural to be the public face of the police department. The media always seemed to enjoy getting quotes from her. Her long auburn hair and dark brown eyes further complimented her delicate features and made for attractive video and photos. But it wasn't just her looks. The diminutive, former patrol officer was also sharp, well-versed in policy, and could respond quickly and believably to any media inquiry. She had an air of authority and knowledge which helped disarm even the most persistent reporter.

She was also responsible for presenting case information to department personnel. As part of this morning's presentation, she had written out the last names of the victims across the top of the board. The first letter of each name was in uppercase, and was easily four times larger than the rest of the name. Next to the name, in numbers as large as the first letters, were the numbers associated with them—Charles 67, Coleman 60, Harrison 10, Hill 4. She had also added several bullet points of information below.

"Thanks, Alyssa," said the lieutenant. "Okay, everybody. Take a seat or find a place to stand. We've got a lot of stuff to cover this morning."

For the next thirty minutes, Richardson, Wayne, and McDonald shared the similarities and differences of the four victims. Timelines were broken down. The sketchy video from the first scene and the clearer one from the hotel were shown and discussed. The killer appeared to be of average height and relatively thin, but the waist-to-shoulder ratio indicated a muscular build. Pictures were passed around.

Connor raised his hand. "I know it's early, but I noticed—"

"I don't see gloves on his hands," a booming voice said. "Did we get any prints?"

"None yet," McDonald said. "Seems like everything had been wiped down. He has been thorough about not leaving any evidence behind so far."

The intern said, "I don't know if it matters, but—"

"So basically we should just look around at everyone in a sweatsuit and see if they look like some crazy-ass whack job," someone said. "Maybe we should send someone over to Forest and Grant to see if the psych center lost any guests."

"Hardly," said a woman's voice. "I highly doubt you'd be able to see this kind of psychosis."

"Most of you know Doctor Taylor," the lieutenant said, as the psychiatrist walked to the front of the room. "I've asked Kaileen for assistance, and perhaps give us more insight into his mind."

"Thanks, Bill."

The cadence of the doctor's hard sole shoes offered a rhythmic tapping as she strode to the front of the room and placed a folder on the podium.

"With all due respect to your fine observation skills, this probably isn't going to be something that jumps right out at you. As a matter of fact—and it may seem odd—but over eighty percent of serial killers are deemed psychologically and legally sane. So if you're just looking to find a *crazy-ass whack job*, as you so eloquently put it, you are probably going to come up empty. Think more Ted Bundy than Charles Manson—not everyone looks the stereotype."

For the next twenty minutes, Dr. Taylor gave more background on the psychology and possible motivations of the killer. The audience's jovial attitude from earlier had disappeared. Each member of the team followed with rapt attention, and asked questions to further their understanding.

"Remember that there is something personal going on in this killer's mind," she said. "Some sort of trauma has caused this break and sent him in this direction. But trauma is subjective. What may be a normal event, or a trivial problem to some, may have had a devastating impact on this person. In fact, he may not even know about this himself."

Wait a second." Finch furrowed his brow. "Are you saying he might not know what he's doing?"

"Part of him may. But consciously, he may be completely unaware. Without sounding like the twist from an M. Night Shyamalan movie, there has been a great deal of research into dissociative identity disorder—or as it used to be called, multiple personality disorder. Some doctors are quick to dismiss it, but other scholars are seeing that individuals can sometimes operate in two different states of mind. One intended for daily living, and the other as a defense to perceived threats or problems."

The room fell silent as everyone in the room looked at her.

"I came across an impressive article written by Arnon Edelstein in 2015," she said. "He is in the criminology department at Kaye College in Israel. Doctor Edelstein has cited numerous research in his article. Over and over again, there has been evidence through MRI testing which shows that some people have had different parts of their brains working when they shift from one personality to another. Edelstein also points to the Van der Hart study, which shows that the *fantasy* personality can overpower the *neutral* personality without them even knowing it. This fantasy personality will do things it sees as fixing a wrong, but the main, or neutral, personality is completely unaware these things have been done. After the fantasy personality is satisfied it has avenged something or someone, it relinquishes control back to the normal personality. This is why so many serial killers can appear normal and lucid in everyday life. As far as anyone can tell, they *are* normal—until the other, unknown personality takes control."

CHAPTER 11

A PREDATOR WAS ON THE HUNT AGAIN.

He slipped his hood on and let it rest just below his eyebrows as he dropped down from the four steps at the back door. His running shoes made little noise as he hit the street. The high, thin clouds muted the moon's best efforts of illumination. The dull yellow glow from the streetlights did little as well. He kept his head tipped down where he could still see about ten feet in front of him. With the poor lighting and the black hood, no one would be able to clearly see who he was. The few people who were out this late generally tried to avoid eye contact and confrontation. That was the way he preferred it.

It really wasn't all that late. Just a little after ten o'clock, but he was being more ambitious with this hunt. This monster lived in the suburb of Orchard Park. It would be a little over a ten-mile run just to get there. He felt he would still have enough time to take care of business and then run back in time to get other things done.

This was a first. He was pushing it. He had not run over twenty miles in a night yet. He didn't think it would be too much of an issue, though, especially since he would be able to rest his legs for an hour or so while he took care of the night's prey.

He glanced at his watch—be there by 11:30 at the latest, leave about 12:30. Even if he slowed his pace a little, he should still be able to make it between 2:00 and 2:30. He thought it should work out just right.

Running gave him focus. The rhythmic pace of his soft-soled shoes hitting the sidewalk was hypnotic. Everything else was shut out, allowing him to think of the task at hand while he approached his target. Afterward, the endorphin rush gave him a peaceful feeling of accomplishment as he traveled back.

Running in South Buffalo at night was much easier than during the day. In this part of town, most people punched a clock from 8:00 to 4:30, went home and spent some time with the family before heading to bed and starting the whole process over the next day. Traffic at night was light, and a focused killer could continue running, crossing against the lights with few stops or delays.

He traveled down South Park Avenue until he could merge on to Abbott Road. He headed south on Abbott a few more miles, until he hung a left on Lake Avenue in Blasdell, and headed to 5 Corners at Southwestern Boulevard. As he approached the multiple intersections, he dipped his head lower—too many businesses with video cameras around. He couldn't see them, but he wanted to make sure they couldn't see him either.

After he crossed over onto North Buffalo Road, there were even fewer intersections. This was an affluent suburb. People here probably thought working third shift was just an urban legend meant to scare kids into staying in school. Night was for sleeping or socializing. On a Tuesday night, few people here ventured out for any kind of activities.

As he slowed and walked up a concrete driveway, he glanced at his watch. It was 11:28. He had easily hit his goal. He gave himself an approving nod. Ten miles in about eighty-three minutes. Eight-minute miles weren't going to set any records, but considering where his times were a few months ago, he took a moment to be proud of it.

He pretended to stretch against a utility pole as he surveyed the surrounding houses. No one seemed to be around to notice him. He continued up the driveway and peered into a window. The curtains in the kitchen were open a little more than an inch. Wasn't much, but he could see clearly across the breakfast island, into the living room. On the television, Adam Benigni had the Buffalo Bills logo over his left shoulder. After a couple minutes, the gregarious anchor tossed it back to Maryalice Demler and Scott Levin. He couldn't hear it, but he could tell all three were laughing at whatever witty comment Maryalice had made. Perhaps it was the same joke he had heard her say earlier on the six o'clock version. The Channel 2 logo came up, and the image switched over to a commercial break.

He still had plenty of time to get in place. Years ago, the major networks had decided to start their late night programming at 11:35 instead of 11:30. In lieu of filling that extra time with informative news, events, and topical stories, viewers had the privilege of seeing another few minutes of car dealers screaming about how great their prices were.

After the news, there would be a few more minutes while Jimmy Fallon performed his opening monologue. After that, he would be ready. Soon the back door would open, and his opportunity would be there. He wondered if people realized just how much information they put out on the Internet. Habits are sometimes so easy to find and exploit.

Did Kelly Hallock realize just how predictable she was?

Hallock laughed and smiled at Fallon's latest parody song as she clicked the television off.

"Come on, Chilly. Wanna go out?" she said, in a high-pitched voice.

The chubby pug looked up with an air of indifference. The couch was way too comfortable, and he had little desire to go out just yet. Rolling over, he grudgingly placed his front paws out as far as he could, stretching all the way from his stubby tail to his long rolling tongue that curled out of his yawning mouth.

"Let's go, Chilly. It's time to go out. Momma needs to get some sleep."

The nurse practitioner, still in her blue scrubs, shook the leash as the black pug waddled out to the tiled kitchen floor. Hallock was tall and thin, and looked as athletic as she did twenty years ago in college.

After dropping to one knee, she hooked the leash on the collar and stepped out onto her back patio. Looking up at the overcast moon, she stretched her neck back and forth in the night air. Chilly tugged at the leash as he growled.

"Aww…looks who's a tough guy. What do you see, little buddy. Is it another squirrel." She laughed and muttered, "Anything bigger, you'd run and hide."

She continued looking into the shadows, but saw nothing. A few moments later, Chilly dropped his back leg and ambled past her, toward the door. Kelly held open the screen as she pushed the house door open. She strolled back through the door, and gasped as her body lurched forward and her head snapped back. Two arms wrapped around her waist as someone pushed her across the kitchen. With her elbows pinned at her side, she let go of the leash and raised her hands to brace herself before hitting the edge of the counter. She clasped the set of keys she had tossed there earlier. Chilly ran into the other room, jumped on the couch, and began barking.

"Hello, Miss Hallock," growled the voice behind her.

He slid his arm around her narrow waist. With her arm clamped in his elbow, he slid his forearm across her tight stomach and settled his hand around her right arm in a vise-like grip.

"Maybe you shouldn't be so happy to inject your poisons into people."

As she began to scream, he shoved a foul-smelling rag into her mouth. Hallock's muffled cries could not get through the rag being held in place. The strong hydrocarbons burned her nose as tears flowed in a futile attempt to flush away the irritating fumes.

The attacker was about her height. She could feel his chin digging on to her collar bone.

As a former gymnast, Hallock had been flexible, agile, and wiry most of her life. Weekly yoga classes had helped to maintain that.

She collapsed her elbows in front of her waist as she pivoted to the left. The move created just enough room where she was able to jerk her right arm out of his grasp. With all her might, she pulled her arm up and out as she swung her hand around, trying to reach a spot just above her left shoulder. Still holding onto her car keys, her aim was true. She could feel the jagged edge of the key rip into his flesh, and heard a startled grunt as the attacker briefly relaxed his grip.

She spit out the rag and turned to run toward the front door. She only made it three steps before a hundred eighty pounds landed on her back, driving her down onto the hardwood floor. With the wind knocked out of her, she tried to draw air back into her lungs—unable to move any closer to the door, unable to call out for help.

From behind, she heard, "I can't believe you did that. This changes things. This isn't good. No, not good at all. Now I have even more to do."

She felt the man's weight against her back as he brought his arm up around her throat. Air was finally starting to expand her lungs as a muscular bicep and forearm were constricting across her throat.

With a mixture of resignation and fear, she gasped, "Please don't hurt my do..."

Everything went dark.

He turned toward the living room strode toward the yelping pug. The dog tried to get away, but one step onto the leash halted his efforts.

He picked the dog up and stroked its head. "It's all right, little fella. You didn't do anything. But I'm going to have to put you somewhere. Can't have you waking up all the neighbors."

Kelly Hallock woke in the middle of her living room. She could feel the straps holding her in place. Her mouth was gagged. A man was standing over her, wearing a pair of knee-length shorts and a black T-shirt. Her eyes widened and grew wet with tears as she saw the craft knife in his hand. She shook her head and uttered a muffled, "Noooo!" as he stepped closer.

"I'm sure you've been keeping up with all the news lately," he said, in a low monotone voice. "You know what happened to your fellow busy *professionals* in the last couple weeks. Normally, I would never hurt a woman. But I need to stop you monsters, and I can't be biased with who I make pay. You're about to experience it yourself. But first you're going to find out why. Oh, and don't worry about your dog. I like dogs. Unlike your kind, they've never done anything to me. He is safe in the basement. He stopped barking as soon as I started petting him. He's a sweet pup, and he's cuddled up on a throw pillow I took off the couch."

The predator stepped over the terrified nurse and knelt down, holding her head between his knees.

"I give you credit. You were surprisingly harder than the others. I can't believe you did this." He brought his hand up to the gash on his left cheek. "I didn't see that coming. Literally. Let's just say, I'm glad you had a full bottle of bleach by your washer. Much better than the little one I brought with me. I'm going to have to do some extra cleaning and sterilizing tonight. Let's get busy. I'd like to spend more time explaining all this, but I'm on a tight schedule."

Thirty minutes later, Nurse Kelly had a newly carved *47* near the bottom of her sternum. He stood and walked back to the breakfast island to grab the bottle of bleach. He liked the fresh meadow scent. It smelled clean and pleasant. Reminded him of the smell in springtime at Tifft Nature Preserve when the blossoms were in full bloom.

With a shake of the head, he brought himself back into focus. He had no time for a walk down memory lane.

He went through the kitchen, starting at the back door. He needed to make sure there were no traces of his blood anywhere. After pouring a small amount of bleach into a cup, he dropped her keys in to soak. He had wiped it down, but you never know if trace amounts made entered any scratches or crevices in the metal. Attention to every little detail and scenario was even more imperative now.

He still could not believe he had messed up like that. He had to admit, she was a fighter and had briefly got the better of him. He had to make sure it never happened again.

He peeled off the shorts and t-shirt, placed them into the trash can, and poured the remaining bleach over them. After grabbing a spatula from the dish rack, he moved the clothing around in the can to make sure they were evenly coated in the fresh-smelling bleach.

He pulled his watch out of his backpack and glanced at it as he got dressed. It was just after 1:10 in the morning. He hadn't been able to spend as much time with Nurse Hallock as he'd wanted, but he was still able to get the job done. He was running behind, but not too badly. He had wanted to be in the Old First Ward by 2:30. That would be tough, but he should be all right, even though he was tired. He had run an eight-minute pace to get here. Even if he slowed to a nine-minute pace, he would be a little late, but should still be close.

After slipping out the back door and wiping the handle clean, he started his run toward Maple Drive. From there, he turned on Webster, headed back to North Buffalo Road, and headed back into the city.

With sweat stinging and irritating his cheek, he kept running. There was no endorphin rush. No peaceful feeling of accomplishment. His focus was only on the error he'd made. Sloppiness could not be tolerated. He had a mission he needed to see through to the end. He could not be derailed by mistakes. He would need to make sure it did not happen with any of the next ones.

After winding through the Old First Ward in South Buffalo, he stopped in front of a modest, but nicely landscaped, home on Mackinaw Street. This was the home of Paul Schon.

Standing back in the shadows, he glanced around. As expected, the street was silent and vacant at this time of night. He walked up the driveway, toward the back deck. After glancing around again, he picked up a flowerpot on the deck rail. He knew the key was underneath. He had used it before.

After putting the key back under the pot, he slipped off his shoes and padded through the house. He placed a hand against his cheek a couple times. The sweat stung like hell, but he had things to do and he needed to go upstairs.

Paul Schon's bedroom was the first door on the left at the top of the stairs. As usual, the door was slightly ajar. He opened it a little bit more and slipped in. There was a glass of water on the nightstand next to Paul's bed. He grabbed the glass and drank half of it. It had been a tiring night already, and he had to get things all set.

Slowly, he stripped the sweatsuit off, folded it and set it on a chair next to the closet. He needed to rest, and morning was still a few hours away. Perhaps he could relax for just a little while.

Beep...beep...beep! the alarm clock blared.

Paul rolled over and slammed his hand down to shut off the annoying squawk. He sat up, and with a groan, swung his feet onto the floor. He gave a quizzical look at the half-full glass of water.

Shaking his head, he stood with a groan and muttered, "Man, this getting old sucks. I'm beat."

He stood on shaky legs. Something didn't feel right. He was tense and anxious, his heart beating way too fast for this early in the morning. He had a knot deep in his stomach and felt nauseated, as if his body wanted to expel any remnants of last night's meatloaf.

He finished the other half of the water and then, licking his lips, shuffled to the bathroom, where he closed his eyes against the unwelcome glare of the light while emptying his bladder, and then drifted over to the sink. Once his eyes grew accustomed to the light, he looked up at the mirror.

"What the hell…" Paul reached up to touch the gash on his left cheek.

CHAPTER 12

"SHIT, I HATE EARLY CALLS AND INTERDEPARTmental bullshit first thing in the morning," Richardson growled at Wayne, as they pulled up to Kelly Hallock's home in Orchard Park. "Just look at all these friggin' cars. I don't want to deal with some big pissing match over this."

"Me either. Just look this crap. OP police, Erie County Sheriffs. And for good measure, it looks like we have a few state troopers here, too. So why would you think there's gonna be a pissing match?" Wayne laughed.

"I hope not. I'm not here to step on anybody's toes." Richardson as he took the last swig of coffee from his brown cardboard cup. "Hey, there's Tommy. Let's talk to him first before we go in."

Tom Carter had been an Erie County deputy for more than twenty years. Richardson and Wayne had met him several times over the years, at various law functions. He had also been in some of the same bowling leagues as they had, and would sometimes join them for karaoke nights. He was always a straight shooter, and never seemed the territorial type.

"Hi, Tommy." Richardson shook the stocky deputy's hand. "This is some crazy shit, ain't it?"

"Hey, Rhody. Hey, Jon. Sure is." Carter smiled. "Man, am I glad to see you two here for this."

"Really?" Richardson returned the smile. "That makes one of us. Just unbelievable, isn't it? Glad to see you're here, though. Who's in charge of the scene?"

"Um, that would be you guys." The deputy gave a puzzled look.

"What do you mean," Richardson aid.

"Didn't you hear? It came all the way from the top this morning. And I mean way up at the top. We're talking the governor's office. This case has some big-time juice behind it. The governor himself, the sheriff, the troopers, the mayors of Buffalo and Orchard Park have all been tele-meeting this morning. All the major players have agreed—you two are running point on this one, and we're supposed to handle all support roles. You have full access to everything—all the databases, all the labs. Damnedest thing I ever saw. Everyone was quick to accept it and offer their help. This is big."

"Yeah, it is," Wayne said. "But I think we all know why they're stepping aside."

Carter nodded and shrugged.

"Yup," Richardson said. "They all want to show how hard they're trying. Looks great in the press. But if anything goes south or it gets worse, they point the finger at us and say we were the ones at fault. If it goes well, they come out rosy. If it goes bad, we are the ones who look like shit. Oh, well. Not gonna look a gift horse in the mouth. I wanna catch this piece of shit. Whatever works. I'm glad to get any extra help we can."

The two detectives walked in with Carter. The deputy introduced them to the other people bustling around inside. Kelly Hallock's body lay in the center of the living room floor. Her blue scrub top was cut halfway up and folded back, and a number 47 was carved into her abdomen just below the center clasp of her bra. Yellow plastic tents with numbers on them were placed around the body as a photographer made moved around, snapping shots from every angle.

Richardson inhaled deeply and then squinted against the fumes.

"Hey, everybody," he said. "I appreciate your efforts here, but please don't clean anything up until we go through everything. Tom, I'd really like to get Jeff McDonald and his forensic guys in here. They're on the way." He turned around. "Has anything been moved? This place smells entirely too sterile. Whatever your guys are using is strong as hell. What is it?"

"Not us, Rhod," Carter said. "These guys know what they're doing. They wouldn't have tampered with anything. We're thinking your guy did a little clean up duty while he was here. There's an empty bottle of bleach in the kitchen. He went through and wiped everything down. Not only that, but he dumped a bunch of it in the trash can over there, on some clothes. The smell is overwhelming, but you'll get used to it in a few minutes."

"Great. Sorry about jumping to conclusions." Richardson walked over to the body. "Can you tell us everything you've got so far, Tom? I see she's wearing scrubs. Was she a doctor, too?"

"No, she wasn't." Carter flipped open his notebook. "Kelly Hallock, forty-two. Nurse practitioner at AllNewU med spa here in OP. It's one of those medical day spa places where ladies can go for all kinds of spa treatments, including facial goop, nutrition advice and exercise clinics, therapeutic massage—all the crap my wife tells me she wants to do. They also do some medical stuff, too, like laser surgery for scars, wrinkle treatments like Botox, tattoo removals, and a whole bunch of other things."

"Tell me about the scene here," Richardson said. "Who called it in?"

"Next door neighbor. Said something didn't seem right. She always brings her dog out at the same time as he does every morning. Her car was in the drive, but he could hear the dog's muffled barks for quite a while. The dog was shut down in the basement. We think your boy did that, too. Anyway, he called, and the local PD sent a car around. When no one answered, they looked in through that front window there, and they could see her on the floor. Front door was deadbolted and chained from the inside. Looks like the perp may have come in through the back door."

"Any sign of forced entry?"

"No. None at all. But if he'd been stalking her, he might have been watching. Neighbor said she was like clockwork. She'd watch the news, watch some of the Tonight Show, take the dog out back to do his business, and then go to bed. He said she did that same thing pretty much every night."

"Well, that goes along with what we've been thinking. I don't think it's random. He knows who his victims are. He is choosing them for some reason. He would've left a poem, too. You guys find anything?"

"Sure did," Carter said. "It's there in the middle of the dining room table."

Richardson and Wayne walked over to the table. In the center was a sheet of white copy paper with the same block lettering.

An unknowing host with a broken heart.
A life of love lost from the start.
Five monsters dead, with five to go.
Ten years gone with nothing to show.

—Levon Moore

"Damn it," Richardson said. "Another name to add to our list. Who the hell is Levon Moore—or any of these people he's referring to?"

The door opened again as Jeff McDonald and his team poured into the room and opened their forensic suitcases. Richardson and Wayne spoke with the team and shared the information they'd received from Carter. They also introduced them to their new partners from the other agencies. McDonald's team finished setting up their equipment and started processing the evidence.

"Hey, Rhody. Come over here," McDonald called, a short time later. "I think we have something a little different here."

"What's up, Jeff."

Wayne followed closely.

"There already seems to be plenty different with this one," McDonald said. "She's a woman, her shirt is only cut halfway up, and the numbers are lower down and quite a bit smaller than the others."

"What else did you find?" Richardson said.

"I found a few fibers around her torso." McDonald held up his hand, and in a pair of tweezers appeared to be a small black thread. "You can also see a few of these around her face and next to her head. We didn't have a single thing like this at the other crime scenes."

"Her dog is black," Wayne said. "Could it possibly be dog hair."

"Not unless she has a polyester dog." McDonald gave an apologetic look. "Sorry. Not trying to be a smart-ass. But no. Up close, you can tell it's from some type of clothing."

"Well, then I wouldn't be surprised if it came from the shorts and T-shirt in the garbage can," said Deputy Carter, who was standing about five feet away.

"What do you mean," Richardson said.

"Remember I said he dumped a bunch of the bleach into the trash can? One of the state boys took a look at it. There was a pair of shorts and a T-shirt soaked in bleach. They're mostly white and gray now, but it looks like they were probably black at one point. We left them in there for your team."

"This is getting weird," McDonald said. "I know for sure there was nothing like this at the other four scenes. Why change things up now?"

"You gotta be shittin' me. He's a shy boy." Richardson spun around and yanked his smartphone off his belt.

He walked back over to Harrison's lifeless body. After scrolling through his phone, he found a name on his contact list and hit send.

"Hello, Doctor Taylor. It's Rhody Richardson. I really need you to come out to Orchard Park. Yeah. We have another victim. And if I'm right, we're going to need your expertise on this one."

CHAPTER 13

"I have to give Detective Richardson a lot of credit on this one," Dr. Taylor said, into a speaker phone. "His observations will take us into a new direction on the killer's psyche. With this new direction, it may help us narrow down or eliminate some potential suspects."

In the station meeting room late that afternoon, Taylor, the two detectives, Finch, McDonald, Dr. Matthews, Captain Reynolds, Alyssa Joseph, and Connor Patrick were seated around a rectangular table. Joseph was taking notes. Dr. Taylor and Richardson sat across from one another, with the phone in between them.

"This is Don from the governor's office," an over-modulated voice boomed from the speaker. "Do we have any suspects or leads yet?"

"No, Don." Finch cleared his throat. "But you both said you wanted to be kept up to date with any developments. We have another task force meeting scheduled for first thing tomorrow morning, and we wanted to give you a heads up on what we're working on."

"Detective Richardson, this is Dante from the mayor's office. What exactly did you discover?"

"Well, I didn't really *discover* anything. It's more of an educated guess on what this guy does, and maybe some of the psychological issues he might have." Richardson drank from a bottle of water. "We now believe he kills most of his victims in the nude. But based on our latest victim, I also think he has issues with women."

"Why is that," an unidentified voice said.

"The big clue for me was the polyester threads that Jeff found on the one from this morning. There weren't any at the other four scenes. That got me thinking that if there were no threads, there were probably no clothes. He may have killed the first four while he was naked. This guy is too precise—I could see if he missed one thread, but this one had several threads visible around her head. We know that he toys with his victims for a while before he finally kills them. They were alive as he tortured them. They could see what was happening. I don't think he wanted a woman to see him in the nude."

"Maybe a little self-conscious about the size of his parts?" Don said.

Richardson rolled his eyes as he pictured the governor's smug little political appointee sitting there with a smirk on his face.

"I have no idea, but I don't really think so," Richardson said, in an irritated tone. "He also wore a t-shirt. Who knows—maybe he had an over-bearing mama like Norman Bates. Maybe she told him he was a dirty boy if a girl saw his body. Don't know why he also made sure he wore a shirt. That's more Dr. Taylor's area. But I think his issues also extended to the victim herself. She was handled different, and the one big difference between her and the other vics is that she was a woman."

"As I said, I think Rhody is right." Dr. Taylor leaned in toward the phone. "He also made some other poignant observations which support his theory. Miss Hallock had the same cuts around her eyes and mouth, and the same slashing of the throat that killed her. I'm sure Doctor Matthews's autopsy will also confirm that the numbers cut into her were done postmortem, just like the other victims."

"So what would the difference be," said the mayor's rep.

"All the male victims were the same, Dante,'" said Richardson. "Their shirt was either unbuttoned or sliced open to about an inch from the collar. The numbers were around five or six inches tall, and a little more than three inches wide. Except for Hill, who only had one number, the cuts went across the entire chest, from nipple to nipple. Not this one, though. Miss Hallock's shirt was cut only halfway up. And here's what was interesting to me—her bra was never moved. He left it in place and cut the number forty-seven into her just below the center clasp, with much smaller numbers. It seems to me that, even in death, he couldn't bring himself to touch a woman's parts."

"You think he might be gay?" said the governor's aide. "You said you thought he liked to get nude with the men he killed."

"Ugghh." Dr. Taylor sighed, with a look of disgust.

Richardson boomed, "I can't believe that in this day and age, you would say something so friggin' stupid. What the hell is wrong with you?"

"Richardson, ease up," said Lieutenant Finch.

"Why the hell should I?" the detective growled. "I don't give a shit what this political kiss-ass thinks." He turned to the phone. "Did you even look at the file? Or do you think you're too damn important for that?"

"You're right, Detective. I'm sorry. That was a stupid comment, and way out of line. Sorry I said it. Wasn't really thinking straight, I guess. I will leave the observations and assumptions to you from now on. And yes, I have read the file several times."

"Then you know there has been zero evidence that there was anything sexual about any of this. This guy is smart and seems pretty well-educated on our forensics. And let's be clear. At no point did I ever say he *liked* to get nude with the men. I only said he *did*. I think he does things in the nude to hide any blood evidence, and it looks like one of Jeff's team members may have been able to prove it."

"Hello, gentlemen. This is Jeff McDonald. I'm the lead forensic investigator. I am here with Connor Patrick, a newer member of our team. We think he may have found out a little more about how the killer does things. And it seems to back up what Rhody was thinking."

"What is it?"

"Detective Richardson invited Doctor Taylor to the scene this morning," said McDonald, "and was going over his thoughts on the motives and reasons of the killings. After that, Connor decided to go upstairs again, although we had found no evidence that the killer had been up there at all. Bed was made, everything was still in place. Perhaps the killer didn't want to be in a woman's bedroom. Doctor Taylor is exploring that angle from a psychological side. Anyway, Connor went into the bathroom and did a swab test in the shower. Although most of it was destroyed by a bleach solution, he was still able to find a small amount of blood hidden deep down in the drain. After showing me what he found, he and I drove back to Doctor Harrison's house, and then to the Lenox. Both scenes are still secured. In addition to being a math whiz and a science guy, it turns out Mister Patrick is a pretty good amateur plumber, too. He was able to take apart some of the drain pipes and bring them in for further examination. They both have blood evidence in them. We still have some testing to do, but we're fairly certain that it is the victim's blood."

Captain Reynolds said, "So what do you think this means, Jeff?"

"Like Kaileen, I think Rhody is right. This guy is killing them in the nude as a means of concealing blood evidence. DNA means so much these days. Once he's finished, he takes the time to wash himself off and let the blood evidence wash down the drain. With the latest victim, we think he didn't want to be naked with a woman and had to take the extra step to soak his clothes in bleach to destroy any evidence."

"We also believe that none of this is random," said Lieutenant Finch said. "He knows who he's going after."

"Why is that," said a voice from the speaker phone.

"He needs privacy," Richardson said. "All the victims had some sort of tie to the medical community, and there were no collateral victims. He was able to kill and then clean up without disturbing anyone else. He knows when they're alone. He makes sure he has a place to take his time, torture them, and then wash himself clean. This guy is precise in everything he does. Random doesn't seem to fit his style."

"Rhody, this is Dante again. How could he know all this stuff?"

"I think he does his homework. The first two doctors were at work in their building late at night. Apparently, it was common knowledge when they kept late hours and stayed afterward. They both had blog sites where they talked about what they were working on. From what we've found, Doctor Harrison was on a couple dating sites and mentioned that he lived alone. Isn't too hard to find addresses on the Net these days. For the other two, I think social media had a big hand with things as well. Hill, the salesman, had a Twitter account and a blog site for Pharmer-Grown. He would give updates on his travels—where he was, and the doctors he was meeting with. Like Hill, Miss Hallock is—or rather, was—another one of those people who feels it necessary to share every little detail of her life. At least a dozen times in the last two months, she has had Facebook posts where she mentioned that Jimmy Fallon was done with his opening, and that it was time to let her dog out and then go to bed. Pretty easy pickings for a psycho to know when her back door would be open."

"Damn, you can bet I'll be talking to my wife and daughter as soon as I get home," Don said. "Thank you everyone for your time this afternoon. Again, my apologies for speaking out of place. I am very sorry about that. Please let me know if I, or the governor, can do anything to assist."

"That goes for me and the mayor as well," Dante said, and both parties dropped off the line.

"Anyone have anything else to add?" The captain looked around the table. "And Rhody, I understand and agree with your feelings. But remember, it's not what you say, it's how you say it. Try to use a little more discretion with your comments. Yes, he may be a political kiss-ass, but he is a direct line to the governor, and we don't need to piss off a possible resource."

"Sure thing, boss. I'll do my best, but I have severe allergies to stupid people. Causes me to lash out with Tourette-like symptoms."

Richardson smirked as the captain shook his head, smiling, and walked out the door.

He then turned across the table. "Hey, Connor. I meant to ask you before, but the other day during the first meeting, you started to speak up, but then people were talking over you. What were you going to say?"

"Yeah, man," said Wayne . "Around here, you have to stand your ground if you want to be heard. You gotta speak up sometimes and force the issue."

"I'll try. But I'm just the lowly intern that some of these guys really don't want to hear from."

"Well too damn bad for them," McDonald said. "I should've come back to hear what you had to say. That's on me. What was it?"

"Well, Rhody and Jon seem pretty sure this isn't random, and that he is selecting them for a reason. So I guess I'm just trying to find a reason. It may not really be anything, but I noticed it when Alyssa wrote their names on the board. I thought it was interesting that both of the first two victims' last names started with a C, and the next two started with an H. Now today we have a third person, and her name started with an H, too. It might be a coincidence, but I just thought it was worth mentioning."

"Hmm…I didn't notice that." McDonald looked back at the board. "I'll be sure to bring it up at our meeting tomorrow.

"Unfortunately, it looks like I'm going to have to make room for another name on the board." Joseph closed her notebook.

She and most of the others got up to leave. Richardson and Wayne walked over to the sink in the back of the room and rinsed out their coffee cups. Patrick stayed in his seat, staring at the whiteboard with the names and numbers of the first four victims written across the top.

"C'mon, kid," Wayne said. "Time to head out. Don't let this job eat you up. You're too young, and you've got enough going on."

"Yeah, you're probably right. Otherwise, I'm going to start looking like you two pretty soon." Patrick wore a shy grin, and laughed.

"I hope you do, kid, Richardson said. "I've had a pretty damn good life. Been a lot of fun." He touched an index finger to the crow's feet near his temple. "Maybe someday you'll be lucky enough to have a million laughs and smiles permanently etched into your face."

CHAPTER 14

"Hello, Paul. Come on in."

He walked through the door and turned to face Dr. Taylor.

"Oh, my!" She stared at his bandaged cheek.

The beige square had a dark patch that had soaked through.

"What in the world happened to you?"

"Well, to be honest, I really don't know. Woke up like this. Surprised me, too. I must've raked my face with my nails or something while I was sleeping."

"I'm sorry to hear that. Did you have someone look at it?"

"No, it's all right. A little antibiotic ointment and a bandage, and I'll be fine in a couple days."

"Okay, but please keep an eye on it. You're going to want make sure it doesn't get infected."

"Really, Kaileen?" He chuckled. "Like I should be so lucky. I am the poster child for knowing exactly how bad an infection can get and what it can do."

The psychiatrist blushed. "I am so sorry, Paul. That was a poor choice of words. I should have been more mindful. Please have a seat, and let's talk."

Paul took a seat on his usual side of the large couch. He sank back into the deep brown cushion and let out a long sigh. He had both a look of frustration and exhaustion as he stared at the shaded window. Dr. Taylor noticed that his left ring finger, with his wedding band, was fluttering.

"You look pretty tired today, Paul. Did you get much sleep?"

"I don't know. Thought I did. But going by the gash on my face, I'm pretty sure it was another restless night. I woke up tired and drained. I know I had another one of those nightmares again."

"Do you remember what it was about?"

"Not really. I just remember lots of blood…knives, a dog, crying, and just an overall bad vibe. Remember last week when I told you I had a bad dream, but woke up refreshed and felt kinda focused?"

She nodded.

"Not this morning. Not at all. I woke up in a bad mood, and felt beat up. I was nervous and out of sorts, my heart going a million miles an hour. I couldn't even eat any breakfast. My stomach was just too upset."

"This might be part of your healing process, Paul," she said, in her soothing tone. "As we've talked about, there have been a lot of things you haven't successfully dealt with since Sheila's death. These violent images in your dreams may be the manifestation of the anger you have. Feelings are coming to the surface. I think your subconscious is coming to terms with your loss, and it is something painful and personal. You may be making real progress here, Paul. Some days you will feel refreshed. Others you may feel anxious. It is all part of your healing. Your mind is telling you it's ready to start dealing with some of this a little more."

"Maybe. But it's unnerving, and still hurts like hell."

Kaileen looked up from her notebook. "Have you opened the envelope yet?"

"No. Right now it's hard enough to focus on how she lived. I don't want to read about how she died."

After Sheila had lightly squeezed his hand, she slipped into the next world. The doctors had said it was an involuntary contraction, but he knew better. She had given him one last *I love you* before she left him. In a numbed haze, he'd signed the autopsy request and investigative inquiry. The doctors wanted to pinpoint the cause of the infection that took his angel from him.

A couple months later, his letter carrier left him a peach PS 3849 form to let him know she had a large certified envelope he needed to sign for. He had no desire to go to the post office, and he was in no hurry to see it. He signed the back of the form and authorized the carrier to sign the green return form for him. He put it back in his narrow mailbox and flipped the flag up. Two days later, he saw the thick red, white, and blue priority envelope sitting behind his screen door. His letter carrier was a conscientious woman and always made sure his deliveries arrived in pristine condition. He wished she had dragged this one through the mud and let a Rottweiler tear it to shreds.

With a heavy sigh, he set it on the desk near the front window—the desk where his sweet Sheila would write love notes to him. The envelope sat there, untouched, for half a year. A little over three months ago, on her birthday, he decided to break the seal on the autopsy report. Part of him needed to know. Most of him didn't. What difference would it make? She was still gone, and he would never hold her soft skin against his again.

Inside, he found a thick yellow envelope. It looked similar to an interdepartmental office envelope. At the top were two maroon paper buttons with a white string wrapped between them to keep the flap closed. As Paul grabbed at the thin string, he drew a deep breath. The small part of him that needed to know conceded to the majority, which did not.

With shaky hands, he placed the manila envelope back inside the desk drawer, dropping it on top of an array of paperclips and pens. He slowly closed the top drawer and sat in her chair to cry.

"It's still sitting in the same place since her birthday. She would be thirty-two now. I just don't have it in me to read through it just yet, Doc."

"I know. But I think it may hel—"

"Oh, my God, I just miss her so much." Tears streamed down his face. "I'm sorry, Kaileen, but it hurts so damn much. Every damn day. I try to focus on all the good times, but sometimes that makes it even worse. Makes me realize just how much I've lost."

He slammed his fists onto his thighs over and over again. He hoped the physical pain would lessen the emotional pain and rage that tortured him. But as usual, it didn't.

"Paul, please. This is hard, but remember, Sheila wanted you to go on living. Sheila wanted you to do well. Sheila loved you."

Hearing her name had the desired effect. Paul gathered himself, took several deep breaths, and then reclined against the back of the couch.

"I'm sorry. I know better than that. You're right—she was always more worried about me than herself. God, I love her." He sniffled as he forced a small smile. "She was always focused on taking care of me. One time, I hurt my back doing some gardening. Right away, she booked us for a couple's massage at this spa she liked to go to in Orchard Park. It was so nice we made it a regular thing. She was wonderful right from the start. Did I ever mention to you that she was a couple years older than I am?"

The doctor shook her head.

"Yeah, she was. She took a couple years off after high school and worked for AmeriCorps down in the Appalachians. She was such a good person. Always cared about others. We both graduated from Buff State the same year, but that's why she was older. It always seemed to bug her, and I'd joke with her that she was my hot cougar." He looked up at Dr. Taylor, with a smile. "She kept saying she was worried I'd trade her in when she became a wrinkled old hag. Oh, my god, that is too funny! As if I would ever want anyone else. The thought of even touching any other woman intimately is something I find repulsive. I could never be with another woman."

Paul was fighting back tears and laughter as he continued to take his mind back to a wonderful memory.

"After she turned thirty, she was freaking out." He giggled uncontrollably. "Against my wishes, she wanted to get those shots to get rid of wrinkles. I don't know why. I never noticed any, but lord knows she thought she could. Anyway, she went to a place, and whoever did it messed up and blew through some veins or something. She would never tell me who did it to her, but it was just ridiculous." He wiped tears off his cheek. "She had these black eyes that made her look like she'd gotten beat up. I kept calling her Ricky Raccoon. She got so mad at me, but it was just hysterical. Aah, it was too funny." He sighed deeply and wiped his eyes once more. "She didn't need anything. She was perfect just as she was. She was always the most beautiful woman I'd ever laid eyes on."

"That is a very funny and sweet story, Paul, but I still think it would be good for you to finally face the report and read through it. It could bring you a sense of closure."

"I doubt it. The only closure I'll ever have is when they drop the lid on my casket."

CHAPTER 15

ALYSSA JOSEPH WALKED INTO THE MEETING ROOM first thing Thursday morning. She held several folders containing notes from all the crime scenes. As she set them down on the table, a new box of bright-colored dry erase markers slid off.

"Well, good morning Connor." She looked confused. "I'm usually the first person here. Surprised to see someone else here so soon."

"Good morning, Alyssa. Guess I just wanted to look at the board without any distractions. The numbers are really bugging me. The detectives are sure they're a message. I can usually pick patterns out pretty easy, but this one has me stumped."

"Wait a sec. You were in here when I left yesterday afternoon. Please don't tell me you've been sitting here all night."

"No, not at all." Patrick tugged on his collar. "See, clean shirt. Fresh as a daisy. I just woke up early. All this stuff keeps swirling around in my brain, so I figured I'd just come in early."

"Okay there, boy genius. But with all due respect to your brain and your serious skills with numbers, I'm going to have to erase this board for now. I need to make some room to add our latest info."

"Of course. Please go ahead."

He sat back and watched as she erased the board and then opened the files to get the information she needed. The different scenes played through his mind as he recalled as much of what he'd heard, as well as what he'd seen.

His high school wrestling coach had constantly reminded the team of the importance of listening. *"That's why you have twice as many ears as you do a mouth."*

All these years later, Patrick still lived by those words.

Joseph was writing across the top of the board in her same pronounced style. The huge first letter was followed by the rest of the name, and then the large number was placed at the end. Charles 67, Coleman 60…

Patrick stared at the names. He furled his brow and squinted as he thought back on the images. Then, with a grin and a shake of his head, he leaned back and relaxed his face. The detectives were right. He needed to relax, or—as Wayne had said—this job would eat him up. He could hear Richardson's voice echoing in his head. *"Maybe someday you'll be lucky enough to have a million laughs and smiles permanently etched into your face."*

He looked up at the white board again.

Harrison 10, Hill 4…

In his mind, letters began to fade, gaps started to shorten.

"…a million laughs and smiles permanently etched into your face."

The picture in his mind was becoming clearer. Could it be?

Hallock 47.

"*...permanently etched into your face.*"

"Oh, my God! That has to be it." Patrick jumped up and ran toward the door. "I'll be back, Alyssa. I gotta call Rhody."

"Um...okay," she said to an empty room, as she turned and saw the back of the running intern shove open a door in the hallway.

After dropping down two flights of stairs, four to five steps at a time, Patrick ran toward the CSI lab. He logged onto a computer, pulled up Google and did a quick search. He knew he was right, but he wanted to see the confirmation.

"Hello, Rhody? This is Connor. I think I found something."

For the next few minutes, Patrick laid out his thoughts and conclusions to the detective.

"Wow! That is something else, kid," said Richardson. "Jon, Jeff, and I are on the way, but we're probably going to be a few minutes late for the meeting. We went back to the hotel this morning. The lieutenant knows about it. He'll be running the show until we get there. I want you to get the whole team up to speed with what you found."

"I'll try. But maybe we should wait. They don't exactly listen to me."

"C'mon, kid. Grow a pair. You can't let people push you around." Richardson exhaled. "Look, we've all been there. I understand. We shouldn't be too late. If they're giving you a hard time, I'll handle it."

Patrick grabbed a sheet of paper off the printer and strode back up to the meeting room. As he climbed the stairs, he rehearsed how he would present it. He knew he was right, and he knew he would have to show the others what he found.

As the hinge on the door moaned, several members of the task force, glanced up at Patrick. After seeing it was just the intern, they turned back to their conversations. He headed toward the front of the room, where Lieutenant Finch was speaking with Joseph as she finished writing out a few details.

"Good morning, Connor," said Finch. "I just got off the phone with Rhody. He wants you to start things out this morning. Says you had some sort of an epiphany. Looking forward to hearing it. It's all yours. Get them together."

As his stomach churned, Patrick swallowed hard. "Okay, everyone. Please take your seats. I have some things I'd like to share with you."

A voice called out, "Like what? You've been playing Blue's Clues, and you found a paw print?"

Laughter ran through the rest of the room as they turned back to one another.

"Yeah, that's cute. Used to love that show as a kid. Please, though. I'd like to share a few things I found with you."

Another voice said, "Just because you caught all the Pokémon on your iPhone doesn't mean you're a detective now."

More snorts of laughter echoed through the room.

Bill Finch started to step forward, but stopped as a window-rattling voice boomed.

"God damnit! Sit your asses down and listen up!"

A roomful of people turned and looked as Connor Patrick glared back at them, his jawline set, his dark steely eyes piercing. He no longer looked like the carefree kid who would shrug off a joke or a backhanded comment.

They began moving to the tables.

"Look, I am tired of this. If you want to make fun of me later, it's fine. Go ahead. I really don't give a damn. But you can at least listen to me for a few minutes. I deserve that. Some of you like to make fun of me because I'm good with numbers. Maybe you didn't do so well at math, but yeah, I did. And now we have five people dead, with numbers on them. Five people gone, and maybe another five to go. So just maybe it might be worth listening to the *numbers guy* for a moment, because I think I have an idea on how he selects his victims."

As they continued to sit, a derisive snort was heard.

"Yeah, right."

"What's that, Randy?" Patrick said. "I haven't heard you offer a single thing to this case yet. You like to just sit there on your high horse and mock others. Tell you what, if Tim Horton's is missing a few buckets of doughnut filling, I'll call you, because that's your area of expertise. But right now you can listen to me, because science and numbers are *my* thing."

Nervous laughter ran through the room as they all looked at the red-faced officer. Randy Shea was not blushing. The veins throbbing in his neck and temples indicated that his blood pressure was through the roof. The muscles on the thick, tattooed forearms of the former Navy man rippled as he clenched his fists. He glared back with an intensity that would've frightened many men.

But not Patrick. Not then.

Joseph dipped her head down as her shaking shoulders gave evidence of her laughter. Patrick continued scanning the room until he looked at the back door. McDonald, Richardson, and Wayne were all standing there. Richardson closed his eyes and gave an approving nod. The corners of McDonald's mouth formed a small smile as Wayne offered a thumbs-up.

"All right, then. Can we get busy now?" Patrick said, in an even tone. "We know that all five of the victims are somehow tied into the medical profession. That's a broad field, though. If we look at it from a different angle, we can see that they are all in the medical *beauty* business. The first two were in a plastic surgery center. Those one's are obviously about beauty. Doctor Harrison ran a dermatology center. Again, dealing with skin and some beauty issues. Mister Hill at the hotel was a drug rep. Along with other things we found in his trunk, he deals with Botox, Dysport, and Xeomin. Those are all beauty products used for removing or reducing wrinkles. The nurse from yesterday worked at a medical spa where they do a bunch of out-patient things— again, procedures dealing with beauty." He turned and walked up to the board. "Alyssa, I'm sorry, but would it be all right if I erase some of this?

"Sure. I have it all on handouts they're going to get."

Patrick erased the bullet points. "I don't know if I would have even noticed this if it weren't for the way Alyssa writes those huge letters at the beginning of the name. That, coupled with something Detective Richardson said, got me thinking about what the killer is trying to tell us.

Leaving the first letters, Patrick erased the rest of the names across the top of the board.

C 67, C 60, H 10, H 4, H 47

"Okay, I know that doesn't look like much, but let's bring them together," He wrote below them.

C67C60 H10H4H47

Lieutenant Finch's eyebrows were drawn together so they almost touched as he tried to see where this was all going. He started stepping forward.

"Just bear with me." Patrick held a hand up. "Let's get rid of the repeating letters."

C6760H10447

"Look, I know I'm a science nerd and a numbers geek. I see things, especially numbers, differently than a lot of people. But I knew I had seen that combination somewhere before. Somewhere in one of my medical books."

The other task force members looked around at each other to see if anyone else had a clue. The confused looks throughout the room let them know they were not alone in their ignorance.

Finch said, "I don't get it yet. I'm not seeing anything there, and you said you think you know how he is selecting them."

"Yes, I do. His next victim's last name will start with the letter N, and he, or she, will probably have a seventeen marked into them."

A murmur went through the room as they looked around at each other again.

"Okay, I'll bite," Finch said. "How do you know that?"

Patrick turned back, and after briefly looking at his sheet of paper, continued writing across the board.

$$C_{6760}H_{10447}N_{1743}O_{2010}S_{32}$$

"Ladies and gentlemen," he turned back with a confident smile, "I would like to introduce you to the chemical formula for botulinum toxin type A. You probably know it by its commercial name—Botox."

CHAPTER 16

THE NEXT MORNING, RICHARDSON AND WAYNE WERE pouring through notes. With the new focus, the task force had been busy reaching out to area spas, clinics, hospitals, and doctors' offices. Any threats or issues were documented, as well as any malpractice allegations or lawsuits. While a few doctors were not inclined to divulge such problems, most offices were glad to assist if it meant they might be able to sleep a little easier once the killer was caught.

"Hey, guys," said a bright voice.

"Hey!" Richardson said. "There's that bad-ass kid who put a room full of tough guys in their place. What's going on, Connor."

"Like I said yesterday, my young amigo," Wayne said, "that was perfect. Good to see you lay it down like that."

"Well, I still feel like I stepped too far over the line. That's not really my style, but I was getting so aggravated when they wouldn't listen."

"I have to admit, part of that falls on me." Richardson laughed. "When I called Bill, I asked him to leave you hanging out there just to see how you would handle it. Gotta say, kid…you really caught a lot of people's attention. And for the better. Don't worry about stepping on any toes. They're big boys and girls. They'll be fine with it. From what I hear, you impressed a lot of them."

"Thanks, I guess. But I still didn't like doing it. What are you guys working on this morning?"

"Same damn thing we were doing yesterday afternoon," Wayne said.

"Doing the shitty work," said Richardson. "All the crap they don't show on the TV shows. I don't think my ass has moved from this chair. Boring shit—going over statements and reading about lawsuits. Now on top of everything else, a couple of the medical offices have announced they're putting up a twenty-five-thousand-dollar reward for information leading to the arrest and conviction of this asshole."

"Yup." Wayne flipped through a stack of papers. "Now every idiot with a grudge against his neighbor is calling in with bullshit information. It's all a big ass waste of time."

"I'm glad nothing was released about the jogger yet," Richardson said. "We want to keep that in-house for now. Otherwise, we will get calls from anyone and everyone who sees someone running down the street."

"Doesn't sound fun," Connor said. "Rhody, can I ask you a question?"

"You just did."

"Huh? Oh, yeah. I get it. Funny." Patrick smiled. "I was wondering about your Glock nine millimeter. I have my pistol permit, and I've been looking at getting something a little better than the twenty-two I have on it now. I see you still carry the Glock seventeen."

"You've got a good eye, kid. Sure is. What do you want to know about it?"

"Well, the seventeen is an older model, and I was wondering why you don't use the newer model thirty-seven, like the troopers use. It's a forty-five caliber."

"Because he's an old fart and is set in his ways." Wayne laughed. "The state boys stopped even replacing those seventeens back in 2007. Now, if they need a new one, they get the thirty-seven whether they want it or not."

Richardson pulled the black gun from his holster and set it on the desk.

"You never have to replace it if you take care of it. I use it because this is the gun I like. I'm comfortable with it. I know it, and it knows me. We seem to work pretty well together. The forty-five cal is quite a bit bigger, too. You can only fit ten rounds in the magazine. With this one, I can put seventeen rounds per mag. I like the idea of having those extra shots available if I ever need it."

"Yeah, I know the forty-five is bigger," Patrick said, "but isn't that part of the point? Doesn't it have more stopping power? I read how it is more powerful and creates a bigger cavity in the body."

"Hmmm...a bigger cavity in the body, huh? I guess that's true. But I want you to think about something an old prostitute once said."

"What did she say?"

In unison, Richardson and Wayne said, "It ain't the size of the hole, it's where you put it!" They laughed and high-fived each other.

Patrick blushed and began laughing as well.

"Look, kid, just don't be cheap and buy a piece of shit," Richardson said. "Power is nice, but let's face it—it's not like you are ever going to be shooting a pistol at something one hundred fifty yards away. Look for something that is good and accurate for your shooting style. Get something you can depend on, and make sure you take good care of it. It's not like buying a pair of sneakers that eventually wear out. If you get a decent gun and take care of it like you're supposed to, you'll have it for a lifetime. Hell, at home, I still have some of the same shotguns my grandfather used to hunt with when he was a kid."

"Thanks. Good advice. What are you guys going to do now? More sifting through papers?"

"No," Richardson said. "I gotta get out of here and breathe some air that hasn't been through these other cops lungs a few hundred times." He stood and stretched his arms and neck. "Jon and I are going to start tackling this from a different angle. We'll keep asking about lawsuits and disgruntled patients, but honestly, you'll find that CEOs and lawyers won't tell you jack-shit. They like to act like everything is all rosy and their turds don't stink. We're going to go out and visit some offices and the crime scenes again. We'll show some of the stills around, see if any of the real workers recognize anything. Maybe we'll get lucky."

Wayne said, "In a perfect world, we'd have this wrapped up in a couple hours."

"Yeah, but in a perfect world," Richardson said, "George Strait would never have retired, and he'd still be putting out CDs and going on tour every year."

Wayne nodded as he followed him out the door. "I hear that, brother. I hear that."

CHAPTER 17

THE TWO DETECTIVES WALKED OUT AND CLIMBED into the department-issued black sedan. They had decided to visit the four crime scenes again, in reverse order. Before heading to AllNewU, they stopped for lunch and grabbed some suicide wings at Duff's in Orchard Park.

A half-hour later, Wayne looked across the platter of bones.

"Guess we should get heading out. I'm gonna hit the little cowboy's room before we go."

As he headed to the restroom, Richardson pulled out a credit card and placed it in the server's folder. She walked past, grabbed it, and let him know she would be right back with it.

Hearing a gasp, Richardson looked up. The waitress stood frozen at the register. A gaunt-looking man had a knife in his hand. He held it down low, but his intent was clear.

"I said open the register, bitch." He grabbed her arm. "Just do it."

Richardson covered his phone laying on the table. He tapped it a few times and stood. With his hands out in front, he took one step toward the register.

"Hey, do we have a problem here?"

"Shut up, asshole. You trying to be some sort of hero?"

"Nope, not at all. Just a cop trying to do his job. I know we're in Orchard Park, but I'm Detective Richardson from Buffalo."

The man yanked the waitress in front of him. "I don't give a shit who you are! Just sit your ass down, or I will cut her up. I just want the money. Leave me alone, and we ain't got a problem."

"Now I don't quite see it that way. I do think we have us a bit of a problem," Richardson said, in a sing-song sarcastic tone. "Here we are in OP, enjoying a little lunch at Duff's, and you're holding a knife to my waitress. You see, I am a cop. I even have the gun and badge right here on my hip. So in this scenario, I'm the good guy. You, on the other hand, are not. You're the bad guy. Judging by the track marks on your arm, I'm thinking you're probably Jonesing for some heroin. And looking at those few green and brown teeth you still have, I'm thinking you're a meth-head, too. Looks like you're having a pretty shitty day. Trust me, it's about to get a whole lot shittier if you don't let her go."

The guy held his arm around the waitress's throat and pointed the knife at Richardson.

"Shut up! You think you could shoot me before I cut her up?"

"Yes."

"What did you say?" He narrowed his eyes and stretched his arm out even more toward Richardson.

"You asked me a simple question. I gave you a simple answer. Yes. I think I can draw my gun and pop a new hole right in the middle of your forehead before you even get close to hurting her. And remember, I don't have to pull my gun and rack the slide—

this ain't Hollywood. I know it makes a cool sound in the movies, but trust me, a real cop always keeps one in the chamber. All I have to do is pop the safety off, and I'll do that before the gun is even halfway up to your beady eyes."

"Just try it!"

"Now I don't want to do that, but I want you to know I will if I have to. I'm just a cop, sworn to uphold the law under the constitution. But I think another document is more important right now. Let me give you a little bit of a history lesson. The Declaration of Independence says everyone—even crackheads like you—is entitled to life, liberty, and the pursuit of happiness. And I'm starting to think you are depriving this young lady of her happiness. Miss, are you happy right now?"

The woman rapidly shook her head. Tear-streamed cheeks waved back and forth.

"See, I was right. You are interfering with her happiness, and that means we have us a problem here. A big one." Richardson held up a finger. "Ask anyone who knows me. I don't judge people based on their lifestyle choices. Love whoever you want. Doesn't matter to me. Pray to whatever god floats your boat. I don't care. Your political views? Nope, don't care about that either. Do your own thing. Just don't interfere with someone else's right to pursue happiness. I try to never judge anyone based on their personal choices. Well, except if they think ranch is better than bleu cheese on their wings. That's just wrong."

Pulling the waitress in even tighter, he continued holding the knife out toward Richardson.

"Just shut up, man! Give me the money, and no one gets hurt."

"Come on. Haven't you seen those westerns where the law man steps in and saves the damsel in distress from the bad guy at the very last second?"

He sneered. "I suppose you think you're John Wayne?"

The extended arm with the track marks came crashing down. The knife bounced off a stool and skidded across the tile floor. A hand came around behind, grabbed the addict's other wrist, and spun him around as the waitress ran behind the counter. With his arm pinned up behind his back, the gaunt, hollow-faced man slammed down onto the floor.

"Nope. That would be me," said a voice from on top. "Nice to meet you. I'm Detective Jon Wayne. But I spell it a little differently."

The front doors to the restaurant flew open. Erie County Sheriff's deputies rushed in with guns drawn. They lowered their weapons as they looked at Wayne, who was still sprawled over the man's back.

"Hey, Tommy." Wayne smiled as another deputy slipped cuffs on to the supine suspect. "Fancy seeing you twice in one week. How's it going?"

"Better than the shit you guys seem to find yourselves in." Deputy Carter laughed as he extended a hand to lift Wayne up off the man. "And Rhody, nice job dialing 911 for us. I love how you dropped in your name and location so nonchalantly. We knew right where you were. Good job. Dispatch had it patched into our cars. I know it was serious, but I couldn't help but laugh half the way here. I swear you and Jon are two of the biggest smart-asses I know."

"Well, I was trying to stall for time," Richardson said. "Jesus, Duke. Try adding some grains or something to your diet. It'll help you go a little quicker."

"Or I could hold it in and try to be as full of shit as you." Wayne smiled.

"You guys are a hoot," Carter said. "But Rhody, I do have to say, you were definitely right about one thing."

"What's that, Tommy."

"Who the hell would think ranch is better than bleu cheese for their wings." Carter laughed. "Just goes to show there are some sick-ass people in this world."

CHAPTER 18

AFTER GIVING THEIR STATEMENTS AND SHAKING hands with the deputies, Richardson and Wayne headed to AllNewU med spa. In the lobby was a large picture of Kelly Hallock holding her black pug. The picture was already surrounded by flowers, cards, and stuffed animals.

As they moved through the building, they spoke with any of the staff and patients who knew her. Over and over again, the detectives showed the picture of the man with the black hood. Each time, they received the same response—a headshake and a no. Her co-workers and patients all agreed that Kelly Hallock did not have any enemies, and no one had caused any problems for her at work, nor had anyone heard of Levon Moore.

The hotel offered similar results. No one recognized the photo. The front desk had no record of Mr. Hill having any problems. The police who had spoken with his wife in Syracuse, and she said she wasn't aware of any issues or threats. She had never heard of anyone named Odel Ives.

Dr. Harrison's co-workers and neighbors had the same observations. No one was aware of any problems, and the name Herbert Noak did not sound familiar to any of them. There had been no issues for any of his neighbors on the affluent street. After viewing the photo, several residents pointed out how Nottingham Terrace was flat, beautiful, and so close to Delaware Park that it made an attractive detour for runners. There were so many joggers, cyclists, and walkers that no one person would ever stand out from the others. In their neighborhood, joggers were just visual white noise.

"Well, this is getting us nowhere," Richardson said, as they walked back to the car. "But at least we're not chained to the desk. Let's head back over to Nia-Buff before we call it a day."

Fifteen minutes later, they stepped out of the late afternoon sun, into the shaded, air conditioned comfort of the glass building. The receptionist, who looked like a walking billboard for some of the services they offered, recognized them and came out from behind her desk.

"Hello, detectives. Did you catch him?"

"Unfortunately, no," Richardson said. "Not yet. We're here to ask some follow-up questions and show some pictures. I hope that isn't a problem."

"No, not at all. Doctor Mitchell told all of us that we are to cooperate as much as possible. I can get someone to cover the desk for me. Would you like me to get Kim, too? She just came back to work yesterday. She's doing a little better, but it's still so upsetting for her."

"That would be great. Thank you."

The four of them sat in a small meeting room just down the hall from the lobby area. After exchanging pleasantries, the detectives offered their sincere condolences for the loss. Kim forced a smile as she dabbed a tissue on her red, puffy face. Ample amounts of makeup still could not adequately cover the dark circles under her eyes. The shock and sadness from the last couple weeks was obviously still weighing on her. The loss of her friend, boss, and part-time lover had shattered her world and transformed her into a torrent of emotional pain.

"Mike—I mean, Doctor Mitchell—asked me to go through the call book," said the receptionist. "We try to keep a log of every call we receive through the day. Nothing much, just quick notes of what was asked about, who the calls were for…stuff like that. Kinda gives us an idea on what people are interested in. I couldn't find any complaints or problems. I'm not aware of any accusations or concerns any of our customers had."

"Have either of you heard of an Arthur Seth," Wayne said.

"No," said the receptionist. "I heard the other cops mentioning that name being on the notes. I would've definitely noticed if I saw that on our call list."

"It may not be anything, but could you take a look at this picture?" Richardson said "He's just a person of interest at this point."

"Is this Mister Seth?" Kim said.

Richardson shook his head. "We don't know. Might have nothing to do with Doctor Coleman and Doctor Charles at all. This pic was taken from another crime scene, and there was someone who looked similar on your security video that night. We were wondering if either of you had noticed this man around."

"You can't see his face at all," said the receptionist.

Kim picked up the picture and tipped her head. "Looks a little like it could almost be Sheila's husband, doesn't it? But he is such a sweet guy."

"Hmm, maybe," the receptionist said. "It was sad. He is so nice."

"Who is Sheila?" Richardson said.

"Sheila Schon. S-C-H-O-N."

Richardson wrote her name is in his notebook and gave it a puzzled look.

He turned back to the two women. "Does she work here, too?"

"No. She worked at the office on the other side of the parking ramp." The receptionist pointed out the window. "I would see her almost every day. We worked at the same times and were parked near each other. We would talk. She was such a sweetheart. She died just about a year ago. It was just awful."

"Really?" Wayne said. "How did she die."

"She got sick," Kim said. "Some kind of infection. She fought it for about a year, before it finally took her. I felt so bad for her husband. He was so dedicated to her. He was just lost without her. He took it really hard."

"That's understandable." Richardson wrote in his notebook. "But if it was Sheila that worked over here, how'd you know him?

"We'd run into them sometimes when he would visit her or leave little things on her car," Kim said. "We both met him a few times. His name is Paul. Paul Schon. Such a nice guy. They were the cutest couple. After she died, he would sometimes just come down near here after-hours and walk around. I guess he just wanted to be around the places she had been. Maybe it helped him feel closer to her."

"Yeah, there were a couple mornings I came in and he'd be sitting on the ledge where she used to park," the receptionist said. "But I haven't seen him around in quite a while. I know he took some time off. I just assumed he went back to work. I hope he's doing better. I know he was getting counseling, but I truly believe the only reason he made it through was because of the promise he made."

Richardson looked up from his notepad. "What promise was that?"

"One morning, when I came in, I could see how upset he was. It looked like he had been crying. He mentioned how he didn't know how he could possibly go on. Said the only thing that kept him going was that he promised Sheila that he would go on living. He loved her so much and would never break a promise to her, even after she was gone."

"How about you, Miss Thatcher? Have you seen him around?"

"No. I don't think so, anyway," Kim said. "A month or so ago, there were a few nights I thought I saw him jogging by. That's what made me think of it when I saw the picture of that guy in the sweatsuit."

"But it wasn't him?"

"I don't think so. I thought it was him. But when I called out his name, he just ignored me. That's not like him at all. He's very nice. Who knows? I wear earbuds when I go for a run. Maybe he just didn't hear me. But then again, it was dark, so maybe I was mistaken. It was one of the nights I worked really late with Dave. So it would've probably been a Tuesday night."

Richardson finished writing and looked up. "Did Sheila ever have anything done here? Was she a patient?"

"Not that I know of." The receptionist looked down at the strained buttons of her blouse. "She used to joke with me before she got sick. She would say she'd like to get some of the same enhancements I have. She thought Paul would love them."

"She wanted to get some wrinkle treatments a couple years ago," Kim said, "but we didn't do it. We were booked out at least a few months, and she wanted to have it done right away. Even if we weren't booked, she wouldn't have had it done here. I remember that Dave and Doctor Mitchell were in the lobby when I was talking to her. They looked at her and told her it was a waste of money. Dave said she didn't need it, and that maybe she could stop by in another fifteen or twenty years."

"I remember Doctor Mitchell saying something about you being able to turn away work you didn't think was realistic," Wayne said.

Richardson nodded. "They do sound like a cute couple. You wouldn't happen to know how long they were together, do you?"

The receptionist said, "Would've been...eight years? Yeah, eight.

"You sure?"

"Yes, because Sheila got sick not too long after their seventh anniversary, and she was sick for a little more than a year. I remember it was their seventh because he got her the sweetest gift. Did you know that copper is the traditional gift for your seventh?"

The two detectives looked at each other and shook their heads.

"Neither did I. But Paul did. Have you ever seen those sheets of hammered copper where the artist is able to forge a picture on it? I don't know where he had it done, but Paul was able to have their wedding picture done in copper, and had it framed for her." The receptionist sighed. "It was so beautiful. Sheila was crying when she was showing me the pictures on her phone."

The two detectives thanked them for their time. They handed them a few of their business cards and asked them to feel free to show the picture around to anyone else in the building.

"What do you think about all that," Wayne said, as they headed out to the car.

"Not too sure. There's something familiar about that guy's name. Can't think of what it is, but something about it is bugging me. The guy sounds pretty nice, but I hate him. He's making the rest of us husbands look bad."

CHAPTER 19

It was another Friday night in Buffalo, and the hunt was on again. A hooded predator was running through the streets of South Buffalo. The American and Irish flags decorating most of the houses in the Old First Ward indicated a light breeze was coming from Lake Erie. Smelled like rain could be moving in over the water.

Rain would be fine with him. He was too focused to be bothered by it. As a benefit, rain meant even fewer people out and about. Those who did venture out tended to hustle along with their heads down. He could run right next to someone and they wouldn't notice a single thing about him. That was exactly the way he liked it. For now, though, it was just overcast and gloomy. The dim streetlights did their best to alert him of hazards along the sidewalks as his black running shoes kept their rhythmic pace.

Tonight's run wouldn't be as long. He had someone to visit in Sloan, another working-class section of the city. It was only about six miles there. Not too bad, especially after his previous effort.

Before he realized it, he was on Reiman Street and getting ready to turn down Griffith. He slowed as he saw Sloan Village Park on his right. Directly across the park was the home of Dr. Saran Nadeer, a dentist who would not have a nice smile for long.

•.•.

"Damn it, Bill. I used to like Saturday mornings. Not so much lately."

"Me, too, Rhody," said Lieutenant Finch. "You're not the only one who would rather be home with family."

"About the only good thing is that I get to listen to Clay Moden doing Wide Open Country on the radio while I'm driving here."

"Oh, yeah, you like all that older country music." Finch walked up the front steps and opened the door.

"What's going on with this one," Richardson said, as the two walked into the house.

Wayne was already in the living room, standing near the body.

"First thing off, Connor was right," he said. "As you can see, Doctor Nadeer has the number seventeen. I guess that means the next one will be another N-name and have a forty-three."

"Not if we can stop him first." Richardson grimaced. "Is this one in the beauty business, too?"

"I suppose. Guess a nice smile is a thing of beauty. This one is a dentist."

"No shit? Our guy is all over the board, ain't he? Three doctors, a nurse, a salesman, and now a dentist."

"Yeah, and this one is small potatoes, too, like the salesman and the nurse. Nothing fancy. He runs a little dental office off of Jefferson Ave.—deep in the hood. From what we've found out so far from the neighbor, it's just him and a dental assistant there, Monday through Friday. Neighbor is the one who found him. Said they were supposed to golf a round over at Caz Park this morning. When he stopped by, the back door was unlocked. He walked in and saw all this. Oh, and sitting over there on the middle of the coffee table is our latest issue of Poetry Digest."

The two detectives went over to the sheet of paper. The same block lettering pronounced its cryptic message.

> *Pain and anger boils in a lost man.*
> *Searching for answers the best he can.*
> *Nothing to lose with a soul that is lost.*
> *Six are gone, with more to pay the cost.*
>
> *—Findley Moise*

"Great. Another poem and name to add to our list," Richardson said. "And what the hell is up with these names? Findley? Levon? Odel? Not exactly normal names around this area."

"Oh, okay, *Rhody,*" Wayne laughed. "Like you never heard of someone having an unusual name."

"Hey, I'm named after my grandfather. Our family brought that name from Ireland." Richardson smiled. "It's not so much that they're unusual, but why is he choosing them? I think there is something going on with these names, and not so much the poems themselves. Hell, he even changed the rhyming pattern after the one on the first night."

"Good catch there, partner. I didn't think you knew anything about poetry that didn't involve the word Nantucket."

"Very funny, smart-ass," Richardson smirked. "Cheesy poetry aside, there has to be a reason he's choosing these names. We haven't been able find anything that relates with them. They're practically Google-proof. Out of all the names in the world, why these ones?"

Richardson and Wayne made way for McDonald and his team to process the scene. As they walked out the back door, they noticed the two trash cans laying on their sides in the wet grass.

Wayne motioned to the bins. "Neighbor said they were like that. They have problems with stray cats and raccoons knocking over the cans all the time."

"Well, maybe our guy knew that and made some noise to draw him out here. Once we get the TOD, let's see if any of the neighbors saw any cars or people moving up or down the street. There isn't much cross traffic here, so maybe someone saw something. Woodrow Wilson Elementary School and Sloan Supermarket are fairly close by, too. Let's see if we they have any video we can use. Maybe we'll see that jogger again. Since this case blew up, I swear I've seen about a thousand black and gray sweatsuits all over the damn place."

"I heard one of the CSI guys say those sweatsuits are from Walmart," Wayne said. Probably a gazillion of them around here. Talk about blending in. He might as well be wearing Bills or Sabres gear in this town."

The two detectives stepped back in and watched McDonald's team go through the scene. All the evidence was being marked, photographed and bagged for further analysis. Connor Patrick stood as they approached.

"Hi, detectives. I think we found something a little different with this one."

"What's that," Richardson said.

"Well, I'm not sure. I was just about to show it to Jeff. I may have found some DNA—or at least, some kind of bodily fluid—on the back of his left pant leg. It's not a lot, but there is something along the calf area. I'm not sure, but I think it's urine. I was going to test it to be sure."

"Just the back of his left leg," Richardson said.

"Yes, it seemed strange to me. Our killer has been so precise. Seems odd he would clean everything up, but forget to do that. Why would he even do something like that in the first place? It's like he marked his territory."

"I doubt that's it," Richardson said. "Do me a favor Connor. I see Nadeer has a pair of dress shoes over there by the door. Do a quick check on his right shoe and see if you come up with a similar result."

A few minutes later, Patrick approached them. "You were right. There were trace amounts on the right shoe, too. How'd you know? And what does this mean?"

"It means we don't have to waste a lot of time and resources analyzing it. How'd I know? I was just playing the odds."

"What do you mean?"

"Well, it looks like our dentist here is in his mid-fifties. I'm thinking Dr. Matthews's autopsy is going to show he has a prostate almost as big as my partner's mouth."

"Hey," Wayne said. "Tell you what, buddy. You are more than welcome to let your mouth kiss my prostate anytime you want."

Richardson laughed. "I think I'll pass. Anyway, kid. I once a saw a post from some celeb griping about the perils of growing older. He showed a picture of wet spots along his khakis and made a comment about how it used to come out as one-way fire hose, but now it was more like a multi-directional sprinkler."

"Okay…" Patrick raised a brow.

"So the good doctor here probably took a whiz and had an errant stream shoot off in another direction and onto his shoe. So I'm thinking he hooked the top of his shoe around the other pant leg and wiped it off. It would be his DNA on both, so we don't need to spend a lot of time looking at it."

"Is this, uh, something you have a little experience with." Patrick beamed.

"Not yet. But I'm thinking, in another ten years or so I will be approaching the bowl with a much wider stance."

"Hmm, maybe you should go with a narrower stance and keep your shoes under the porcelain." Patrick laughed.

Wayne snapped his fingers and pointed at Patrick. "Now that is why they call you the boy genius. Good thinkin' there, kid."

"Come on, guys," said Richardson. "Let's head out and make some room for Dan's guys to get him loaded up."

As the CSI team was wrapping up the scene, the medical examiner drove away with Dr. Nadeer's body. Dr. Matthews would have a preliminary autopsy report by Monday morning, but they all knew what the report would say. The cause of the dentist's death was all too familiar to them by this point. After an extended time of torture, someone holding a knife in their left hand had slashed his throat before proceeding to cut the number into him after he died.

Richardson and Wayne were standing in front of the house, talking about it with Lieutenant Finch and Jeff McDonald.

"Hey, detectives. Hold up a minute," someone called out, coming down the sidewalk.

As he waved his hand, he broke from his stride into a loping jog, hopping over several puddles in the sidewalk.

"Dave?" Richardson said. "Hey, I hardly recognized you in street clothes."

"Yeah, how about that." Pawlowski shook hands with them. "Every now and then, they let us uniforms have a Saturday off."

"What's up?" Finch said. "What would bring you out here."

Pawlowski pointed across the park. "I live just a couple streets over. I'm on Wagner. This is a good area. Everybody pretty much knows everyone else. We are all shocked. Didn't take long for this to make its way through the neighborhood. Anyway, I have some information about Doctor Nadeer that I think would be relevant, especially considering what we learned this killer is focused on."

"Thanks, Dave," said Richardson. "we need all the info we can get. What do you know about him?"

"Well, I really don't know all that much about him, but he seemed to be a stand-up guy. I know his assistant pretty well, though. Her name is Shaniqua Robinson. She's a really good person. Babysits our kids sometimes to make a few extra bucks. She lives just the other side of me, over on Schiller. I like helping her out. I try to drive the patrol car past their dental office whenever I can, just to be seen. She said they've had problems with people trying to break in to steal pain pills, equipment, whatever they can get their hands on."

"I imagine it's a pretty rough crowd around there sometimes," Richardson said.

"Yeah, sure is. Like I said, my wife and I like helping her out. She works hard, so we throw her a few extra bucks when she watches the kids for us. There was a time when she didn't get her paychecks regularly. Doctor Nadeer would always get caught up, but that didn't help put food on the table for that week."

"So the business wasn't doing very well?" Wayne said.

"No, not at all. Not a lot of folks in that area have dental coverage, and those that do tend to go to the fancier places unless they have an emergency or something. But things started turning around during the last year or so. Not exactly like they're rolling in the dough, but at least she was getting paid every week, and he took down the *for sale* sign in front of his house. He must've been able to get caught up on the mortgage."

"That's good," Richardson said, "but how does that fit in with our case? Why do you think it matches up with our killer's MO?"

"I was getting to that. Sorry about taking the long way around. I remembered talking with Shaniqua a while back, and she said how much better things were going. Turns out, to help things along, Doctor Nadeer started doing a little side business."

"Side business?" Wayne said.

"Yeah, Jon. He started going all over the city for private Botox parties. As a dentist, he's allowed to do the injections. Turns out, it's a pretty big industry, if you look it up. Hard to believe. People have a party right in their homes and invite a bunch of friends over. They all pay the doc for the shots they need right there. I guess if the money won't come to you, you have to go to the money. That's how he started making enough money to cover the bills. Thought you guys should know about it."

"Damn, Dave, glad you stopped by." Wayne shook his head.

"Me, too," Richardson said. "We were thinking this may be tied into the beauty angle of a nice smile, but this ties in more directly to our theory of the chemical formula that Connor showed us. This has to be why he was selected."

"That's what I thought, too," Dave said. "I feel bad for Shaniqua. She'll be out of a job now. Hopefully she can land something soon. I'm going to go over there and talk to her now. I'll let her know you guys will probably be reaching out to her, too."

"Thanks, Dave," said Richardson. "I'm sure she is going to be very upset. Let's give her a little time. Tell her we'll talk to her at some point on Monday."

As Pawlowski started walking back across the park, Richardson and Wayne stood by their vehicles.

"Did you know dentists could do that shit?" Wayne said.

"Nope, not at all."

"Well, that certainly puts a new wrinkle into all this."

With a half-smile and a head shake, Richardson opened his truck door.

"Ugh. Really, Duke? That was brutal."

"Heh-heh-heh. I got a million of 'em."

CHAPTER 20

MONDAY MORNING, RICHARDSON AND WAYNE entered the station. After grabbing a cup of coffee, they sat at their desks, facing each other. Several files were flipped open as they poured over the facts from the scenes of the six murders. Each detective also had a stack of phone messages from people hopeful of getting the twenty-five grand in reward money.

Wayne looked up from his pile as he sensed someone approaching their desks.

He smiled. "Hey, Alyssa. Saw you on the news again. Nice job with the press conference. God bless ya. I don't know how you can hear the same questions over and over without telling them to go to hell."

"Thanks, Jon. It's not that bad. I know most of them, and they know me. They know how much I can share and what I won't, but it's still a game we play."

"Good article in the Sunday paper, too," Richardson said. "They had quite a few of your quotes in there."

"Thanks. Hey, I was just over talking with Randy. He says he was able to locate some guy you wanted to talk to. He was looking for you earlier when you were in with the captain. He's across the hall, at his desk. You may want to head over there if you can. He's hitting the street again in a little bit."

"Thanks, Alyssa," said Richardson. "We're heading out in a little while, too. C'mon, Jon. Let's go see what he has."

He and Wayne headed over to Randy's desk. Talking on the phone, Shea held up a finger to indicate he was almost done. The two detectives stood over the desk and looked at the array of files and empty coffee cups littering the top. On the far side of the desk was a small square board with a toy policeman standing under a spindly, plastic tree. Underneath it, in large letters was written, *Near Shady.*

"Hey, Rhody. Hey, Jon." Shea put down his phone. "I was looking for you earlier."

"Yeah, that's what Alyssa said," replied Richardson.

"Hey, Randy." Wayne pointed across the desk. "I've been meaning to ask you for years about your little toy cop there."

Shea smiled. "That's from my wife. It's me."

"Oh, yeah, of course," Wayne said. "I can see the resemblance. But you're gonna need a much bigger tree if you're going to be anywhere near shady."

Shea turned and picked up the toy cop. "Back when I met my wife, she was an English major and really into anagrams. You know, where you mix up the letters to make other words. Anyway, when I told her my name was Randy Shea, she said my name made *Near Shady.* Been her pet name for me ever since."

"That is too funny," Wayne said. "Perhaps you should introduce her to Rhody here. They have something in common. Back in college, he was the anagram king. He would mess with signs that people had out. He was a natural."

Richardson shook his head. "That was long time ago, and generally after the consumption of a few too many PBR's."

"Oh, really? Do tell." Shea chuckled.

"Some were a little warped, but others were just hysterical," Wayne said. "One time, in November, this sign outside a polling place was marked *Election Results*. Rhod walks up, and just as quick as can be, changes it to *Lies—lets recount.*"

"Come on, Duke," Richardson growled.

"Oh, but the best was the church thing at the legion hall, remember? That was awesome."

"What happened?" Shea said.

"So Rhody and I are stumbling along past the American Legion after a few too many, and we see this sign that says *Presbyterians Fundraiser*. Rhody looks at it for a few seconds, pulls the letters off. Then the next thing you know, it says Britney Spears far side run. The best part—no one seemed to notice, and the sign stayed up for a couple days. On Sunday, the day of the fundraiser, a bunch of people showed up in their running gear for a race."

"Holy crap. That's some funny shit." Shea laughed.

"C'mon, Duke. Can we get back to work? I'm sure Randy has better things to do this morning. I know we do."

Wayne pointed his thumb at his partner. "You believe this guy? Look what this case is doing to him. He's turning into some sort of stoic introvert, just like one of those characters from the David Baldacci books he's always reading."

"Hardly. I know I'm not a sure-shot CIA sniper. Maybe a little like a dogged Army investigator…but I know I sure as hell ain't some kind of memory man. I can barely remember my own name these days. So let's get back to the case before I forget that I like you. Randy, what did you find out for us?"

"Oh, yeah. That guy you said you wanted to talk to—Paul Schon. I left a card at his office, and he called. Said he can come in tomorrow morning to talk with you. Be here about nine."

"Good deal," Richardson said. "I appreciate it. Did you get a feel for him?"

"Everybody where he works seems to think he's a good guy. Sad and quiet were the words used the most. I don't know, but from talking on the phone he seemed like a nice guy. Pretty accommodating. Didn't seem like he was trying to hide anything."

"Yeah, that was the impression we got from some people that know him," Richardson said. "I really appreciate the follow through. Thanks for asking him in."

"No problem. I hope it leads to something."

The two detectives got up and started across the room, when Rhody turned back.

"Hey, Randy. One other thing. I know you don't mean much with it, but try not to be too hard on the new kid."

"Oh…like when the two of you were bustin' my balls ten years ago?"

Richardson dipped his head and smiled. "Touché, my friend. Good point."

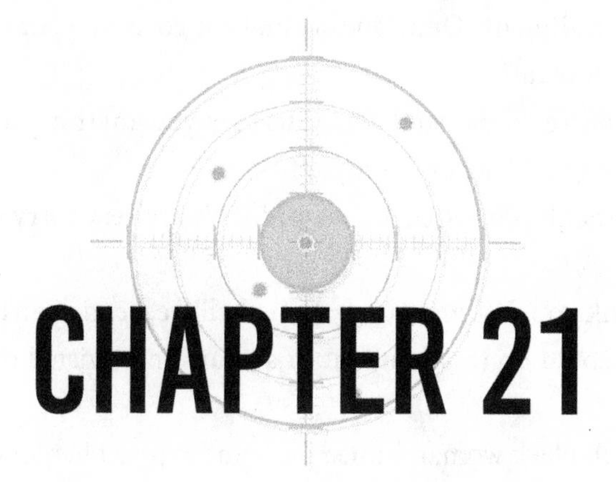

CHAPTER 21

LATER THAT AFTERNOON THE TWO DETECTIVES turned off Broadway, onto the 400 block of Schiller Street in Sloan. Japanese Maples lined both sides of the street. Branches full of burgundy leaves indicated a light wind. The modest houses were close together, with narrow driveways barely wide enough to drive a car through, but not wide enough to open the doors until it flared out behind the homes at the garage. The houses were all in decent shape, with manicured lawns. Flower beds in front of each porch offered a dazzling burst of color. Wind spinners and decorative flags in the small gardens concurred with the maples' announcement of a warm summer breeze.

"Good afternoon, Miss Robinson. I'm Detective Rhody Richardson. This is my partner, Detective Jon Wayne."

"For real? Like the cowboy?"

"Yeah, my dad was a big fan. But spelled differently. I get that a lot." He rolled his eyes and lifted his chin at Richardson. "And this guy calling me Duke doesn't make it go away. Can we come in for a moment?"

"Of course. Please sit down. Can I get you anything to drink? I'm going to grab a pop for myself."

"No, thank you," Richardson said. "We are very sorry for your loss."

"Thank you. I'm just numb. I cried all weekend. Can't believe anyone could do this." She sat in a chair and twisted open the bottle.

The tall black woman leaned back and crossed her long legs at the ankles. Her straight black hair went just below her shoulders. Dark purple strands along the sides of her angular face and high cheek bones sat in a stark contrast to the lavender of her bangs. The sadness in her eyes countered the smile she tried to offer.

"It must be very hard for you," Wayne said. "And on top of everything else, Dave said this means you're going to be out of work."

"I'm not worried about it." She wiped a tear from her cheek. "I've had quite a few good job offers for more money over the last couple years. I'll be able to get something else."

"Why wouldn't you take a new job before," Richardson said. "I understand things weren't going very well for a while."

"Because I was raised to be loyal to those who are loyal to me," she said, with an air of indignation. "Doctor Nadeer was good to me. I'd be nowhere without him. When I was a teenager, I was cleaning his house once a week to make a few bucks. After high school, I had nothing. He was the one who helped get me into Erie Community so I could get certified to be a dental assistant. He even gave me a scholarship to help pay for it. Hired me on the day I was certified. And then he helped me again when I decided to go back. This summer, I'm finishing up my last class, and I'm going to get my degree as a dental hygienist."

"That's very impressive," Richardson said.

"Yeah, I'm pretty proud of it. First one in my family to go to college. And I owe it all to Doctor Nadeer. I would've ended up a street punk going nowhere fast. Anything I get in this life, I owe to him. So to answer your question, that's why I never would have taken another job offer."

"Loyalty is an admirable quality," Richardson said. "Doctor Nadeer was a lucky man to have you working for him."

"Thanks, but I'm pretty sure I got the better end of what could've been."

"Do you know if Doctor Nadeer was having problems with anyone in particular," Wayne said. "Dave said you had some issues at the office."

"Yeah, if by *issues* you mean crackhead losers and junkies." Shaniqua wore a look of disgust. "People try to break in 'cause they think we've got all these painkillers or something. Doctor Nadeer kept a record in his computer of everything going on. We gave up on reporting them all to the police. Wasn't much they could do. It did help when Dave would drive by and scatter the roaches a couple times a day."

"Have you ever heard of someone named Findley Moise," Wayne said.

"No. Never heard of him. Maybe Doctor Nadeer had."

"You said he kept records of everything," Richardson said. "Could you get us a copy of it? Probably has nothing to do with this, but we'd like to check out every angle."

"To be honest, I'm scared to go back there now. But I have a bunch of my stuff in there. I gotta get it sometime. I can try, I guess, but I really don't want to be there. I have keys, and I know his password, but I have no idea where the file is. He has, like, a zillion files all over the screen, and files inside files. But if it'll help catch whoever did this, I'll try to find the needle in that haystack."

Wayne turned to Richardson. "You thinking what I'm thinking?"

"Sure am." Richardson looked back to Shaniqua. "Tell you what. Detective Wayne and I have to go to city hall and meet with the mayor this afternoon, and we have a few things going on in the morning. Could you meet us at your office tomorrow afternoon? That'll give us a chance to have a judge sign off on it, and we can stay there with you while you get all your things. I think we'll bring along a new guy we have. He's one of those techie guys, and he's pretty good at finding things in a computer."

"Oh, that sounds a lot better than me trying to find it. I'm glad to help. I'll meet you there at three?"

"Sounds good. See you then."

CHAPTER 22

"MISTER SCHON? GOOD MORNING. I'M DETECTIVE Rhody Richardson. This is my partner, Detective Jon Wayne."

"Oh, that's an easy name for me to remember. My dad was a huge fan."

"Mine, too—hence, the name. I spell it differently, but I still get a lot of comments and jokes about it."

"I'll bet." Paul smiled. "Just be glad he didn't name you Bruce."

"Hey, I didn't think of that." Wayne laughed. "Yeah, the Batman jokes would've been a lot worse."

"Can I get you some coffee or anything." Richardson pulled out a chair in the interview room and motioned to another.

Mr. Schon shook his head and sat, looking around at the room. The gray and light blue walls offered a cold, lifeless feel.

Catching his reflection, Paul ran his fingers through his hair and patted down a few wayward locks.

"I've never been in a police station before. Looks a lot like what you see on the TV shows. Is someone watching us on the other side of that mirror?"

"No, not at all," Richardson said. "It just gets way too noisy out there on the floor. It's nicer to talk back here. Quieter, and less distractions."

"Okay. What can I help you with? As I told Detective Shea, I have no idea why the police would want to speak with me."

"We're just looking to follow through on background information for a case we're working," Wayne said. "It's just one of those things where we're talking to anybody whose name has come up. And you'd be surprised at how the tiniest bit of info from someone can help. Some people have no idea they know what they know."

"Of course. I'd be more than happy to help if I can, but how did my name come up?"

Richardson cleared his throat. "We were talking with the folks at Nia-Buff Plastic Surgery, and they..."

"Oh, wow! This is about those doctors who were killed." Paul's jaw dropped, and he raised his eyebrows. "I was at Doctor Chandler's office just a block away that morning and saw all the police cars. Later, I heard what happened. It was just awful. But how does this have anything to do with me?"

"As I was saying," Richardson replied, "we spoke with the staff. I am very sorry to hear about the loss of your wife. They said that you would sometimes be around there after-hours. It must've been very difficult."

"It still is difficult." Paul placed a hand over his other, shaking one. "Sometimes I do go out that way just to be near some of the places Sheila used to go. She worked near there."

"That's what we heard, too," Richardson said.

"Were you there the night things happened? We are trying to see if there were any witnesses who may have seen something or someone that night."

"No, not at all. I had a doctor's appointment first thing in the morning, and I saw all the police cars out front when I was going to see Doctor Chandler. But these days, I go to bed pretty early. One of my prescriptions kinda knocks me out."

"Must make it pretty tough to go to work some mornings," Richardson said. "The people at your office said you don't come around as much anymore."

"My company has been very understanding. They have let me take off as much as I want. I can do some work from home, and I can work as few or as many hours as I want. I make and design models for the engineering and product development departments. A lot of my work is stuff I can do right at our house—carving and painting plastics, clay, and wood to make prototype models."

"Wow, that's nice for you," Wayne said. "I wish I was artistic like that. But it still must make it tough to pay the bills sometimes, depending on how many hours you're able to put in."

"Well, that's really not much of an issue. Sheila had life insurance through her work, and on top of that, we got policies for both of us right after we married. Not that I care about it, but there's more money than I will ever need."

Paul's chair creaked and groaned as he shifted. He placed his hands underneath the backs of his thighs and swallowed deeply as he looked back at the detectives with a sullen expression.

"Are we making you nervous, Paul," Wayne said. "I can't help but notice you seem to be just a little jittery.

"No, not at all. Why should I be nervous? You've both been very nice." Paul placed his shaky hands in his lap and looked down at them. "I think it's another side effect from my medicine. Another one of the reasons I don't spend a lot of time at the office. Makes people uncomfortable. Maybe that's why I go to sleep so early now—my muscles are probably exhausted from twitching all day long."

Richardson said, "Do you like to go running, Paul?"

Paul looked back and forth at the two detectives with a sense of amusement.

"No…I used to. I was on the track team in high school and college, but I don't do it anymore. Why do you ask?"

"Just wondering," Richardson said. "We have a picture of a man about your size, wearing a black sweatsuit. He was seen near Nia-Buff the night the doctors were killed. The staff there thought he might have resembled you. We were hoping you may have been there and maybe saw something."

Wayne slid the picture from Hotel Lenox across the table to Paul. He picked it up to look at it, and a small, tight smile formed on his face. As he looked up, the fluorescent lights bounced off his glistening, misty eyes.

"Is something wrong," Richardson said.

"No, not really. I'm sorry." Paul wiped at his eyes. "Everything still brings back memories. I can see why they thought it might've been me. I have the same exact sweatsuit. I think I wore it when I stopped by Sheila's office to pick up some of her things while she was in the hospital. She made me buy it. We had been spending so much time in the hospital, and she kept insisting that I needed something comfortable to wear while I was sitting there all those hours. When they took her away for more tests and scans, she implored me to run over to Walmart to buy a sweatsuit, or something more comfortable to lounge around in. She was always trying to make me feel more at ease. She really liked the way it looked.

Said I looked sporty. Haven't been able to bring myself to wear it since she..."

"I understand," Richardson whispered. "Again, we are very sorry for your loss."

After Paul left, Wayne turned to his partner. "He seemed like a nice guy, but a little too jittery and jumpy to me. What are you thinking?

"Not sure. Tough to get a real read on him. Something there I can't quite figure out yet. But part of me is thinking Tardive Dyskinesia."

"Huh? What does Travis Tritt in Asia have to do with this?"

Richardson laughed. "You're an idiot. Tardive Dyskinesia is where certain drugs cause that uncontrollable shaking. It's usually after long-term use, but it could be something else. He said he's having issues with one of his scripts. Some anti-psychotic meds can cause tremors. I wonder what he's taking and what the side-effects are? Did you notice it only seems like his left hand shakes, and his ring finger moves the most? Maybe it's a coincidence, but he's still wearing his wedding band. He might be on something pretty strong to help him with the emotional issues."

"We should go to Doctor Chandler's office. That's where he said he was at that morning."

"Sounds good, but I'm not expecting too much. HIPAA laws and patient privacy will probably prevent them from saying much of anything. But it wouldn't hurt to try."

CHAPTER 23

LATER IN THE AFTERNOON, RICHARDSON, WAYNE, and Connor pulled up to a dilapidated brick building. Trash was billowing down the street. Stray dogs and stray men standing along the uneven concrete cast sideways glances at the unmarked car.

"Looks like Shaniqua isn't here yet," Richardson said.

"I still can't believe you were able to get the captain and Jeff to agree to this." Patrick looked around, wide-eyed, from the backseat. "This is awesome."

"Easy there, country bumpkin," Richardson said. "We have permission to be here from an employee with authorized access. Nadeer has no relatives, and the information we're looking for isn't part of any investigation against the doctor. We're just looking to find a file. That's it. You're only here to help her find it."

"Yeah, there's nothing official about this," Wayne said. "You're just here to make it easier to find the info." He laughed. "Hey, it's not like the BPD is the first company to ever take advantage of free labor from an intern."

"Sure. Of course. I understand."

"But this is a good thing, too, kid," Richardson said. "Pretty big deal, and unusual, to be including you in so many parts of this investigation. The bosses must like you. Bodes well for your future if you want one with us."

"I sure do."

The brakes on Robinson's dark blue Escort squealed her arrival as she pulled up behind them. The three of them stepped out of the car and greeted her. Richardson cast a knowing look at the rail-thin man leaning against a light pole. Long black cargo shorts hung so low he could see at least six inches of red plaid boxers in the back. The grungy wife-beater tank top had probably been white at some point early in its life. The man refused to meet Richardson's gaze. He finished typing a text, hit send, and then turned away and walked back toward Jefferson Avenue.

Richardson looked over at Patrick. "Pretty safe to say everyone in the area knows we're here now."

"Please come on in." Shaniqua slid her key into the door. "Be careful on the steps. Narrow stairs. We're on the second floor. No one else is around. We're the only ones who use the building. All the other offices are empty."

As the four of them stepped just inside Dr. Nadeer's office, they halted. Standing in the far corner was a husky man in his early twenties. He methodically turned and held both hands up. Shifted his gaze back and forth across the room.

"Hey, man, it's cool. I ain't doin' nothin!'"

Shaniqua shrieked as another man stepped out from behind the door. Before he could turn around, a baseball bat caught Wayne with a glancing blow off his shoulder and up to his right ear. He was out before he hit the floor. Richardson kicked the door, sending the man with the bat crashing into the wall. The back of the attacker's head painted a red streak down the wall as he collapsed in a crumpled mess next to Wayne.

Richardson whirled around, grabbing at his hip to draw his Glock. Before it cleared leather, he was tackled as two more men jumped from behind the half-wall separating the entry from the reception desk. Black metal skittered across white tiles as the 9mm hid under a desk.

Richardson threw his right arm out and made a sweeping arc back to bring it around the neck of the man on his back. He pushed off with his foot and rolled over, flipping the man onto his own back as Richardson twisted to lay across him, chest to chest. He reared back his left arm to deliver a crashing blow, but his arm stopped. He looked back to see the other man holding it. Out of the corner of his eye, he could see a foot coming toward his head, but the angle was wrong. Too high.

As he dipped his head, the foot flew past, swinging up and over Richardson's back. Connor Patrick's ankle landed squarely on the other man's throat. With his larynx crushed, the man dropped to his knees and fell to his side. Curled in a fetal position, he laid there making gasping and gurgling noises.

Richardson turned and smashed his fist into the face of the man he was holding. As he reared back again, he caught a glimpse of metal as the afternoon sun bounced off the blade. The man had pulled out a knife. Richardson gripped the man's wrist as the two locked in a stalemate.

Two other men burst from a doorway on the other side of the office. Patrick whirled around as he heard the heavy footsteps coming toward him. A large man in a blue T-shirt was bull-rushing straight at him with his arms open. Dipping down and to the left, Patrick swung his arm around and caught the man in the middle of the back as he brought his knee up into the man's abdomen. With a loud gasp and his lunch spewing from him, the man dropped to the floor. Then, as the other man in a red-striped rugby shirt rushed at him, Patrick dropped to a crouch, swinging his leg around. His shin landed on the side of an approaching knee. With a *pop!*, the patella dislocated and shattered. The anterior cruciate ligament ripped apart, allowing the femur and tibia to go their separate ways. The red-striped shirt crashed to the floor, screaming and clutching the disabled limb. Patrick continued spinning around as his hand found its mark on the man's chin. Patrick could feel the unmistakable pop as the lower jaw disconnected from the upper. The attacker was unable to feel any of it, as he immediately lost consciousness.

The room went silent for a short moment.

"I'm gonna kill you, you son of a bitch!" Blue shirt was back up and rushing toward Patrick.

He was a big man, maybe an inch or two shorter, but easily fifty pounds heavier than the wiry intern. While rage, size, and strength can be useful at times, they were no match for quickness, discipline, and training.

Stepping aside again, Patrick hooked his arm into the armpit of the blue shirt. Thrusting his hip into the rushing man, Patrick used the momentum to catapult the man up and over as the back of the blue shirt slammed onto the white tile floor. After landing on the big man's chest, the intern unleashed a barrage of four punches into the man's temples until he stopped moving.

It had been less than a minute of fighting, but he felt like it had been much longer. Panting, he jumped up and looked around to assess the situation. Wayne was looking at him and trying to sit up. Shaniqua had finally stopped screaming, but sat there with a look of dazed confusion. Shock, fear, and disbelief erupted through her tears. Richardson was still grappling with the man holding the knife.

Patrick stepped over to help him.

"C'mon, asshole!" yelled the first young man. "Let's go."

He was still in the same corner, but his hands were no longer held up in surrender. He had them out in front, waving a six-inch blade.

"I'm gonna cut you up, shithead."

"Easy, man," Patrick said. "No one else needs to get hurt." He held his empty hands out in front and slowly stepped sideways to the middle of the room.

He knew it was a pointless conversation. The attack was going to happen, and he wanted to have options on which direction to move in.

With fire in his eyes, the young man lunged at Patrick with the blade slashing through the air. Patrick spun to the left as the knife caught the billowing side of his polo shirt. He continued spinning to the side as he threw his fist around and caught his attacker on the cheek. The man stumbled a few steps and turned back toward Patrick, who knew it wasn't over yet. This wouldn't end without someone going down.

"Dude, if you come at me again, I will break your arm," Patrick said, in a calm cadence. "I don't want to do that, don't make me do it. Just put the knife down."

"Oh, you think you're all that." The man sneered as he jumped across the room.

With the knife coming straight at his heart, Patrick knocked the man's forearm. The knife passed across the front of Patrick's chest. He gripped the man's wrist, spun around and locked out the man's arm, with his elbow pointing to the ceiling. Patrick jerked his arm up, and as he dropped to his knee, slammed the back of his own elbow down onto the man's exposed joint. Screams echoed off the walls while ligaments, cartilage, and bone shattered and tore apart. The man's arm snapped to a right angle in the wrong direction.

Patrick looked up as he heard another knife hit the floor. Richardson landed a punch to his attacker's face. The man went limp for just a moment, but it was more than enough time. In one fluid movement, Richardson rolled the man to his stomach, yanked his wrists together, and clamped on handcuffs so tightly the folds of skin instantly started turning purple.

After securing the other assailants, Richardson grabbed his radio and called it in. He made sure they knew Wayne had been hurt and that they would need several ambulances. He then ran over to his partner, who was sitting up but still looked dazed. Before joining them, Patrick reached his long arms under the desk and retrieved the Glock. He came over and handed it to Richardson.

"Thanks, kid. Shaniqua, are you all right? Did you get hurt."

"No, I'm okay." She sniffled through the tears.

"Hey, Duke!" Richardson shouted. "Are you okay?"

"Jesus, Rhod, I ain't deaf. But I have a hell of a headache."

"Just sit still until the ambulance gets here, Sundance. How're you feeling?" Richardson looked back and forth at Wayne's pupils.

"Not sure. My shoulder took most of it, but he still got me pretty good." Wayne rubbed behind his ear. "I'm thinking I might be hallucinating, though. Did I really see that shit that just happened?"

Richardson turned and looked up at Patrick as well.

"Yeah, holy shit! What was that, kid? I had no idea. Where'd you learn to do that?"

Patrick blushed as he shifted his weight back and forth.

"My old man had a gym with a heavy bag, in the basement. I really liked kicking and hitting it. Dad thought I was pretty good at it. When I was ten, he bought me my own bag and gloves and stuff. He showed me a bunch of moves. I kept it up and took some classes."

"Maybe he isn't Connor Patrick," Wayne said. "Maybe he's really Conor McGregor, MMA champion." He gave a weak laugh.

"Damn, kid. Glad you were here to help. I had no idea you could fight. Never would've guessed it."

"Well, just because I know how to fight, doesn't mean I need to act like I can. I save that for occasional competitions. Or for guys who give me no other choice, like these ones."

"No shit," Richardson said. "You do MMA tournaments."

"Sometimes."

"Ever win them?"

"Most times."

CHAPTER 24

Dr. Aaron Nigel stepped out of the shower. With a towel wrapped around his waist, he continued to dry his hair with another towel while his Versace flip flops padded across the tiled floor to his locker. As he spun the combination on the lock, he rolled his neck and shrugged. It had been a tough workout. He knew he would have that good muscle soreness coming in a day or two after this one. He'd earned it—his shoulders and arms were already telling him how much he had pushed it.

From the bottom of his large locker, he pulled out a pair of leather Ferragamo's and set them on the floor. He slipped his hand in one to lift it, and used the dry corner of his towel to buff out an almost imperceptible scuff. The thousand-dollar shoes felt as soft and supple as velour in his hands. Sure, they were pricey. But they were only about a third of the cost of his Armani coat and pants. For Aaron, it was an investment that paid off well.

He glided his legs and arms through the two-piece offset windowpane wool suit. Long ago, he had learned to slip into his clothing with the air of a man accustomed to wearing the finer things.

Every now and then, he would think back to the first time he drove six hours down the New York Thruway, to the Neiman Marcus store in White Plains. It was his first venture in surrounding himself with what he perceived to be the best. Of the many things he had learned in life, he realized money recognizes money, and successful people want to be with other successful people.

He longed to become the plastic surgeon of choice for anyone who could afford his services, and desperately wanted wealthy people to recognize him as a success and as a peer. He wanted patients whose first question was, *When can you do it?*, not *How much will it cost?* Looking the part was an important step in attracting the kind of customers who had bank accounts even larger than their egos.

These days, being draped in the finest clothing and softest leathers was who he was. But it hadn't always been that way. After his father had walked out, his mother crawled into a bottle and stayed there even after Child Services pulled Aaron out and placed him in foster care.

It wasn't all bad, though. Some of the families he stayed with were decent. At least it was better than growing up with a mother who was usually passed out.

Growing up poor in rural areas wasn't unusual, and certainly wasn't a bad thing, but he always knew he wanted more. As a foster child, he grew accustomed to bouncing around in the system and living his life feeling as if nothing was truly his own. He always felt as if he was just a guest user in someone else's life. His young eyes were drawn to the things that seemed unattainable to a poor young ward.

One thing he did have was a brain. Even at a young age, he knew he was smarter than most, and he could absorb information quickly. Perhaps it was because he didn't have many personal relationships or friendships to interfere. Even though he had been bounced around to several small rural schools in Western New York, he was always able to get up to speed quickly and had a knack for taking tests.

Great grades and a 1580 on his SAT had helped him earn a full ride to the University of Buffalo. After earning his pre-med degree in biochemistry with honors, he stayed at UB for his medical school training. When he began, he made the conscious choice to become a big fish in a smaller pond. Instead of competing with the crowds of doctors in New York, Miami, or LA, he decided to remain in the Buffalo area and live the prominent lifestyle he had always longed for.

The first few years were tough. He knew he was overextending himself to portray the image. A fancy office in the affluent suburb of Williamsville was pricey, but worth it. Expensive shoes and high-end suits also ate into his budget. And of course, he needed the car to complete the illusion. Right outside the entranceway of his office, in his reserved spot, sat a beautiful Mercedes-Benz. Clients walking in could easily read DR N1GEL across the license plate.

At first, he couldn't afford to buy luxury cars outright, but no one needed to know that. He had been willing to cut back on non-essentials, such as food. When he first went out on his own, he still had a decent credit score and was able to find a dealer who would make it happen. A leased vehicle fit his monthly budget better, but looked just as good wrapped around him.

It had all worked. A few lean years lead to a successful practice and a waiting list of clients begging for his services. The contacts list in his phone had become a who's who from all across Upstate New York. He was beginning to enjoy the life he had built for himself.

"Hi, Aaron. Getting another late workout in?" said a cheery voice.

Dr. Nigel returned the smile and gave an appreciative look at the two women walking along the hallway. Yoga pants hugged their toned legs. Tight tank tops clung to glistening, tan skin.

"Of course. Every Tuesday, when you're teaching your class, Rachel. I'm afraid it's the only way I can see you around. You are far too beautiful to ever need my services professionally." Aaron winked.

After years of effort, his voice had an over-enunciated, well-practiced mix of British and Boston accents. Childhood reruns of Dr. Frazier Crane from Cheers, and Dr. Charles Winchester from MASH, had served as the benchmark for how a young Aaron Nigel perceived the speech of the wealthy and successful. Countless hours of reading to himself with his hand cupped to an ear had helped to erase any trace of his rural, hick-town drawl.

"Aren't you just the sweetest." Rachel giggled. "Who knows? Perhaps I'll stop by sometime just to say hello."

"And if she doesn't, maybe I will." Her friend giggled as they continued down the hallway.

Aaron spun around and walked backward a few paces as he admired the sway of the two ladies before they disappeared into their locker room.

He stepped into the parking lot and pressed the buttons on his key fob. Eight cylinders of German engineering roared to life as layers of the hard-shell convertible top began to slide into the trunk.

About twenty minutes later, he pulled into downtown Buffalo. The scanner read his parking permit and lifted the gate to the private parking lot for residents of the Lofts on Ellicott. The apartments were retro chic, paying homage to the history of the Queen City, but having a modernized classy style. A nice place to live, but to Aaron it was just another hand-me-down. It belonged to someone else, and others had lived there before. He didn't like being a guest user.

He still had another six months remaining on his lease, but the timing should be just about perfect. His new mansion should be completed by then. Several acres, with a large pond in Clarence, was overrun daily by construction crews building his dream estate. A long, winding driveway would lead to a massive brick home with twelve-foot windows. It would be his. Only his. No one else's leftovers.

Using the keypad, Aaron opened the side door and strolled across the lobby. He never noticed the black running shoe that stepped in to prevent the door from closing. Just as the elevator doors were about to shut, a hand slid in between the doors and they opened back up. A man, panting, stepped in. He raised his hand to the buttons, but stopped when he saw the number 5 was already lit up.

"There's plenty of streetlights," Aaron said, "but running in all black and gray at night has to be risky. You have to be either a brave man, or crazy."

The man nodded beneath his hood. He kept his head down as his chest continued to heave.

"Yeah, you're right," he said, breathlessly.

"About which one." The doctor laughed. "You should also make sure you tie your shoelace before you trip."

"Oh, yeah, thanks," the man said, as the doors opened.

About halfway down the hall, Aaron paused for a moment and looked back. The events over the last couple weeks had made him suspicious and nervous. The runner had taken his advice and was down on one knee, tying the loose lace.

Aaron turned back and slid the key into the loft door. As he entered, he dropped his gym bag on the floor and heard footsteps rushing up behind him. Arms slammed around him, pinning his elbows to his waist. As he was launched forward, a left foot wrapped around his ankles to trip him. The floor was now coming at his face at a dizzying speed.

With a killer's hands clasped into his stomach, and a shoulder driving into his back, Dr. Nigel slammed onto the floor. He felt several of his ribs crack as his lungs expelled their contents.

Gasping for air, he could feel himself being rolled over. The cracked ribs let him know just how unhappy they were with this type of movement. The pain was unbearable, but with minimal air in his lungs, he could do little but utter a few pain-filled gurgles and gasps. His breathing became even more difficult as he tried desperately to draw air through the damp, acrid rag that was now pressed against his face. Through watery eyes, he could see a blurry image of the black hooded runner leaning over him.

"Hello, Doctor," he hissed. "To answer your question, I think I'll go with...crazy. Wouldn't you agree?"

Just over an hour later, a killer stepped out of Dr. Nigel's shower. He ambled back out and placed his towel into the backpack sitting on the table, then turned and walked back to the lifeless body. The number 43 had turned a reddish brown as the blood had thickened and dried in the cool air conditioning.

After lacing up his running shoes, he threw his backpack over his shoulders and left a sheet of paper in the center of Dr. Nigel's glass coffee table.

So many more of them deserve to pay
For the lost and broken heart I feel today.
Seven are gone, with more monsters to kill.
My rage still grows, and more blood will spill

—Gene Vance

CHAPTER 25

"THIS IS BULLSHIT!" YELLED THE SCRAWNY MAN in the dingy wife-beater.

The front of his grungy tank top was now decorated with bursts of vivid red droplets. The black cargo shorts were still the same, hanging low and revealing the same dirty boxers as the day before, and probably several days before that.

"I want me a lawyer. This is police brutality!"

"Shut up, bitch," Richardson growled, as he shoved the handcuffed man through the police station hallway. "I already said you have the right to remain silent, but you're too stupid to use it. Shut your face, or I'll shut it for you."

The grimacing detective continued to push him to the front desk. With one quick movement, he crunched the rail thin man over and slammed his chest onto the oak. A muscular forearm was pressed across his bony back, pinning him to the desk.

"Well, good morning there, Rhody," said the desk sergeant. "And a happy hump day to you. What little bit of sunshine did you bring us this morning?"

"This is the douche-bag who set us up yesterday." Richardson reached into his sport coat pocket with his free hand.

"That's bullshit! He's lyin'. I didn't set up nobody." The man squirmed against the desk.

"Yeah, that's probably accurate, considering you used a double negative, you illiterate piece of shit." Richardson winked to the sergeant.

"Kiss my ass, motherfu—"

Richardson went up on his toes and drove more weight down onto the center of the man's back. With a grunt, the pinned man continued to breathlessly give his opinion of the situation. Most of these opinions revolved around the premise that this situation involved various forms of bovine excrement, and how Detective Richardson had an unusually close relationship with his maternal parent.

"Here, Tony." Richardson pulled a cell phone from his coat pocket. "Have a judge sign off on searching this. I'm sure we'll find a text message to the dickheads who attacked us. It's password protected, and I don't believe Mr. Sunshine here is going to give us access. Once you get a warrant, get it to the boys in IT. Won't take them long to get into it."

"Sure thing, Rhod. What do you want to do with Mr. Happy in the meantime?"

"Toss his ass in a cell. For starters, charge him with assault, conspiracy, and resisting arrest. You can also charge him with being an asshole in the first degree, and felony stupidity."

Two officers escorted the swearing man down the hall.

"Hey, Rhody. What do we have going on here?" Lieutenant Finch walked up.

"Good morning, Bill. I thought I'd take a little side trip on the way in this morning. Got lucky and noticed the guy who sent the text to set up Jon and me. I was kinda surprised. Didn't think scumbags got up before noon."

"Was he the one who popped the pink spot under your eye?"

"Yeah. Can you believe that shit? After I chased him a while, we had us a little discussion. I told him I wanted to bring him in to talk, but he said he wasn't inclined to do so. I let him know I didn't care what he thought. Next thing I know, he caught me with a shot, so I had to take him down and bring him in."

"Mmm-hmmm." Finch raised an eyebrow. "I highly doubt it. I've seen you fight, Rhody. There's no way some scrawny street thug like that could lay a hand on you unless you wanted him to. You're too damn quick. Just save me the bullshit. More than likely, you let him tag you so you could be justified with IA for tuning him up."

"C'mon, Bill. I am getting older." Richardson laughed. "Maybe I'm slowing down a little."

"I doubt it. Please just remember department policy is to use only necessary force when bringing someone in."

"Hmm…my mistake. I thought it was *all available force.*"

"Very funny. Just try to keep it within department policy."

"I'll try. But when someone gets my partner hurt, my policy says to take him down."

"Just cover your ass. By the way, Doctor Taylor is here. Said she needs to speak with you. She's waiting up by your desk."

Rhody nodded and started down the hall.

"Hey, Richardson," the lieutenant called.

He stopped and looked back over his shoulder.

Finch nodded. "Good job getting the guy. Well-done."

Dr. Taylor was coming out of the break area, holding a steaming mug. She smiled at Richardson. As she stepped up to the cluttered desk, she took a sip of the bitter brew and scrunched her nose.

"Honestly, I don't know how you guys drink this swill. I should've hit a Tim Horton's on the way in."

Richardson smiled. "I think the bosses buy that cheap stuff to make us mean and keep us from going soft. Tell you what, though. It does the job when you have to pull an all-nighter."

Kaileen smiled briefly before narrowing her slate-blue eyes. "I wanted to talk to you and Detective Wayne—hope he's doing okay—about something I noticed with the poems. It's causing me some concern about the direction he's heading in."

The room erupted with cheers, whistles, catcalls, and applause. Richardson and Dr. Taylor spun around to look at the door. He laughed and clapped as well. Standing in the doorway, with his arms raised up like Rocky Balboa, was Wayne. The gregarious detective was soaking up the moment, exchanging high-fives and taking a few bows as he drifted through the workroom.

"Hey there, Louisville Slugger," Richardson said. "I can assume this means your doctor appointment went well?"

"Yup. The hit didn't do much damage." Wayne rapped on the top of his head with a closed fist. "Unfortunately, it didn't make me any smarter either. But the doc still has me riding a desk for the rest of this week. Even with the bruised shoulder, I should be able to go back to full duty next Monday."

"You were hit in the head," Dr. Taylor said. "I can't believe they would let you come back at all."

Richardson said, "I'm sure he probably reminded the doc that he has a gun and a badge and can make life tough for him if he didn't let him come back to work."

"Now, now, now," Wayne said, in a sing-song voice. "It doesn't matter how I got it. But I gave Bill a sheet of paper that says I can be here. I can do the desk work for a couple days, while you do the leg work. We have a case to get through, Doc. You didn't think I was going to let this yahoo have all the fun, did you?"

"Kaileen says she wanted to discuss some concerns she has with our Robert Frost wannabe. Says she noticed something with the poems."

"Yes, I did." She sat back down at the end of his desk. "I'm becoming more concerned with the verbiage, and there is a vagueness in the latest one which makes me think this may continue longer than we thought. Rhody, just like you're convinced the names mean something, I'm worried about some of the content and what it may mean."

"What are you thinking," Richardson said.

"Well, for one thing, the latest poem is vague. The others were clearly defined, with hard numbers. But now this one was open-ended." She looked at her notes. "The first two were together. He used the same poem, but it specifically mentions that there would be a total of ten victims. There was a consistency each time with his use of numbers in the next few. With Harrison, he says three are gone, and there will be seven more. Same with Hill—four are gone, and six to go. With Hallock, he does it again—five are gone, and five to go. But it changed with this last one though. I'm not sure if it's just a coincidence, or now that he's halfway through his original goal, he is getting a taste for this and doesn't want to stop at just ten. With Doctor Nadeer, he simply acknowledged that six are gone, but he only says *more* will pay the cost. Why does he say more, not four? He stopped giving us a countdown. It's not like he needed to condense syllables or something. They're the same. You noticed that he changed his rhyming patterns. With any of them, it's not as if he needed to keep a certain meter or cadence going with it. The poem patterns aren't exactly consistent. He doesn't seem to be OCD with that. Even so, he wouldn't have to edit to make it fit. I'm concerned that he now feels justified and comfortable with doing this. I'm having doubts he will want to stop when he gets to ten."

"I'm hoping we catch him before he gets to ten," Richardson said. "Actually, he's already at six, so I'd like to stop him before he gets to seven."

"You said you noticed something else with his words, Doc," Wayne said. "What else is going on?"

"Oh, yes. Something else that is troubling me—the words he's using. Or more precisely, one particular word." The psychiatrist placed her notepad back on the desk and folded her hands in her lap. "I realized our killer feels lost. I believe this feeling of being lost will make his twisted agenda and rage continue to grow."

"Okay, Doc. But how do you know he feels lost?" Richardson raised his brows.

"Because he told us." Kaileen picked up her notepad again. "First poem—*each of those years I've lost.* Second poem—*All those years loved and lost.* Third poem—*Tears flow free from a lost man's heart.* Fourth poem—*A life of love lost from the start.* In the fifth poem, he uses the word twice. First line says, *Pain and anger boil in a lost man.* And then the third line says, *Nothing to lose with a soul that is lost.* He has left five different poems with five different names, but each one of them has the word *lost* in it. His feeling of being lost has me even more concerned about the potential for escalation and continued killing."

"Why is that?" Wayne said.

"Feeling lost is a feeling of hopelessness, with no escape. It's like a caged animal and needs an outlet as the pressure builds. Did you ever wonder why so many prisoners work out so much and get stronger?"

Wayne smirked. "Because they'd rather play pitcher than catcher on the ol' ball team."

"Huh. Excuse me?"

Richardson laughed. "Because they'd rather lead than follow at the prison prom?"

"Oh, I get it. Real cute. Not funny." Kaileen shook her head. "I suppose survival and being able to stand your ground are part of it, but I would wager that the primary reason is because of the need to relieve the growing pressure of feeling trapped. People put under intense pressure need an outlet. Some turn to physical activity to vent their emotional strain. All this would be fine if it actually dissipated the rage, but it doesn't. It's temporary. The rage can continue to grow, even with this outlet. Plenty of prison attacks and riots are proof enough for me."

"And you're thinking our killer is experiencing this," Richardson said.

"Yes, I do. I was thinking back to our first task force meeting. It was stated that the killer was of average height. But as Jeff pointed out, his shoulder-to-waist ratio indicated a muscular build. Our killer is strong. He uses some sort of physical activity to vent his anger, but this is like being in a pressure cooker—even if you do something to lower the heat, the pressure will still continue to build and build. If the venting isn't enough, it will explode. I believe his feeling of being lost, and the anger with his so-called monsters, is building more and more. Killing is the way he vents some of the pressure, and I don't think he can, or even wants to, stop."

Lieutenant Finch walked toward the trio. "Hey, Rhody. We have another plastic surgery doctor who was a no-show at work this morning. Nurse says phone is going straight to voicemail. His name is Aaron Nigel. He lives in the Lofts on Ellicott, fifth floor.

Sending a couple uniforms there now. I want you to head over, too. Let's hope it's nothing, but my gut is telling me otherwise."

The two detectives jumped up and got ready to head out.

"Detective Wayne." Finch scowled. "That shiny gold badge looks mighty nice hanging on your belt. Unless you want me to take it away, you will sit your ass right back down in that chair."

"But Bill!"

"Don't you *But Bill* me, Jon. I have a piece of paper that says you will be parking your butt in this office all day, for the rest of the week. I don't know what bunch of bullshit you gave the doctor to get released, but this is non-negotiable. Plant your ass."

"Sorry, partner." Richardson gave a half-smile. "I'll let you know what we find. See if you can come up with anything more on those names. Well, Doc? Sounds like he may have got to number seven. Want to come along and see if there's anything you notice with this one?"

"Sure. I'm free until this afternoon."

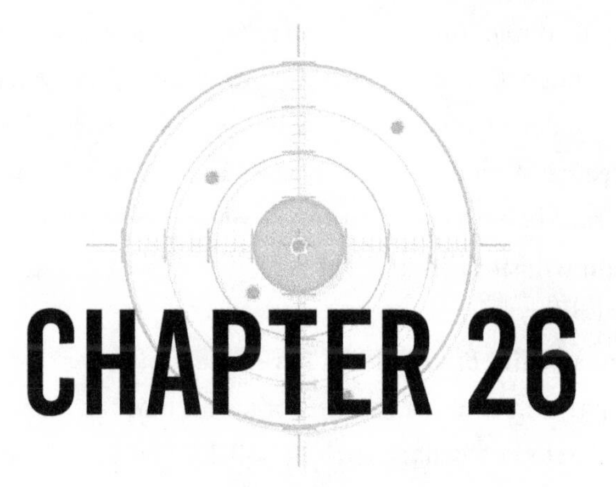

CHAPTER 26

PAUL SCHON PULLED INTO THE PARKING LOT. HE was a few minutes early for his appointment with Dr. Taylor. After turning off the ignition, he looked at a pair of exhausted eyes in the rearview mirror. It had been another restless night of nightmares revealing horrific images he couldn't remember. Dark circles under his eyes echoed the wear and tear his body felt.

"Look who's a Ricky Raccoon now." He put on a pair of sunglasses.

"Good afternoon, Paul," said Dr. Taylor. "Nice to see you again. How are you feeling?"

Paul sat in his usual spot. "Absolutely exhausted. I feel like I'm sleeping half my life away, but I'm still so tired. Another rough night last night, I guess."

"Another nightmare?"

"Yeah, I think so, but I don't really remember much about it. Blood and knives. Seemed like I was watching it from above, but then it was if someone was grabbing at me. When I woke up, I was drenched in sweat again and felt like I'd been run through the mill."

"As I recall, you've had similar dreams before. You mentioned you also had one last week, too. I see your cheek is healing nicely."

He reached up and brushed it with his hand. "Yes. It still hurts if I smile, but that doesn't happen too often now, does it?"

"How often are you having these dreams?"

"Well, I think I have them nightly. But you seem to see the worst of it. I noticed lately that the days I come to see you are the ones I'm the most tired." He blushed. "I'm sure it's nothing personal against you, Doc. Saturdays are a little rough, too. But at least on the weekends I can just lounge around, so it doesn't hit me as hard. Between the rough nights and my shaky hands, it's a wonder I can even function at all."

"I'm sorry to hear you're having such a hard time lately. I know this is going to be a stressful time of the year for you."

"Yeah, I know. Seems like the upcoming anniversary is getting to me. I seem a nervous wreck to everyone at work. I can tell they're trying to be understanding, but it's also obvious that they're trying to avoid me. I try to not go into the office too often anymore. They're probably glad I work from home a lot more these days. Between my shaky hands and baggy eyes, I would avoid me, too, if I could. I must look insane."

"Paul, you do not look insane. But I am truly concerned about you. This is something we can get through. You can do this—and I'm here to help you. I can't help but notice the tension and anxiety building up within you. This is all part of the healing process. I have been going through our past sessions, and I've noticed a few things which may explain some of this. You need to stop being so hard on yourself. We can, and will, get through this."

"I sure hope so."

"Do you remember what day of the week it was when you lost Sheila?"

"That's an easy question. It was late Tuesday night. Worst night of my life. Last night marked the forty-ninth Tuesday night since she passed." He sighed and chuckled. "And for those keeping score at home, the day after tomorrow will be the forty-ninth Friday since she was laid to rest. It was also the very last time I was able to kiss her and see her beautiful face before we went to the cemetery."

"Yes, I realized it when I was taking a look at our notes. I'd like you to think about that. You just said your worst days are Wednesdays, when you meet with me, and you also said Saturdays are rough, too, but you can sleep in."

"Yeah, I know."

"I think the reason you're so exhausted on Wednesdays and Saturdays is because you are struggling with Tuesdays and Fridays. Subconsciously, you may be associating those days with what happened with Sheila."

"Wow. I never put that together, but it sounds right."

"I truly believe it. This could be why you are so tired and worn out the day after. In your mind, it may seem like fresh, new pain. I wouldn't be surprised to discover that you have been very active in your sleep. Thrashing, tossing and turning could explain why you wake so sweaty, sore, and thirsty. In your mind, you are in a painful and emotionally raw place."

"That does make a lot of sense, Kaileen. Where do we go from here, then?"

She looked back with her sweet and caring smile. "This is a good discovery for us, Paul. But remember, it's still a process. It won't just go away. This is something we have to work through, but now we have a direction. Now that we know you're dealing with the trauma you associate with those days, we can begin to heal and move past it. I'd like you to keep a diary, like we talked about with your nightmares. Especially on Tuesdays and Fridays, please write down everything you feel—what upsets you, what you're thinking about. Try to journal all your thoughts before you go to sleep at night. Things like that can help us find out what triggers these restless nights."

"Sounds like a plan, Kaileen."

"Well, among other things, I've also been thinking that maybe we should try something other than the Pentozipratol for a while."

"No!"

Dr. Taylor jumped back in her chair. She looked up from her notepad, and her surprise melded into fear. Paul was now sitting on the edge of the sectional, glaring at her. His left hand was fluttering violently. His jawline was clenched, and he appeared to be grinding his teeth.

What scared her the most was his eyes. They had always been sad, but remained kind and gentle. Now she felt as if she was facing a cornered animal ready to attack. The soft brown eyes were now cold, hard, and pulsing back and forth as rapidly as his spasmodic hand. His gentle, caring voice was replaced with a harsh, gravelly tone.

"I don't want to change them. Not yet."

"Okay, Paul," Dr. Taylor replied, in a smooth, even cadence as she set her notebook in her lap.

She sat back, composed herself, and tried to erase any traces of her fear.

"It was just a suggestion as we look at some of our options."

With a shake of his head, Paul's eyes stopped their ping pong match. He cleared his throat and returned to a more normal tone.

"I'm sorry, Kaileen. I don't know what came over me. I guess I'm more tired than I thought. Must be making me just a little edgy. I just don't want to make any big changes right now, if it's okay. Let's keep working on your new focus. I really think you may be onto something."

"Okay, Paul. We can keep it as is for a little longer, and then we will see how you're doing."

At the end of the session, Dr. Taylor stayed a few paces back, but still followed him to the door. For the first time in her career, she locked the door as soon as her patient was out. She hurried to her desk, grabbed a pen with shaky fingers, and began writing in his file.

Paul walked back to his car and placed the keys in the ignition. Before firing up the engine, he looked in the mirror and blinked a few times. He shot his eyebrows up so high folds of skin jammed across the top of his brow. He looked to the left and to the right. Shook his head and closed his eyes, then slowly opened them again.

With wide eyes, he wondered why was he in his car and when he had left Dr. Taylor's office.

CHAPTER 27

IT HAD BEEN ANOTHER LONG AND FRUSTRATING WEEK for Richardson. He sat on his living room couch with papers, files, and pictures spread across the coffee table.

The scene at Dr. Nigel's loft had been just as gruesome and perplexing as the others. No signs of forced entry. With everything in the news lately, why would anyone just let someone into their home? Was it someone they all knew? Aside from the medical profession, there didn't seem to be any connections between the victims.

Once again, Jeff McDonald's team hadn't been able to find any useful forensic evidence. Dr. Matthews was going to have the autopsy results as soon as he could, but Richardson wasn't in a rush to see it. He knew exactly what the report would say. Nigel had bled out after being tortured with various cuts on his face and a lethal throat slash.

Dr. Taylor's concerns were also weighing on him. She had pointed out the vagueness and the use of the word *lost* in Nigel's poem as well. This time, the killer was lamenting *the lost and broken heart I feel today,* and again said that *more* would be killed. Not three. He had simply stated *more monsters to kill.* Richardson couldn't help but wonder if the psychiatrist was right and the killer had a taste for it. Was he planning to continue his homicidal wrath beyond his original pledge?

This case was getting to Richardson. He knew he was missing something. Was he so immersed in the case that he couldn't clearly see things in front of him? He could feel himself becoming obsessed. Even though it was a late Friday afternoon, he knew his mind would be working all weekend. It seemed all his waking thoughts, and most of his non-awake ones, were on the case.

He took Kerry out to grab some dinner and relax a little. They climbed onto the motorcycle and headed out to Uncle Joe's Diner in Hamburg. Nothing fancy, but it was one of their favorites. Something about casual conversation over a grilled Rueben and a pile of fries could usually melt away Richardson's concerns.

But this time it didn't work. As usual, lately, their normal, friendly banter about their family, their puppy, and NASCAR turned into a conversation revolving around the aspects of the case. His wife listened attentively and asked good questions. Kerry always had a calming influence on him and helped him to become more centered when he went too far. Having a husband who recites poetry to you may sound romantic, but when the words are from the ramblings of a psychopathic serial killer, it takes on a much different aura.

Through it all, Kerry was a good sounding board, and many times offered a fresh perspective.

After dinner, they continued to go riding for a while. It helped a little. The evening was sultry and sticky. The humid air blowing in their faces was hot and refreshing at the same time. Leaning back and forth through the curves, the husband and wife worked together as one rider on the bike. The rumble of the V-twin engine under them, and his wife's arms wrapped around his waist with her chest pressed into his back, reminded him how nice life could be. While cruising along, he would tap the front brakes on the big bike just to feel her firm breasts mash even tighter against his back. It was a game they had played since they were dating. As nice as it was, the details of the case had continued to creep into his thoughts.

Now, hours later, he was eyeball-deep in papers, pictures, and theories.

Kerry came in and joined him on the couch. She put an arm around him and rubbed back his upper back with her small hand.

"Hey, babe," she said. "I love these big strong shoulders, but I hate feeling them so tense. You really need to relax a little. This is eating you up."

"Yeah, I know. I'll relax when we catch this son of a bitch."

Kerry stood with a sigh and drifted across the living room.

"I know you will, babe. You'll get him."

Richardson turned his focus back to the array spread out on the coffee table. Papers, pictures, and theories—a labyrinth of information, but none of it helping him get any further. With his head buried in his hands, and the noise of the case bouncing around in his brain, he heard a familiar soft and sultry voice.

"You sure you can't think of anything to help you relax a little?"

He pulled his hands from his forehead and looked up. Standing in the archway was his bride. She was leaning against the opening, one knee slightly bent, holding a hand up under her soft pouty lips as she batted her deep brown eyes. Red lace with black trim caressed and complimented her perfect, petite figure. The coquettish, come-hither look was too much for anyone to resist, let alone a man who was madly in love with her.

"Mmmmm." Richardson wrapped his hands around her small waist. "I think there is definitely something. You always seem to know just what I need."

Smiling at the several inches of deep, creamy cleavage below him, he pressed her back against the wall, bent down, and began passionately kissing her soft lips. Hands were all over one another like a couple who had never forgotten how to act like newlyweds.

She tipped her head back and offered her throat. As Richardson kissed and nibbled along the sensitive muscles on the side of her neck, Kerry clawed at his shirt buttons. With mouths and hands exploring each other, they moved down the hallway to the bedroom. Several articles of clothing, including the red lace, never made it that far.

"Whew! That was awesome." A glistening Kerry sighed, as she collapsed next to him. "See, I knew I could get your mind off the case for an hour or so."

Panting, Richardson smiled. "You certainly did, babe. I needed that more than you know."

"You're not the only one," she cooed, as he peeled back long strands of hair clinging to her shimmering face and shoulders.

She traced the raised marks across his chest with her fingernails.

"Oops. Looks like I gave you quite a few welts with these nails."

"You didn't give me anything. I earned 'em."

"Mmm-hmm, you sure did." She nuzzled up to him and laid her head on his chest.

He wrapped his arm under her neck and down to the small of her back.

"Let's hope it gives me a whole new perspective," he said.

"I hope so too, babe," she said, in a sleepy voice.

It wouldn't be long before she drifted off into her usual, blissful sleep after making love.

"I know I shouldn't bring it up now," she said, "but do you and Doctor Taylor have any ideas on why he used a noun instead of a name with this last one?"

"Huh. What do you mean?"

She yawned. "With this last doctor, he used a noun instead of a weird name. He signed it as *Vengeance*."

Richardson chuckled. "No, babe. It was a name. He signed it Gene Vance."

"Oh, my mistake," she said, in groggy voice. "I must've misheard you. Gene Vance. Vengeance. They're kinda the same. To-may-to, to-mah-to. I guess my ears just heard it wrong."

Soon, the rhythmic sound of her light breathing confirmed her departure into the land of nod. Richardson smiled and turned to kiss the top of her head. He continued to stroke the smooth, supple skin of her lower back and rear. He was much more relaxed and in a better place now. She always did that for him.

His mind was still on the case, though. He wished he could shut it down, but it wasn't going to happen.

He clicked on the bedroom TV and searched for something innocuous enough to help his mind drift away. Listening to some man rave about amazing and incredible non-stick pans could certainly make most people catatonic. He left the infomercial on for background noise, but found himself watching the circling ceiling fan. How appropriate—just like the fan, I'm constantly working. Moving in circles but not getting anywhere.

While keeping his sleeping bride covered, he lowered his part of the sheet to his waist. The fan did its job and forced cool air onto his glistening chest. The combination of the cool air from the fan, his wife's warm breath against his chest, and the droning from the infomercial began to have a hypnotic effect on him. Even with thoughts of the case spiraling in his mind, he could feel himself drifting further and further into sleep.

Richardson jerked awake. "Holy shit! That's it."

He sat up, bringing along a hundred pounds of blond-topped confusion up with him.

"Oh, my God," Kerry mumbled. "Huh? What's going on?"

"Thank you, babe." He kissed her on the top of her head.

"For what?"

"You said, *Gene Vance. Vengeance. They're kinda the same.* Hell yeah, they are! You're the best."

He jumped out of the bed and rushed to the dresser under the television. After an embarrassing lesson from a few years ago, he remembered to slip on a pair of sleep pants before running back out in front of the picture window and sitting on the couch. He flipped open a file and grabbed a pen, then began reading, thinking, and writing.

Tying an oversized robe around her waist, a bleary-eyed Kerry padded out to the living room a few minutes later.

"What is going on, babe?"

"I was right. He was talking to us through the poems."

"What do you mean?"

"They're anagrams! Every one of these stupid friggin' names is an anagram."

CHAPTER 28

THE DARK PREDATOR WAS RUNNING AGAIN. BLACK Asics kept their smooth pace over the concrete sidewalks. His backpack bounced against the black and gray hoodie.

He had been running every night for several months, and he could feel himself getting better at it. Countless push-ups and pull-ups at a neighborhood park had him feeling stronger, too, but running made him feel the best. Listening to the rhythmic pace of his shoes over the pavement helped clear his mind. In some ways, it pulled him completely out of himself.

Most nights, he ran just to relieve the mounting tension that built within him every day. The anger. The confusion. The sadness. The raw emotions raging inside him needed an outlet. He wished the pain could leave him as easily as the sweat that poured from his pores.

Some nights, he ran to not only relieve the tension, but also to scout for information on his newest target. Some things you just can't find on the Internet. Information, and attention to all the little details, was important.

But on a Friday night, it wasn't just about running. It wasn't about relieving pressure or scouting information about his prey. Friday night was a night for action. A time to hunt. A night to rid the world of another monster.

This run would only take him three miles from South Buffalo. But in terms of lifestyles, it was a galaxy away. The homes along the waterfront, especially the townhouses on Rivermist, belonged to people completely out of his realm. On top of the million-dollar mortgages, people here paid as much in monthly homeowner fees as others in the Queen City paid for their rent.

But none of that mattered to him. Rich monster or poor monster, he had to eliminate them.

He crept along Exchange Street, heading toward downtown. The air was still hot and heavy, and the sweat-soaked running suit clung to him. Soon he was under the rats' nest of spiraling exits for the skyway and the interstate that passed overhead. After dropping down to Marine Drive, he turned right and ran along the water. The USS Little Rock loomed over him as he traveled through the Naval and Military Park. Before running in front of Marina Market, he pulled his hood down lower to avoid any cameras. He soon cut across Erie Street and went a short way up Waterfront Circle.

Upon hearing music, he decided to make a short detour down Gull Landing. At the end of the circle, he stepped off the pavement and moved closer to the water. Across the basin, he could see a wedding party on the upper roof deck at Templeton Landing. The DJ had the dance floor jumping. Along with the thumping bass, shrill squeals of laughter and revelry danced across the rippling water. He wished the newlyweds all the best and hoped they would cherish what they had.

His mind drifted back to a warm summer night when he was wearing a tuxedo and staring at the most beautiful bride he could ever imagine. The night had been a blur—a swirling cascade of smiles and happiness. To him, it seemed that barely five minutes had passed between the time they were introduced before dinner, until the DJ announced it was time for the final slow song of the night. As Eric Clapton belted out "Wonderful Tonight," he walked to the center of the dance floor with his bride. With family and friends surrounding them, they danced as he sang every word to her.

It had been a perfect night. They said goodbye to their friends and then went to spend their wedding night surrounded by the luxury of Salvatore's Garden Place Hotel. The next morning, they awoke to breakfast before taking the short cab ride to the Buffalo-Niagara Falls International Airport. From there, they caught a flight to begin their forever. He had no idea how short that forever would be.

With a heavy sigh, the predator turned away from the restaurant. With both hands, he wiped the tears from his eyes, and started jogging back along Waterfront Circle. He needed to clear out those pleasant, but painful, thoughts. Needed to focus. He was almost to the home of Dr. Oh.

He did not need to turn up Ojibwa to go all the way to Rivermist Drive. He could clearly see the water side of the houses along Rivermist from here. As he came to an inlet marked Harbor Bay Station, he slowed and walked past another sign that read, *Private Property—No Trespassing.* Despite the sign's best efforts at stopping him, he was going to trespass for the next hour or two.

Hedges, evergreens, and a tall ash tree near the road all spent their daytime hours competing for the sun. He looked up in admiration at the ash. It was one of the few around Western New York that had not been ravaged by the emerald ash borers that had devastated so many others. The adult insects feed harmlessly on the leaves of the majestic trees. But after laying their eggs on the bark, the larvae dig in and feed upon the inner bark, disrupting the transport of water and nutrients. Once infested, the death of the tree is almost certain.

He grimaced at the similarities to the pain he had gone through—a parasite that ravaged and murdered something so beautiful, from the inside.

Behind the dark mulch surrounding the small grove, stood a short brick privacy wall that stopped at the open decks and railing which ran along the inlet. It would be simple and easy to slip in behind the wall and cross the few patios until he arrived at Dr. Oh's. He knew it would be easier, but it would also be far too risky. Even rich people stayed up later on a Friday night. There was too much of a chance that someone could walk out or look through their large sliding doors to watch the moon reflecting in the rippling water.

During last night's run, he felt he had come up with a better way. The decks jutted out above the breaker wall for the inlet. He would be able to creep along the top of the cut stone while remaining less visible.

He edged along the privacy wall and tentatively reached with a foot onto the top of the breaker wall where it angled off under the decks. With eight gloved fingers gripping the top of the deck, he side-stepped along the rock wall. He kept his head low as he inched along. His eyes were slightly higher than the deck, and he could clearly see the expensive tables, chaise lounges, and Adirondack chairs decorating the redwood. He took one hand from the deck to pull his hoodie down lower. It was dark, but with the moon dancing on the waves behind him, it wasn't dark enough to be invisible.

He stopped and remained frozen. A sliding door was gliding across its rails. As footsteps walked across the deck, he crouched lower and reached under the deck to steady himself. With his other hand, he found a floor joist to hold. He leaned in against the angled rock underneath the edge of the deck and held his breath.

"Oh, Mark. It's such a beautiful night," a woman's voice said, from right above him.

"Sure is. But not as beautiful as you."

He thought her light and airy laugh sounded as if it were being batted around on the wings of angels.

"You are so sweet. I love you so much."

"Mmmm. I love you, too, babe. Come on. Let's head back inside, and I'll show you just how much."

"Ooh, I like the sound of that," she purred, and the angel wings seemed as if they had just been scorched with devilish thoughts.

As the sound of footsteps faded to the door, the crouched killer looked at a spider in the dim light. She was crawling across his black leather glove, curious about what had disturbed the web she had spent all day building. He laid the gloved hand along the joist to allow the diligent arachnid to continue her toils.

A few seconds after hearing the door latch, he placed his hands back on top and peered over the deck. Methodically, he began again. He moved his foot and hand over about a shoulder-width. Shifted his weight, then brought over his other hand. He scanned the deck for signs of movement, and stayed alert for sound. Dr.

Oh's deck was only one more over, and he inched toward it, focused on his hunt.

As he shifted his weight, his foot shot out from under him and he began to drop. His knee slammed into the top edge of the retaining wall. As he continued his slide, the corner of the stone caught him in the stomach and marched up to his rib cage, causing a Heimlich maneuver. As his breath escaped him, he continued falling. He latched his curled fingers onto the top of the wall as his feet dangled just above the water.

He clawed at the wall with his feet, searching for a crevice to step with. After finding a toehold, he began to pull himself up on the wall. He was glad he had lost thirty pounds in the last few months. His triceps flexed as he hoisted himself back up to the top of the wall, and he gripped the deck once again. His knee was beginning to swell and hurt like hell. The left leg of the sweatpants had a small tear folded over where his knee had slammed the rough-edged rock. He looked down at the greenish-black smear that had caused him to succumb so quickly to gravity.

"Note to self," he muttered. "Make sure you check for goose poop."

A few minutes later, he was looking across the floor of Dr. Oh's sparsely decorated deck. He scanned across it and along the balconies. No cameras were visible. He grasped the railing and did a pull-up, slid between the top two rails and crouched on the doctor's deck.

The luxury townhouse was three-stories tall, and each level had its own balcony. The first two floors were dark. From the top balcony, ever-changing light patterns indicated a TV was still on.

Dr. Oh's master bedroom was on the third floor. The doctor would often post how much he enjoyed sleeping with his sliding doors open so he could listen to the sounds of the water and breathe in the cooler lake breezes.

With the slightest limp, the hunter walked across the deck. He did several squats, shook his leg, and stretched the aching limb. He was glad it was his left knee that bothered him. His plan would require the use of both legs, but his right knee was going to be doing much more of the work.

Although most of the deck space was out in the open, each of the townhouses were separated by a brick wall that went partway onto the decks to give the illusion of privacy. This wall jutted out the furthest onto the deck before making the ninety-degree turn to become the wall facing the water. Inside these walls was the spacious living rooms tastefully decorated with leather furniture, large oil paintings, decorative vases, and a ninety-inch television mounted on the opposite interior wall. The three windows facing the deck offered spectacular sunsets throughout the year.

Shortly past the third window, the wall angled back toward the house. The short diagonal wall framed a doorway. Just two bricks past the doorway, the angled wall turned back and went straight toward another wall holding a set of wide sliding doors.

Ever-alert and looking around, he checked the door to the living room before padding to the sliding glass doors. After entering the shadowy area underneath the deck above, he reached out with a gloved hand and tried to ease the door open. It was latched tight and wouldn't move.

He expected it. Not a big deal. This wouldn't be the first time he used his newfound athleticism to get to a balcony.

He turned right and walked over to the angled wall. Slid his hand across the two bricks framing the left side of the door. He smiled. The angle was going to make this more manageable for him. Technique and precision were too important, and knew his physical limitations didn't leave a lot of room for error. This kind of thing wasn't natural to him just yet.

He stood at the end of the narrow brick frame and looked up. The railing for the second-floor deck was above him and slightly to his left. He took a small step to the side and then moved up to the brick frame. He needed to decide which brick he would use as his launching point. If he picked a brick too low, his foot would slide down. If he picked a brick too high, he would lose all his momentum and push himself back out on to the deck. He also needed to account for the angle. He would need to make sure he didn't roll his ankle and pop a tendon.

The narrow frame was only about two bricks wide, and he wanted to hit it just to the left of center. He focused on part of a brick that was in front of and a little higher than his hip. He tentatively reached out with a leather covered finger and made an invisible X to create a mark to aim for.

With his gaze locked on the brick, he backed up across the deck, toward the railing. He crouched and placed his hands along the seam of a deck plank. Like a sprinter ready to start a race, he leaned his weight forward onto his outstretched fingers and thumbs. After breathing deeply in through his nose, he exhaled through his mouth, remaining vigilant of any sounds that would alert him of potential issues.

Waves lapped at the breaker wall behind him. A bullfrog was doing its best to attract a lady friend. A motorcycle quietly rounded the bend on Waterfront Circle before going up through the gears. His eyes never moved. He remained focused on the brick.

His mind calculated and recalculated. A multitude of thoughts and concerns were rolling through his head. It was tight. He had never done this with such little space.

Crouched, with his back against the railing, he stayed focused on the brick. He would only have three fast to get up to speed. His fourth step would need to land perfectly on the brick. His paces had to be perfect. If he launched too soon, his leg would be too straight. If he was a half-step too far, his body would be too close and his knee would be pressed against his chest.

Once more, he drew a deep breath through his nose. As he let it out through his mouth, he exploded up from his crouched stance, into a sprint. One step, he was leaning as his arms drove him forward. Second step, he was now halfway across the deck and more upright. Third step, he was in the right place and running tall.

He arched his back as he swung his right leg up. A black running shoe landed quietly on the chosen brick. His left leg continued driving him forward until the foot vacated the deck. The right leg took over as momentum continued driving his body toward the wall. He pushed into and down on the wall at the same time. Quadriceps flexed and demanded the knee continue to straighten the leg. His right knee answered the call to redirect the energy on a new path. He swung his arms up as he drove his body upward. The angled brick helped guide his body to the left.

Black leather gloves continued sailing up into the air until they closed around the bottom rung of the balcony rail. With a smile, he did another pull-up and slipped through the rails and onto the second-floor balcony. He turned back and took in the bird's-eye view of what he had just done.

He walked over to the second-floor slider. It was locked, but the next climb would be less stressful. On the far side of the balcony was a half-wall that was a little higher than the railing. It opened up the view of the lake, but also made it more convenient for a determined killer to reach the next balcony.

The third-floor balcony only came out about half the distance of the second-floor deck. After hopping onto the short wall, it was just a quick jump up as he wrapped his hands around a railing again. He stood in the shadows as he let his backpack slip down from his shoulders.

Sheer curtains in the open door danced in the breeze. As they undulated through the opening, he dropped to a knee and peered into the master bedroom. ESPN was showing baseball highlights. Justin Verlander had pitched eight hitless innings before the Astros's ace gave up a single down the first-base line. Over the excitement of the announcer's voice, light snoring indicated Dr. Oh was asleep.

After stepping back into the shadows, he unzipped the front pocket of his backpack and reached in to pull out a dark washcloth and a small plastic bottle. He folded the cloth in half and then in half again before pouring the liquid over it. Holding it over the palm of his gloved hand, he slipped through the doorway as the curtains caressed and swirled around him. He stopped at the edge of the bed, unfolded the damp washcloth, and jammed it over the sleeping doctor's mouth and nose. Waking with a gasp and wide eyes, Dr. Oh drew the fumes deep into his lungs.

"Hello, Doctor."

CHAPTER 29

Richardson could see Dr. Taylor walking across the diner parking lot. He tooted the horn before he stepped down from his truck.

"Hey, Kaileen. Glad you could meet with us this morning. Just got a text from Bill. He's on his way here, too. There's Jon's car. He must already be inside."

"No problem, Detective. Looking forward to hearing what you've learned. And ugh, I am really looking forward to getting inside for a little AC. Just walking across this parking lot, I feel like I'm roasting. It's only ten o'clock, and it feels like it's already around ninety degrees and about four hundred percent humidity. Couldn't believe it when I walked out this morning."

"Yeah." Richardson laughed as they walked together. "Going to be another steamy one. Last night was comfortable until that warm front moved in and the humidity shot through the roof. Air is so thick you almost have to chew it. They say tomorrow's gonna be even worse. Monday is looking like more of the same, too. My electric bill is gonna be sky-high this month. Ain't it funny how the networks never talk about this kind of Buffalo weather. But let us get just a couple feet of snow, and they're all over the place."

Richardson held the door open for her as they walked in. The cold air hit them, causing a brief, but welcomed, shiver. They could see Wayne sitting in a corner booth, sipping a cup of coffee, before tossing his head back.

They slid into the booth.

"Hey there, Sundance," Richardson said. "You're looking a little green around the gills. How're you feeling?"

"Getting a little better. But sometimes these headaches get to me. I should be good to go on Monday. Doc gave me some new stuff. Works pretty well once it kicks in. Just popped one as you walked in. Right now, though, my head feels like those mornings after we'd go see the Steam Donkeys play out at Club Utica."

"Ouch." Rhody laughed. "That's gotta suck."

"Did you say, the Steam Donkeys?" Kaileen said.

"Yeah. It's a band Rhody and I used to go see a lot. Rhody knew the lead singer, Buck, back when he played for the JackLords. That was before the Donkeys. They're a real good alt-country rock music. Kinda punk-a-billy. Some of the best nights I don't remember were with those guys at the Utica."

"Yeah, good times," Richardson said. "You should check them out on YouTube sometime, Doc. They're pretty good. They were voted into the Buffalo Music Hall of Fame not too long ago. Cosmic Americana is still one of my favorite CDs"

"Hey, didn't you say one of the Goo Goo Dolls had something to do with that CD?" Wayne said.

"Sure thing. Robby Takac recorded and mixed it. Even back then, he had a great ear for music. We should take the girls over to the Sportsman's Tavern sometime. Every now and then, they still play there. I heard they play in Allentown every week, too. Be just like the old times, except maybe now we'd be able to remember what happened."

"That sounds good. Maybe you could get back up and sing a few Dwight Yoakam tunes with them like you used to."

"Hey, guys, sorry I'm late." Lieutenant Finch walked up. "Good to see you guys on a Saturday morning for once, when we're not elbow-deep in another shitstorm."

Julie poured coffee all the way around and took their order.

"So what's all this about the names on the poems?" Finch said.

"Well, last night Kerry and I were talking about things and she misheard me when I said the name on the last one. She thought I said *vengeance* instead of *Gene Vance*. Easy enough to mishear that one. When I corrected her, she shrugged it off and said they were kinda the same. Later on, I was thinking about it and realized they aren't just kinda the same. They *are* the same. It's the same letters, just swapped around. An anagram. So I figured, we've got a guy whining in his poems about his poor pitiful life and needing to make others pay for it. This shithead is looking for vengeance, and he signs it as Gene Vance. That seemed like too much of a coincidence for me. And as you know, I don't believe in coincidences."

"So what else did you find?" Wayne said.

"Yeah, what else?" said Dr. Taylor. "You said you thought they were all anagrams."

"Yup, they sure are." Richardson pulled out his notes. "Some jumped right out at me after a bit. But some of the others took me quite a while to come up with. I ain't quite as sharp at these as I used to be."

"Maybe you were too sober." Wayne laughed. "You were always better at 'em when we were three sheets to the wind."

"Yeah." Richardson smiled. "Maybe that's why it took longer. I stayed up pretty late getting a couple of them, but I think I got them all now."

"Okay, then." Finch smiled. "I'm prepared to be amazed. Go ahead."

"All right, let's go from the beginning and start with the first one at Nia-Buff. He signed that one as Arthur Seth. It took me a little bit to come up with that one, but I had an idea of where we were headed with his train of thought. Check it out—if you rearrange the letters, it becomes *Heart hurts.* I figured I was on the right path with that one, based on Kaileen's diagnosis of someone feeling pain and loss. The second one from Harrison's house, he signed it as Herbert Noak. Right away I noticed the letters for *heart* again in that one. I rearranged the rest of the letters, and it turns out to say, *Broken heart.*"

"Poor baby," Wayne said. "Went from a hurt heart to a broken heart."

With plates of steaming food in front of them, Richardson grabbed a bite and took a sip of coffee.

"The next one we had was the salesman over at the Lenox. This was the *Odel Ives* name. Swap that bad boy around, and we have *Love dies.* We definitely have a sad serial killer here. I thought it was kind of interesting how the anagrams all focus on sadness. Figured you'd have a field day with this crap, Kaileen."

"I have to admit, I don't know how you recognized these, but this is meaningful stuff." She pulled a strawberry from her fruit bowl.

"Well, he got more creative with the nurse in Orchard Park. Instead of two words making another two words, he used the first and last name to make three words. Levon Moore becomes *No more love*, or *Love no more*. Either way, it means about the same. I gotta say, this guy must really be hurting. But you have to give him some credit. This is a unique way to go about it."

"Oh, yay," Finch said. "You can let him know just how creative he is after you toss his ass in prison."

"Sorry, boss. Just sayin'. The one from Doctor Nadeer's probably took me the longest. Must be losing my touch. I probably went through a few hundred combinations before it started to fall in place. With this one, he turned Findley Moise into four words. He is saying, *My life is done*. And that brings us to our latest one of *vengeance*.

"Now I'm really worried," Kaileen said. "We have a killer who is emotionally crushed and feels his life is done. He's said he has nothing to lose, and doesn't seem to care about his life. The only thing he cares about now is vengeance."

CHAPTER 30

EARLY MONDAY MORNING, DETECTIVE WAYNE CAME out of Captain Reynolds office and weaved through the maze of desks and chairs, to their work area. After plopping down with a sigh, he gave Richardson a half-smile and shrug.

"So how'd it go in there?" Richardson said.

"Could've been worse, I suppose. Captain says he's not too thrilled with me being back so soon. I'm sure the lieutenant has probably been in there chewing his ears off. He was nice enough to remind me about the bullshit *other duties, as assigned* part of the job description and let me know he can assign me to whatever shit job he wants."

"Is he doing that?"

"Nah, not yet. But he says if he thinks I'm pushing it too much, he will step in. So I promised him I'd be a good boy and let you chase the big bad guys down dark alleys for a few more days."

"Good thinkin', Lincoln." Richardson took another gulp of coffee. "But I'm hoping there won't be any running down alleyways today. Remember that guy, Paul Schon, we talked to on Tuesday before you got whacked in the head?"

"Yeah, I remember him. It's not like I have amnesia, wise-ass."

"Nah, just normal forgetfulness." Richardson laughed. "I'm thinking I might have amnesia, though. There's something about his name that keeps eating at me. Do you recall us ever having anything with someone named Schon?"

"Doesn't sound familiar. Nothing I can think of. Why? What's going on with him?"

"When we spoke with him, Schon said he had an appointment with Doctor Chandler just up the street from Nia-Buff. I reached out to them, and Chandler's able to speak with us this morning. Let's head over there. I'll drive."

"Big shock."

"Hey, I don't know how brain damaged you are there, Sundance." Richardson grinned. "You might forget which one is the gas and which one is the brake."

"Ha-ha, smart-ass."

A short time later, the two detectives stepped out of their car and toward the medical office. Shadows stayed ahead of them as they crossed the street. Richardson and Wayne looked down the next block, at the plastic surgery center where it all began. They both held a hand up to shield their eyes from the glare ricocheting off the Nia-Buff glass exterior. The blazing sun was already creating hazy waves of evaporating moisture that had settled into the sidewalk during the night.

Kathy, the receptionist, showed them back to Dr. Chandler's office and let them know she was finishing up with a patient and would be right in. A few minutes later, as they were looking at the various degrees framed on the walls, the smiling doctor walked in.

"Good morning, gentlemen. I'm Doctor Chandler. Pleased to meet you."

"Thanks for seeing us, Doctor. I'm Detective Rhody Richardson, and this is my partner, Detective Jon Wayne."

"Well, pilgrim," Chandler said, with an over-the-top western accent, and chuckled. "You must be the law in these here parts."

"Oh, great. A doctor with a funny bone." Wayne grinned as he rolled his eyes and shook her hand. "Yeah, like the actor, but spelled differently."

"No disrespect. Just having a little fun, Detective." She smiled as she sat at her desk. "What can I do for you?"

"We're following up on our investigation into what happened down the street at Nia-Buff." Richardson pulled out a notepad. "I know you gave your statement to the officers, but we would like to nose around a little more and see if anything else has jogged your memory since you spoke to them."

"No, nothing at all. As I told the officers, we didn't see anything unusual. My receptionist, Kathy, and Phil, the nurse, got here a little before I did that morning. Neither one of them saw anything out of the ordinary. Except for a lot of cop cars and flashing lights. That was certainly out of the ordinary around here."

"We were talking to one of your patients who says he was here the morning after it all happened." Richardson flipped through a few pages. "Paul Schon."

"Well, you know I can't divulge patient information."

"Of course not. We're not asking you to," Wayne said. "He was the one who told us he was a patient here. No harm in that. He's allowed to self-disclose if he chooses. Seems like a nice guy. A little jittery, but nice."

"Yeah, he said some medicine he's taking makes him jittery and shaky." Richardson looked at his notes. "What was that med again? Had some sort of long name…"

The doctor tipped her head to the side. "The Pentozipratol?"

"Yeah, that sounds right." Richardson wrote in his notebook. "Pento-zip-ra-tol. He said since you gave it to him, and it makes his hands shake sometimes."

"No, not me. That would be Doctor Taylor."

Richardson jerked his head up. "Dr. Taylor? You mean, Kaileen Taylor?"

"Yes, she was the one who…" Dr. Chandler's eyes widened, and a new awareness came across her face. "He never mentioned Pentozipratol by name, did he? That's why you just wrote it down. And he certainly didn't mention he was seeing Doctor Taylor."

"Don't worry, Doc." Richardson flipped the notebook shut. "No one needs to know where we got our information. It'll be our little secret."

Tucking the notepad in his pocket, Richardson turned to Wayne with a smile.

"Come on, Duke. Let's head out. This ain't the first time I thought I should drive you to see a psychiatrist."

"Okay, wise-ass. Everyone wants to be a comedian today."

CHAPTER 31

"GOOD MORNING, DETECTIVES," DR. TAYLOR greeted them at the door. "I was wondering how long it would be before someone brought Jon to my office."

"Oh, yay." Wayne laughed. "I'm surrounded by jokers today. Must be national gang-up on Jon day."

"Just kidding, Detective. It's good to see you again." Dr. Taylor ushered them in. "I just had an interesting phone call with Doctor Chandler."

"Hmm. I'll bet," Richardson said, as he and Wayne walked into the dimly lit office. "So I'd guess she gave you a little heads-up on what we want to speak to you about."

"Yes, she did. Jessica told me all about it. But make no mistake, detectives—even though you and I work together at times, I will not violate patient privacy for the sake of your investigation."

"Wouldn't dream of it, Doc," Wayne said. "We're just looking for a little info, and thought it was interesting that one of the people we were talking to is a patient of yours. Small world."

"Again, I cannot, and will not, violate HIPAA rules nor patient privacy. I am not going to confirm or deny that I am seeing him."

"Sorry, Kaileen, but I think it's safe to say the cat is already out of the bag with that one." Richardson laughed. "Look, we're not asking you to divulge anything inappropriate. But I'm sure you know, as a mandated reporter, that you are obligated to report if someone is likely to do harm to themselves or others."

As they sat on the couch, Dr. Taylor remained standing, with one hand on her hip as she used the other to pull her glasses halfway down her nose. With attitude, she pointed at Richardson.

"Well, thank you for the lesson in legal responsibilities, Rhody. But as you are well aware, before I received my medical license, I also earned, and still maintain, my law degree. I hope you two would agree that I am eminently, and uniquely, qualified to understand both the legal and ethical obligations involved with my practice."

Richardson and Wayne held their hands up in feigned surrender. "We give."

"Fine." She smiled and shook her head as she walked around her desk. "I will help with what I can. But just know that I will not divulge anything about anyone who may, or may not, be a patient of mine. And while some of them may have difficult issues in their lives, as far as I know, none of my patients present an immediate risk to anyone."

"Deal," Richardson said. "Let's start with a generic topic, then. What can you tell us about Pentozipratol?"

"Ah, yes. One of the things I like about you, Rhody. You cut to the chase."

"You're a busy woman, Kaileen. Just doin' my best to help you get back to your day."

"Yeah, I'm sure that's your primary motivation. Pentozipratol is relatively new, but has shown an incredible amount of promise. It is being prescribed more and more around the world. Seems to be a good combination of the benefits from anti-psychotic medications, antidepressants, anti-anxiety meds, mood stabilizers, and sleep medication."

"Seems like a pretty potent cocktail, Doc," Wayne said.

"It is, Jon. Instead of taking a handful of meds to handle each of those individual issues, patients can take just the one med, diminishing the chances for potentially harmful interactions. It offers all the best qualities, with minimal side effects."

"What makes it so great?" Richardson said. "How does it work?"

"Well, generically speaking, in layman's terms, anti-psychotics work by blocking a specific sub-type of the dopamine receptors in the brain. It's called the D2 receptor. Older meds would also block the receptors in other parts of the brain as well. This would cause more negative symptoms. This one, like many of these second-generation, atypical anti-psychotics, also work to block a specific serotonin receptor known as the 5HT2A receptor."

"Whoa. This is the layman's version?" Wayne laughed.

"Sure is. It is believed that these newer meds, which impact both the D2 and 5HT2A receptors, do a better job in treating both the positive and negative symptoms. Like the anti-psychotics, anti-depressants also work to address issues within the receptors and the chemistry in the brain. Depression is tricky, though. The exact causes aren't known, but it is believed that biological, genetic, and environmental factors play a role in it."

"So it's not just about being sad?" Richardson said.

"No, it's not at all. But that is a common interpretation many people make. Life happens, and sometimes being sad and angry for long periods of time is justified and explainable. There is a big difference between being downhearted and being clinically depressed. Actual, true depression is based on the chemistry in the brain. Whatever the primary trigger, there is usually a biological basis of the depression related to a depletion in the levels of neurotransmitters like dopamine, norepinephrine, and serotonin."

"And the medicines help correct those imbalances?" Wayne said.

"Yes. Even though there are different families of anti-depressants, which each work a little bit differently, they all work in a similar way to increase the brain's ability to generate and increase the brain's neurotransmitters. This helps smooth out and lessen the depressive episodes. Unfortunately, it can sometimes take up to a couple months before the full effects of anti-depressants take place."

"You also mentioned that the Pentozipratol is a mood stabilizer," Richardson said. "Isn't that what an anti-depressant does? You said it smooths out and lessens the episodes."

"Good question. When it comes to mood swings, people can go from feeling really low, or depressed, to feeling really high, or manic. You may have heard of persons afflicted with manic-depressive disorder. Or more common these days, bipolar disorder. Symptoms can change quickly, or evolve more slowly, and someone can be in either phase for short periods, or sometimes for weeks, or even months, on end. Whereas an anti-depressant works to lessen the depressive phase of the cycle, mood stabilizers work in a similar manner to lessen the manic phases."

"And anti-anxiety meds are different from those?" Wayne said.

"Yes. Think short-term versus long-term." Dr. Taylor shifted papers across her cluttered desk. "As I mentioned, those meds can sometimes take weeks, or even months, before the changes in the brain take place. Benzodiazepines, or tranquilizers, work relatively quickly, usually helping the person within thirty minutes. This makes them helpful when dealing with a panic attack or other overwhelming incident. They work to slow down the nervous system, which helps someone relax both physically and mentally. This also makes them an effective tool as a sleep medication during high stress times."

Richardson finished writing in his notes.

"I'm sure the Pentozipratol has a lot of great benefits. Otherwise, it wouldn't have made it to the market. But I'd also like to know about the side effects, too. Anything with this one?"

"As I'm sure you are aware, all medicines may have side effects on some people. But they are rare, and their benefits greatly outweigh the risks."

"Yup," Richardson said. "We always see the TV commercials, and they spend more time talking about the side effects than they do the benefits."

"Yes," Wayne said. "Another big thank you to the lawyers of the world for telling us not to take meds we're allergic to." He laughed.

"Oh, yeah," Richardson said. "And another great accomplishment for lawyers—making sure if we buy a bag of peanuts, the package says, *Caution, this product may contain peanuts.*"

"Hello…there's still a lawyer sitting in the room." Dr. Taylor gave a tight-lipped smile.

"Yeah, we know," Richardson said. "Just having a little fun. So what can you tell me about the side effects with these types of meds?"

"Although rare, all these types of meds have been known to produce some serious side effects in a very small percentage of people. Anti-depressants, for one, are known to cause nausea, vomiting, and diarrhea."

"Well, that would make me depressed." Wayne laughed.

The doctor rolled her eyes. "Some patients have also been known to experience increased agitation, extreme increases in activity, acting on dangerous impulses, aggressiveness and violence."

"What about with some of the other types of meds?" Richardson said.

"Well, anti-anxiety meds are sometimes known for causing difficulty remembering things, nightmares, and muscle pain. Among other things, anti-psychotics can cause restlessness and dry mouth. Patients will complain about an insatiable thirst, especially in the morning, after not drinking all night."

Dr. Taylor quickly turned her head to the side and furled her eyebrows as if a thought just occurred to her. She grabbed a pen and wrote a few things down. As Richardson and Wayne tried to peer across her desk, she slipped the note into the top drawer.

"Anything we should know about, Kaileen?"

"No, Rhody. Just something I want to look into later. It also reminded me that mood stabilizers are known for causing excessive thirst, too."

"Anything else with them?" he said.

"Again, it's rare, but they have been known to cause blackouts, hand tremors, and agitation. Like many types of anti-convulsants, they can sometimes cause rapid eye movements..."

She pulled open the drawer and wrote again on the sheet of paper tucked away. After sliding the drawer shut, she looked up at the two detectives with a forced smile.

"I hope this helps with your questions."

"Sure does, Kaileen," said Richardson, "Good info. You mentioned hand tremors. Would that be like Tardive Dyskinesia?"

"Ah, well-done. You've done your homework, Detective. Tardive Dyskinesia generally happens after long-term use of anti-psychotics, and can become permanent. Tremors from mood stabilizers tend to occur more quickly."

After looking up from his notepad, Richardson tipped his head to the side.

"Hypothetically speaking, Doctor…let's just say someone is in mourning after a loss, and only seems to have pronounced tremors on the hand that still has his wedding band. Would that, hypothetically speaking, of course, indicate there might be some psychological causes, rather than medicinal?"

"Hypothetically speaking, Detective, you are walking mighty close to a dangerous edge." Dr. Taylor gave a stern look. "Please do not *hypothetically* cross that line. But yes, there could be underlying issues. Medicine is not the solution, nor is it the cause, of all mental health issues."

"I agree. What about the sleep meds? I've heard sedative-hypnotics are known to cause sleepwalking in some people."

"Again, Rhody, I'm impressed. You've done your homework. Nice use of the proper term for them."

"What else can you tell us, Kaileen," Wayne said. "Haven't there been reports of people sleepwalking and doing other things, like driving, and they may seem like they're completely awake while under the influence with these?"

"That's right, Jon. It is actually rare, considering the number of people who use them. But when it does happen, it tends to garner a lot of attention in the news and on social media."

"I remember reading some sort of story about a woman who gained a ton of weight because of these meds," Wayne said.

"Oh, yes. The sleep eaters." Dr. Taylor nodded as she returned his smile. "Sleep-related eating disorder, or SRED, is common enough that it has its own name. It does occur naturally in a number of people, but sedative-hypnotics have been known to make the situation even more pronounced in a very small percentage of people. Many of these meds we've been talking about are known to be weight-gainers. But I think the one you're referring to really garnered a lot of attention. The woman gained quite a bit of weight even though she would stick to a strict diet every day. It wasn't until they saw video that they realized she was getting up and eating lots of high-calorie food through the night. It really packed on the pounds."

"Kaileen, you mentioned a couple of these types of meds also cause memory issues and blackouts," Richardson said. "I was wondering—just like the woman who didn't know she was eating at night, and gained a bunch of weight…remember the picture we were showing at the task force meeting? The guy in the sweatsuit? Could someone go running at night and not even know it? Might explain why someone could take a weight-gainer, claim to sleep right after dinner because of their meds, but somehow still stay trim and fit."

"Careful, Detective. You're approaching that edge again. We are keeping this generic. Sure, I would think it could be possible. Highly unlikely, but still possible."

Richardson nodded. "You said the Pentozipratol has all the positive attributes of these different types of meds. So they probably have some of the same negative side effects, too. Could someone have some of the negative reactions to all of them at the same time?

Maybe blackouts, tremors, sleep walking, violent tendencies, dangerous impulses, and stuff like that, all together?"

"I highly doubt it. That would be a stretch, with astronomical odds."

"Really? I don't think it's much of a stretch for someone to have side effects from one type to be more prone to the side effects of the others."

Dr. Taylor bristled. "Rhody, side effects are extremely rare. Maybe just a few tenths of one percent of patients get any at all. Look at it this way—multiply .003 times .003 times .003. That would be three-tenths of a percent for each of just three of those med types. You'd be looking at about one chance in a hundred million. Statistically speaking, it's just about impossible. And you think it could really happen?"

"Yeah, I guess not. Just a thought." Richardson shrugged. "C'mon, Duke. Let's go over to the diner and grab some lunch before we head back to the station."

"Sounds like a plan. Anything that keeps us out of the heat is good by me. Want to join us, Doc? I think they could press some tofu into the shape of real food."

"Very funny, Jon. No thanks, though. I'd like to look up a few things, and also straighten out this mess of a desk."

"Alrighty, then. Hey, seeing those lottery tix you have there reminds me I need to buy some, too. Up to a hundred thirty-nine mill for the next one. I noticed you have a couple numbers circled. Win anything?"

"Just two bucks." She smiled. "I'll just exchange it for another ticket when I get some more later. You never know. A girl can dream, can't she?"

"Hmm. That's interesting." Richardson smiled as he stepped out into the hallway.

"What's that?" Dr. Taylor said.

"Odds of winning the big money are about one in three hundred million. So even if you bought a few tickets, you're still looking at about one chance in a hundred million. Like you said, that would be a stretch with astronomical odds. But you never know. Statistically speaking, it's just about impossible, yet you think it could really happen?"

CHAPTER 32

It was late Tuesday morning as Lieutenant Finch strode toward Richardson and Wayne's desks. They could see by the scowl, and the way he was biting his lower lip, he wasn't bringing good news.

"Hey, you two. You need to head out to the townhouses over on Rivermist. Looks like we may have another victim."

"That's odd," Richardson said. "He's breaking his pattern? Every victim so far has been killed later on a Tuesday, or Friday night."

"Not sure yet. Let me know what you find," said the grim-faced Finch. "Maybe he didn't break the pattern. We had a couple calls from residents about a foul odor that's been getting worse since the weekend. A couple uniforms went over a little bit ago. They called in and said it is definitely decomp reeking up the area. Said it is really strong in this heat. I was hoping it was just some dead fish, or maybe a deer got hit over the weekend."

"Judging by your look," Wayne said. "Doesn't seem like that was the case, huh?"

"No. Officers said it is definitely coming from one of the townhomes. Doors are locked from the inside, and they haven't gone in yet because they think it may be related to your case. They learned the owner lives alone. His name is Doctor Oh. And yes, he is a plastic surgeon. They've secured the scene and are waiting for us before gaining entry. Jeff and the CSI team are already on their way now, and Doctor Matthews is heading over, too."

"On the way, boss," Richardson said. "We'll let you know what we find."

"As soon as you can, please. I think I'll let the captain call the mayor about this one. So much for not being elbow-deep in another shitstorm."

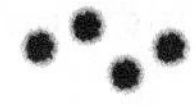

Richardson and Wayne stepped out of the car near the curve where Rivermist hooked to the left before becoming a dead end just short of Ojibwa Circle. Both detectives looked at each other with a look of disgust as the rancid odor assailed their noses.

"Damn," Wayne said. "I can see why the neighbors were calling about this one. That is one nasty ass smell you can never forget. Smells even worse than the salesman's car."

"Yup. They were right. It is definitely decomp. Let's head over and see what's going on."

They walked up as McDonald was speaking with the two uniformed officers stationed out front.

"Jon, Rhody," said a somber-looking McDonald, nodding toward the busted frame of the open door. "We just gained entry about fifteen to twenty minutes ago. The kid is already up there. He volunteered to take the pictures until you arrived, so I have him up there with a couple of our other guys. Just doing a few prelims."

"What can you tell us, Jeff," said Richardson.

"First thing I'll tell you is to rub some of this menthol gel under your nose." McDonald handed them a small white bottle. "If you think the smell is bad down here, it's nothing compared to the third floor. I hope you both have strong stomachs. Even I almost lost it when I first walked in. Looks even worse than it smells. Everyone has been instructed to not touch or move anything until you get here. It is exactly as we found it."

"Thanks, Jeff." Richardson looked at the picture of Dr. Rikichi Oh.

His hospital ID was hanging from a peg on a hall tree inside the door.

"Let's go take a look at what's left of the good doctor."

With each step up the stairs, the smell became stronger and the temperature became hotter, until it rendered the melting menthol to a symbolic gesture. As they approached Dr. Oh's bedroom, two CSI techs exited the room, coughing and retching behind their masks.

"Here. Slip one of these masks on," McDonald grabbed from a stack on a small table set up at the top of the stairs. "Doesn't do too much, but it helps a little. You might want to rub a little more gel on the inside of it. And just a word of caution—if you think you're going to puke, make sure you take the mask off first. Could get even messier."

"Good advice." Wayne slipped the elastic bands behind his ears. "But in reality, a nose full of puke might smell better than this."

The two detectives stepped into the room and looked at each other in disbelief as an oppressive wall of heat and stench slammed into them.

On the bed was something that looked nothing like the trim Asian doctor featured on the ID badge. The blob of engorged flesh didn't look like anything human. Distended, discolored, and disfigured, the distorted remains and features of Dr. Oh were nearly indistinguishable.

Oh's face was grotesquely rendered into a puffy mass of flesh. Flies, maggots, and foaming fluids slithered along the slices around the eyes, mouth, and neck. Like the other victims, Dr. Oh's throat had been slashed. Leaking enzymes from the autolysis process are responsible for producing gases that bloat the body, and normally force blood-filled foam out through the mouth and nose. With Dr. Oh, there was no need to travel that far—the slashed throat provided an easier and quicker exit.

Over his throat, and down to the sheets, was a cascading pyramid of thick, foamy blood bubbles. Some bubbles made it to the top like a frothing volcano, while others worked to expand the base of the pyramid that grew across his shoulders, before popping and soaking into the crusty, reddened sheets.

Below the slash, the collar of his T-shirt had now pulled taut as his bloated torso expanded. At some point after his demise, the constrictive collar became a tourniquet and squeezed his throat closed until the escaping gases created a whistling and hissing noise while the bubbles continued oozing out. The rest of his torso still had the greenish hue which was created as the body went through the initial self-digestion phase. The green torso against the red bubbles created something akin to the center piece of a Manson family holiday table.

Across his expanded, glossy chest were deep cuts filled with writhing maggots. The skin, stretched and mutilated, offered numbers far less pristine than those found on all the previous victims. To the unfamiliar, they didn't resemble numbers at all.

Richardson and Wayne nodded to each other as they recognized what had once been a 20.

Further down the distended doctor, light blue boxers were stretched well beyond the limits of normal elasticity. Adding to the aroma of putrefaction, the swelling body had forced the evacuation of the bowels and bladder into the shorts. The legs had now returned to a reddish color as the blood began decomposing while the deceased's internal organs produced more gases.

"I tried to tell you," McDonald said. "But this is one of those things you just have to see for yourself."

"And smell." Richardson looked around the room. "How do you even start with something like this?"

"Until now, we've just been taken pictures, making preliminary observations, and waiting for you. As I said, we've only been here a little while before you got here. Poor Connor there has been in here the entire time, and has been outstanding so far."

"Hey, kid," Richardson said. "This is a pretty nasty scene. Tough for anyone to come across. You holding up all right?"

"Um, yeah," said the visibly disturbed Patrick. "Just trying to stay focused on the processes and the science of all this right now. It helps me get through. I was hoping I would have some more concrete info for Jeff and the two of you, but some things are just a little off and it's confusing me."

"What's going on, Con-man?" Wayne said. "You seem to be pretty good at picking out details."

"I guess I still have a lot to learn. I really wanted to impress you all." The intern stared at the bed. "I wanted to be able to have some sort of preliminary time of death for you. At least something approximate. But the evidence is throwing me off.

"What is it?" McDonald said.

"Well, take a look at the body and his level of decomposition. The body is severely bloated and has already started turning from green to red. The body turns green during stage one—the autolysis, or self-digesting, phase. As I understand it, leaking enzymes produce a bunch of gases, and the sulfur causes the discoloration. The gases make the body swell up, and cause the bloating and leaking seen in stage two. After that, the body goes from a greenish color back to the red as the blood begins to decompose and the organs in the abdomen accumulate gas. Normally, it would take about eight to ten days to get to that point. And that's the problem—the timeline isn't matching up."

"Not necessarily." Richardson stepped toward the bed. "Remember, Con...our perp has also killed two people in different locations, on the same night—a doctor and the salesman. We don't know much about the victim yet, other than he lives alone. Maybe he was off work and didn't have anyone to report him as missing. For all we know, this could have been on the same night as one of the vics we had from last week. That would put him in about the right timeframe."

"Maybe. But that's not the timeline that is confusing me," Patrick said. "It's the blow flies. Those are the metallic green flies you see buzzing around in here. The ones flying around are the adults. The babies are the ones you see slithering around in his wounds. You can use their larvae to determine an approximate time of death. Granted, we need to do testing in a lab, but just using a rough guess, I'd say the maggots in the wounds would put the death at about only three or four days ago. So one thing is telling me eight to ten days, and the other is telling me three to four. Ugh. I just don't know what to make of it."

"Ah, well-done, young lad."

The four men turned around to see a smiling Dr. Matthews standing in the doorway. The coroner was putting on a pair of latex gloves as he stepped in.

"I can't speak for the rest of the team, but I am impressed with your efforts. You're right, Jeff." Matthews said to McDonald and began slipping on a mask. "He certainly has a lot of potential. Very observant." He turned back toward Connor. "So Mister Patrick, continue to elucidate us with your knowledge of entomology. What else can you tell us about Oestroidea Calliphoridae?"

"Excuse me," Wayne said. "Why are we talking about asteroids in California?"

"Very funny, Mister Wayne," said the doctor. "You're always quick-witted. Oestroidea Calliphoridae are the emerald blow flies Connor was just telling us about. He was accurate with his assessment—their larvae are useful in helping us determine a timeline for a recent death."

"Yes, we are well-aware of that," Richardson said. "But maybe these little guys were just a couple days late to the party. The doors were all shut tight."

"No, that wouldn't happen unless the place was sealed airtight," Patrick said. "And with the stink perforating the entire neighbor-hood, I'd say it's obvious that it wasn't."

Wayne and Richardson turned back to McDonald and Dr. Matthews.

"He's right," McDonald said.

"Continue, Mister Patrick," said Dr. Matthews.

"Well, these little fellas can smell death almost instantly. Hard to believe, and correct me if I'm wrong, but decomposition starts about four minutes after death."

"Damn. Four minutes?" Wayne said

McDonald and Matthews nodded their agreement.

"Yes," Patrick said. "Some of the cells start decomposing and begin emitting the gases almost immediately."

"Didn't realize it was quite that quick," Richardson said. "It really is hard to believe. So you're telling me that all those times you hear about someone being clinically dead for five, ten, or more minutes…their bodies had already begun decomposing before coming back to life?"

"Yeah, pretty wild, huh," Patrick said. "Not too much longer than that, and the adult blow flies can smell those gases from miles away. They can pretty much get into wherever a decomposing body is. The females need protein, not only to eat for themselves, but they need it to lay their eggs. They will lay hundreds and hundreds of eggs near the eyes, mouth, or open wounds so the larvae can have a quick, easy feast as soon as they hatch. They're pretty reliable in their habits and larvae development. That's why we can estimate, within a few hours, the time of death. But this one has me a little confused because of the contrary markers."

"Well-done, Connor," said Dr. Matthews. "You certainly are well-versed on things. You seem to have a laser-like focus. You possess an ability to shut out many things."

"Thanks, Doctor Matthews. I try to stay focused on what's in front of me."

"Hmm. Perhaps too focused." Matthews tipped his head. "Would you like something to drink. You look as if you have been sweating profusely."

"Um, sure. You're right. I didn't really notice. I guess I am thirsty. It's pretty hot up here."

"Exactly." The doctor smiled as he produced a bottle of water from his bag. "Tell me, lad…suppose I offered you a chicken salad sandwich that had been sitting out in this heat most of the day. Would you eat it?"

"No. Of course not!"

"Why not?"

"Well, for one, it would probably taste pretty nasty and make me sick. I'm sure I'd be hugging a toilet before too long. The bacteria would be working in overdrive with this kind of heat, and it would…oh my God! That's it." Patrick looked back and forth from the doctor to the bed. "It's the heat in here. It is so freaking hot. I can't believe I didn't take that into account. It's the heat. An overheated body will produce more bacteria and enzymes. The whole process would be accelerated. Everything would be more pronounced much more quickly. That has to be it. The blow flies are accurate, but the heat is what threw off the other results. Can't believe I didn't think of that."

"That's why we work as a team, lad," Matthews said. "Instead of focusing on what's directly in front of you, you need to also take in what's all around you."

"So gentleman," Richardson said, "can I take it that this now puts our timeline more in line with the perps previous patterns?"

"I will let you know when I know more," Dr. Matthews said. "But preliminary evidence would support that. I would not be surprised to find that this happened Friday night, as we feared. As Connor said, in this case, the blow flies are much more accurate.

They show up as soon as the body dies and begins emitting gases. He was right—judging by the developmental stages of some of the larvae, it would have been three or four days ago. When young Mister Patrick was relating the timeframes for decomposition, he was referring to the standards set in more moderate conditions, at around twenty degrees Celsius, and..."

"Whoa there, Doc." Wayne laughed. "Remember, we're on the south side of the Peace Bridge. For those of us who don't speak Canadian, what's that in American degrees?"

"Again, you are very funny, Detective Wayne." The coroner smiled. "That would be room temperature. Around sixty-eight. But obviously, we are much higher in here. These high temperatures would explain the expedited decay Connor noticed. Jeff, do you know why it is so warm in here?"

"Looks like nothing more than a good old-fashioned greenhouse effect. The doctor had his AC shut off. As you can see, there are lots of windows, as well as these wide sliding glass doors on all three floors, facing west. So the sun was baking this place all afternoon and through the early evenings. And over the last few days, this record-breaking heat has been brutal."

"That's for sure," Richardson said. "I see a piece of paper in the middle of the dresser behind you, Jeff. Is it our latest bit of rhyme with no reason?"

"Sure is," McDonald said.

The two detectives walked over to get a closer look at the newest poem. The same block lettering as before was centered in the middle of the page.

A heart once full, now an empty hole.
A cheated man's lost and broken soul.

The monsters stole my happily ever after.
They took my life, my love, my laughter.

—*Evan Heger*

"Hmm," Wayne said. "He went with another normal first name this time, like he did with the last one."

"Yeah," said Richardson. "And like Doctor Taylor pointed out, he used the word *lost* again. His last couple anagrams have had normal names, but they're also more obvious. This one says, *Avenge her.*"

"Haven't lost your touch at all there, amigo," Wayne said. "Glad you can see them, 'cause I sure as hell can't."

Richardson turned back to the CSI team. "Hey, Jeff. If the downstairs door was locked from the inside, do we know how he gained access into the house yet?"

"Perhaps he can fly." McDonald scoffed. "The only door that was unlocked is right there in front of you. The sliding door was closed, but it was unlocked. Every other door and window in the place was locked or bolted from the inside. So the slider could be his only point of entry, but we're on the third floor. Maybe he's part mountain goat or kangaroo. Difficult, but not impossible, I suppose."

"Jon and I are going to head out and speak with some of the neighbors. We'll see what else we can find out about Doctor Oh. We'll follow up with you and Dan before we go. Give me a shout if anything turns up."

"Of course, Rhody. We'll be here for a while longer as we process everything. If they ask, let the neighbors know we'll have a hazmat team in here to clean up and de-stink the place."

Richardson's eyes smiled above the mask. "Thanks, Jeff. Is de-stink an official techno science term?"

"Hey, whatever works to get the point across. That's the secret to good communication."

"Agreed. Hey, could one of your guys take a look at the one curtain there by the slider? Just caught my eye. It's not much, but if you look at it in the sunlight, looks to me like there's some discoloration on the inside edge, about four feet up. Can you see it?"

"Yeah, you're right. Faint, but I can see it, too. Good catch. What do you think it is?"

"I don't know. But judging how clean he keeps the rest of this place, I doubt it would be something he'd let just stay there. Could be recent. Maybe our killer left a little something for us. See if you can get a read on it."

"Will do."

"Come on, Sundance. Let's see what we can find out from the neighbors. Maybe get a little fresh air."

"Sure thing there, Butch." Wayne pulled off his mask and followed his partner down the stairs. "Doubt it'll be fresh air, but it has to be better than what's in here."

CHAPTER 33

KNOCKING ON SEVERAL DOORS PRODUCED FEW results. The residents who were home had little information about the doctor. It seemed he was a nice and cordial man who kept to himself, and like most of the people on the street, did not engage socially with his neighbors. Most interactions were limited to a wave at the mailbox, or a nod and raise of a finger as he drove past. The few homebodies they were able to interview couldn't recall the last time they saw Dr. Oh.

"Come on, Duke," Richardson said. "Let's head back to the deck at Oh's place and see if Jeff's guys found anything back there. Maybe they figured out how he got up three floors."

"Lead on, partner," Wayne said. "The air was getting too fresh this far out, anyway."

The two detectives walked through the house and out the angled door from the living room to the back deck. Two CSI techs were gathering evidence from the patio planks. Richardson and Wayne heard other voices and looked up to see more techs on the deck above them, and also on the deck leading to Dr. Oh's bedroom.

"Well, partner," Wayne said. "Second-floor deck rail has to be at least twelve feet up. You're six-foot-one and in good shape. Think you could jump up there?"

"Not even close. But I can't dunk a basketball either. Doesn't mean there aren't a lot of people shorter than me who can."

"So any ideas?"

"Not yet. Maybe he used a rope and a grappling hook. Latched it on the railing and then scaled up the wall. But I'd think it would be too noisy, though. Might draw attention."

"Maybe he covered the hook with something like pipe insulation. That would muffle the sound."

"Yeah, it's possible. But I still think it would make some noise and be too risky if he had to make a couple throws to get it to latch on. Maybe Jeff was on the right track."

"With what?"

"He joked that maybe the guy was part mountain goat or kangaroo."

"You really think he could've jumped that high?"

"Yeah. But with a little assistance. I know there's military training that teaches soldiers how to scale a building, and even get to a first-story roof. The secret is to keep your momentum going and push upward on the wall. You and I have seen it a bunch of times in Jackie Chan movies. He didn't have to use special effects. Just used his momentum and went up the wall. Our killer seems to be adept at learning things online. I'll bet there's probably some YouTube videos on how to do it."

"There sure are," said a smiling Patrick, as he walked up. "Watched a few of them myself. Sometimes comes in handy when I train to compete in the octagon. It's not really all that difficult."

"Sure. Of course it isn't, says the athletic twenty-something." Wayne laughed.

"Thanks, Connor." Richardson extended his hand. "Jeff let you out to get some fresh air already? Must be getting soft in his old age."

"Yeah." The intern smiled. "Actually, I was out front putting some evidence in Jeff's car. The neighbor from two doors over just came home. The officers told him you would probably want to ask him some questions. I saw you from above and knew you were out here. I told them I'd tell you. Oh, wait…there's the neighbor right there."

The detectives followed Patrick's outstretched arm and looked along the rail. Two decks down, a man in neat khakis and a light blue button-down shirt was waving to them. Richardson held up a finger to let him know they were on the way.

"Come on, kid," he said. "You want to join us for the interview."

"Of course. Just let me make sure it's all right with Jeff."

Wayne boomed, "Hey Jeff. Connor's coming with us for a bit."

From high above, McDonald stepped out onto the third-floor deck and looked over the railing. He gave a salute and a wave to offer his approval.

As the trio began walking across the deck, Wayne slapped Patrick on the back.

"You owe me, kid. Saved you from wading back up into that mess again."

As they crossed over onto his deck, the neighbor introduced himself.

"Hello, I'm Mark Landers. This is my place."

"Good to meet you, Mister Landers. I'm Detective Rhody Richardson, and this is my partner, Detective Jon Wayne."

"Really, like the cowboy?"

"Yeah." Wayne rolled his eyes and shook his head. "But I spell it a little differently. This is Connor Patrick. He helps with our forensics. Do you mind if we ask you a few questions?"

"Of course not. My wife got a call at work from our neighbor. She said police were here trying to speak with people. I was able to cut away from my job. I'm here to help with whatever I can. Can't believe this happened to Rick."

Richardson said, "Rick?"

"Yeah, Doctor Oh. His real name is Rikichi, but he likes to go by Rick. He said it sounds more Americanized. His parents liked the more traditional Japanese."

"So you knew him fairly well?" Wayne said.

"Not real well. But well enough, I suppose. He and I work at the hospital together, but I'm in the business office and just push papers across a desk. Our schedules are pretty similar, so we leave and get home around the same time. We have some idle chit chat back and forth, nothing too in-depth. I know he was supposed to be in San Diego this week for some big plastic surgery conference. His flight was supposed to leave on Sunday."

"Pretty clear he didn't make that flight," said a grim-faced Wayne. "Do you know if he was having problems with anyone?"

"No, I don't. But we didn't really talk about things like that. I don't recall hearing any scuttlebutt around the hospital. And believe me, those people love to gossip. Very few things stay a secret there. I'll ask around and let you know if anyone else heard anything."

"Thanks," Richardson said. "We appreciate it."

"Hey, detectives," a voice called out, as a uniformed officer walked across from Dr. Oh's deck. "We have something you may want to check out."

"What's going on, Carlos?" Richardson said.

"We have someone who says he has video evidence. He was all about making sure the twenty-five grand reward was still up. He's a pompous ass."

"Well, that's not illegal," Wayne said. "Otherwise, we'd have a lot more people locked away. So did you get a look at it?"

"No, sir. Not a lowly peon like me." The officer took a step back and waved his hands by his shoulders. "I'm not important enough. The guy said he wanted to talk to the lead detectives, and not some flunky with an eighth-grade education."

"Great. He sounds like a real prize," Richardson said.

"You're telling me," said the officer. "My partner made the mistake of placing his hand on the fender of the guy's car. I thought he was going to blow a gasket. Started yelling and carrying on about how his car is worth more than both our salaries, and how dare we touch it and get our finger smudges on it. He has a Porsche SUV."

"Well, that tells us a lot right there." Wayne grinned.

"Um…tells us what?" Patrick said.

"He likes to pretend he's a manly-man by driving a four-wheel drive," Richardson said, "even though it won't ever see the snow. But he's one of those types who needs to scream to the world, *Look at me, look at me. I have money.* Probably trying to make up for his little two-inch pisser."

"He's a friggin' dickhead for sure." The officer turned back to Landers. "My apologies, sir, for the language."

"A Porsche SUV?" Landers said. "He lives right there on the other side of the inlet. Those are his windows facing us." He returned his gaze to the officer. "You're right, he is a pompous ass and a dickhead."

"You know him?" Wayne said. "What's his name?"

"No, I don't know him, but I do know he's about this close to getting his ass kicked. My wife and I just refer to him as Captain Pervo." Landers wore a look of disgust.

"Captain Pervo? That's awesome." Wayne smiled. "Why is that?"

"Whenever my wife was out here sunbathing, she'd see that scumbag leering at her through the window blinds. Funny thing, though, his left hand would hold the blinds open a little more, but you'd never see his right hand, just his shoulder moving back and forth while he was probably taking matters into his own hand, so to speak."

"Seems like a real winner," Richardson said.

"He's a piece of work," Landers said. "Funny how he stopped his Peeping Tom routine after I sat next to my wife and made a point of cleaning my Smith and Wesson. Don't worry, gentlemen. It's all legal. I can show you my pistol permit if you'd like."

"No, that's all right." Richardson smiled. "I'm sure everything is good."

"Thanks. He just pisses me off. Money doesn't buy class. He also has a string of pretty young things coming in and out of there all the time. Most of them look like they'd get proofed to get into an R-rated movie."

"Just lovely." Richardson sighed, then turned to Wayne and Patrick. "Well, boys, let's go see what Captain Pervo has for us."

CHAPTER 34

THE THREE MEN WENT AROUND THE PORSCHE sitting in the driveway and rang the bell. Wayne pointed to the camera above their heads on the front steps. Richardson nodded and pointed to the one above the garage door angled down the drive.

After a few moments, they heard two deadbolts turn back, and the door opened. Framed in the doorway, a man in his late thirties stood stone-faced and looking annoyed. His black hair, which was too uniform in color, was held perfectly in form by copious amounts of hair product. His salmon polo shirt had the collar flipped up. The three opened buttons at the top revealed several gold chains and small tufts of black and gray chest hair. A pair of Ray-Ban sunglasses hung from the V below the last button.

"If you're selling something, or here to talk about my eternal salvation, you can just keep moving your asses down the road. I don't want to hear it."

"You're the one who asked for us." Richardson stared straight at him. "I'm Detective Rhody Richardson. This is Detective Jon Wayne. Connor Patrick is part of our forensics team. Detective Wayne and I are the lead detectives on the investigation next door. We were told you may have something for us."

"Yes. Yes, I do." A tight smile carved across the man's taut face.

He extended a hand, with fingers covered in gold, diamonds, and black onyx. A gold Rolex dangled on his narrow wrist.

"My name is Donald, Donald Winston the Third. Is the twenty-five-thousand-dollar reward still available?"

Richardson's hand engulfed the much smaller one, Wayne said, "Yes, it is. We're still looking for the guy, and we are interested in any information you may have."

"If you don't mind me saying," Richardson said, "it doesn't look like twenty-five grand would be all that big a deal for you, Mister Winston. Beautiful home, car, jewelry. Extra money is always nice, but seems like a drop in the bucket for you. Not necessarily a priority."

"Yeah, I do very well. Soon to be a partner in my law firm. Just won a few big settlements. So no, I don't need the money. But it would make a great story in the press. Be kinda cool in helping me get even more hot little chickees than I already do now." Donald gave a hollow laugh.

Richardson cleared his throat. "Fine. You seemed a little put-off when you answered the door. Did we catch you at a bad time?"

"No. Sorry if I came across a little gruff. You just never know who's around. We're close enough to the lower west side, and some of those people sometimes get bold enough to try and come see how the other half lives."

Richardson narrowed his eyes. "Those people?"

"Yeah, you know what I mean. Hell, I'm sure those types keep you guys in business, though. Am I right, or am I right? That's why I set up video cameras all around my condo to keep an eye on the grounds around my entryways and windows. Can't trust any of those people. You never know what they'll do. That's why I insisted on talking to the lead investigators. I know it's not politically correct, but I wasn't about to hand over anything to those type of officers."

"Officers Rivera and Lopez are good cops and an asset to the force," Wayne said.

"Whatever. I can't understand half the people over there along Niagara Street. If you can't talk English correctly, don't talk to me at all."

Fighting the urge to say what was truly on his mind, Richardson shook his head, sighed, and pulled out his notebook. Winston didn't notice. He was gazing up and down as he admired his reflection in the glass door.

All four men turned toward the street as they heard a car pull up and stop quickly. A young woman jumped out of the car and momentarily got hung up in the shoulder belt. After regaining her balance and closing the door, she hustled as quickly as her miniskirt and high heels would allow her. The clicking of her shoes slowed as she moved past the SUV and toward the steps.

"Oh, my God, Donny," she said, breathlessly. "I was so worried when you weren't at work. We heard the police were in your area for something. And then I pull up and there's all these emergency vehicles right here by your place. Are you all right?"

"I'm fine," he said, with indifference. "Detectives, this is Miss Redfield. She is a new clerk at our firm."

"Hey, Britney." Patrick smiled.

"Wow! Connor. How are you? I don't think I've seen you since we were at UB!"

"Yeah, it's been a while. I heard you went off to law school."

"Yes. Still working toward passing the bar. I'm keeping busy working as a law clerk now. I work right here downtown, with Donny."

Richardson caught the dirty look and quick head-shake Donald shot at the young clerk. She blushed and looked down.

"It's so nice you have new clerks who care and know exactly where you live," Richardson said. "Let's take a look at what you have, Mister Winston. I'm sure we all have other things we'd like to get to today."

"Um, sure. It's upstairs, downloading in my room. I edited out all the extraneous stuff, and I got it all set for you. Had to put together the feeds from two different cameras. I just started loading it onto a thumb drive when I heard the doorbell. Should be done by now."

"Thank you," Richardson said. "Lead the way."

Stepping up into the entry hall, the veteran detective towered over the much shorter attorney. As Donald walked up the carpeted stairs, the two detectives, the intern, and the young clerk all followed. It became obvious to the detectives how much Winston loved the sound of his own voice as he continued to talk. He seemed particularly proud of the quality of furnishings, art, and decorations throughout his home.

"As I said, I wanted to make sure my house, yard, and property are protected. I like being surrounded by the best of everything. I want to make sure no one is trespassing on my lawn, trying to break in, or causing any other kind of mischief. I bought the very best system I could find. I didn't mind how much it cost. If someone is in my yard, I want to know about it So, it's worth it."

"Makes sense," Richardson said. "You said you were able to edit it for us, too?"

"Yes, I did." Donald smiled. "I also bought one of the best video editing software programs available. Uses a whole lot of memory. That's why I keep it on my desktop upstairs, and not my laptops. The cameras record in ultra-high def. Even with wide angle shots, I can zoom in on any part of the video and it is crystal clear. Spent a lot of time teaching myself how to use the editor. Must say, practice makes perfect. I'm pretty good at it now."

As they made their way along the hallway, Winston stopped in front of a dark door.

"Here's where the magic happens. Your edit was pretty simple, though, I just took the raw feed and cut out the sections you need. I then spliced in the feed from the second camera. One camera has him coming in along the stone wall, and the other picks up where the first one left off. On that one, you can see him go right up there on the balconies. As soon as I heard what happened over there, I started rewinding through the DVR. It took me a while, but hey, for twenty-five grand, it's worth it. I think I found something from Friday night that will break your case wide open."

They entered Donald's bedroom as the smug little man continued with a sweeping gesture.

"As you can see, gentlemen, big screen TV, surround sound stereo system, king-size bed. I like to surround myself with the best."

The room had obviously been decorated with great expense, but with no sense of theme or focus. Winston's large screen computer monitor sat on a beautiful walnut desk that would have looked more appropriate in a CEO's office. Tapestries draped alongside oil paintings decorated the open wall areas. Most of the furnishings and decorations looked as if they had been randomly plucked from a Tiffany's catalog. Purchased because they were expensive, not because they matched anything.

Along the right side of the room, a large, ornate mirror gave a full reflection of the king-size sleigh bed. At the far side, underneath the mirror, sat an antique rocking chair. Slumped over in the rocker was an oversized teddy bear with mismatched eyes. The bear's t-shirt proclaimed, *World's Greatest Uncle.*

Richardson looked at Wayne, nodded toward the bear, and rolled his eyes. Wayne nodded back, shook his head in return, and then flipped his chin to the other wall, which held a majestic oak bookcase. He pointed up and to one side of the case. It was an odd array of genres, with no discernible order. Each shelf was filled with hardcover books ranging from law encyclopedias to self-help, pulp fiction, and a few literary classics.

"You have quite the collection in here, Mister Winston," said Wayne. "This bedroom is bigger than some apartments."

"Pretty nice, huh." Winston beamed as he walked toward the computer and took a moment to view his reflection across the room in the mirror. "Like I said, I like to be surrounded by the best. You should be honored. I can safely say you are the first men to ever be in here."

"Yes, it's very nice," Richardson said, with no emotion. "Is this where the video is? Do all your cameras feed into this room?"

"They sure do." Donald sat at the computer and moved the mouse.

After he typed in a password, the screen popped up, announcing the download was now complete. He pulled the thumb drive from the USB port and handed to Richardson.

"Here you go, Detective. If you'd like, I can show you what I loaded on there for you."

"Thank you." Richardson dropped the drive into his pants pocket. "Let's see what you found."

"Um, Donny—I mean, Mister Winston," Britney whispered. "Should I leave?"

"No, you can stay, Miss Redfield," he said, without looking up. "May be nice to have a witness to what I found for the detectives."

"Your faith in humanity is inspiring," Wayne said. "Let's get a look at it."

The two detectives stood over the attorney's shoulders. Patrick and Britney stood to the side and angled their necks to see the screen. The clerk, blushing again, refused to meet the gaze of her former classmate as they stepped up closer.

A swiping star effect soon filled the screen and announced, VIDEO PROVIDED BY DONALD WINSTON III. A DWIII logo then spun to the upper right corner. Across the bottom of the screen, *Video filmed and edited by Donald Winston III*, continuously scrolled.

"Let me guess, Mister Winston," Richardson flashed a cold smile. "You were an only child."

"Yup, I sure am." He laughed. "How'd you know? Is it because I'm used to having the best for myself and like getting accolades?"

"Yeah, sure. Something like that." Richardson kept looking at the screen.

For a few seconds, the video only showed the far wall to the inlet and the patio decks above it. Decorative flags moving back and forth in a light breeze was the only indication this wasn't a still photo.

"He'll be showing up pretty soon," Donald said. "This is the raw feed showing everything. It's exactly what was on the camera. I didn't change anything, but I can zoom in and redo anything you want on there. You can zoom in real tight on any part of the screen. You'll love how clear these night vision cameras are."

Rhody and Jon nodded to each other. They had to admit, it was a good-quality feed and was much clearer than the blurry, grainy video they usually dealt with near crime scenes.

Although the moon had drained the colors from the night, the images in shades of green and black were clear and sharp. They could easily read the logos and designs on the towels left on the Adirondack chairs.

"That looks like our guy." Richardson pointed to the right side of the screen.

Along the top of the inlet wall, they watched as a figure in a dark sweatsuit peered across the deck. He inched across the wall, sliding his left hand across the deck, and then stepping over before bringing the right side. After working to the center of the computer monitor, the hooded man reached under the deck, crouched, and laid on the rocks underneath.

A couple walked across the deck holding hands. When they reached the railing, the man wrapped his arms around the woman's waist from behind as they unknowingly stood directly above the hidden predator.

"Hey, there's Mark Landers and his wife," Wayne said.

Winston cleared his throat and muttered, "Never met them."

After a few minutes of watching the couple nuzzle against each other, the husband whispered into her ear. She smiled, said something back to him, and then turned to kiss him. After the two had drifted back through the sliding doors, the anonymous eavesdropper got back up onto the stone wall and continued his journey along the outside of the deck.

"Here is where I cut to the second camera. You'll see him coming in on the right side again. This camera is focused a little further over."

"Damn! That had to hurt," Wayne said, as both detectives flinched.

They had seen the predator's left leg slip, his knee smashed into the rock, and then he continued sliding off the wall. Now the image on the screen showed a man dangling by his fingertips, just above the water. With his feet flailing around, the man was able to find a foot hold and then use his arms to get back on top of the wall.

"Pause it for a minute." Richardson stood and jerked the phone off his belt.

"Hey, Jeff. We're looking at a possible video of the perp. He made his way along the deck rails and walked on top of the stone wall that's just outside the railing. He took a pretty hard fall against the top blocks. We need to get someone to look for traces of DNA or anything else that might be there. Yeah, hasn't rained for a while, so there might still be something there. It's the deck right next to Oh's. No, the other one, on the road side. Thanks. Let me know."

"Good call there, Rhod," Wayne said. "All right then. We now return you to your regularly scheduled program already in progress. Let's see what else happens."

Winston tapped the mouse to restart. They leaned in closer and watched as the man continued across and climbed onto Oh's deck. They saw him shake out the left leg and stretch it. He then walked into the shadows under the deck, but the dim light showed him trying the sliding door before walking back out into the open, running his finger along a brick on the doorframe, and then backing to the railing.

"Holy shit!" Wayne said. "Did you see that? Damn! He was able to get all the way up there."

"Pretty wild, huh," Patrick said. "Looks awesome, but it's really all about the timing. I'm not saying it's easy, but it is one of those things that looks harder than it is. It's a matter of practice and getting the timing down."

"What do you mean, Con," Richardson said.

"Okay, let's say the bottom rail is twelve feet up. I think it might be closer to twelve and a half. Anyway, you said the guy is around five-foot-nine. So if he holds his hands up…let's say that puts him at around seven-foot, give or take. Did you notice he went over to the wall and picked a point about four feet up? Not too high. Not too low. That's where he launched from. He can already reach seven feet, and then he launches from four feet up. That makes eleven feet right there. He only needs to get about another foot of air when he launches to reach it. I'm sure both of you could easily jump a foot or more. It's all about getting the timing down. It's kinda like the curved wall on the *Ninja Warrior* show. You see regular-sized people all the time, going fifteen, or even eighteen, feet up."

"So when do I get my money and talk to the media," Donald said.

"You get it when, and if, this leads to an arrest and conviction," Wayne said. "Right now, we need to keep this among ourselves and not tip anyone off. Don't worry. You'll get credit if it helps with an arrest."

"If? I practically handed the bad guy to you."

Richardson walked over to the wall at the head of the bed.

"Mister Winston, is this the wall that has that camera on it? I'm sure it will come up in court. You know how defense lawyers can be."

"It sure is." Donald walked over and pulled the blinds up. "Have it mounted right there on the edge of the window frame. And the other one is mounted further over, near the back corner of this wall. I will testify to its authenticity. As you can see, there are no obstructions or anything that could have been edited out of my video. The time stamps also show that both cameras are giving you a continuous, uninterrupted view."

"Yeah, I kind of figured you set them up right there for your entertainment," Richardson said.

"Excuse me? For my entertainment?"

"Yeah, your entertainment. Isn't it amazing how you like to brag about your high-end security system." The stone-faced detective as he stared out the window. "Isn't this the system you bought to make sure none of *those people* are approaching your house or walking in your yard? Yet somehow these two cameras don't show even one blade of grass from your precious lawn. They do, however, show all three floors of that building. Funny how this one seems to be centered right where Mrs. Landers likes to lay in her bathing suit. And I'm betting that when we meet the owners on the other side of Doctor Oh's, we will probably find another attractive woman right where you have the other camera focused. You probably like to zoom in real tight on those third-floor bedrooms. This means you don't have to peep at them through the blinds. I'm sure it made for great *security* videos while you got your jollies."

Winston's face turned red as his breath became shallow and quick.

"Why, you insignificant civil servant. How dare you talk to me like that. I don't like what you're inferring to everyone here."

Wayne elbowed Patrick in the side and whispered, "Oh, yeah. This should be good."

"Listen here, you pompous little prick." Richardson stepped in closer, trapping the diminutive lawyer in a corner. "When I say something, I'm *implying* it. How you interpret it is *inferring.* Any flunky with an eighth-grade education knows that. If you're not going to *speak* English correctly, don't *speak* to me at all. And yes, it is *speak*, not *talk*. Know the difference between a verb and a noun, you jackass."

"We are done, Detective." Donald's face grew a darker red. "I want you to leave m—"

"We are done when I say we're done." Richardson's voice dropped lower and became even more gravelly. "Listen up, because I'm only saying this once. You may have skated by your whole life on your daddy and granddaddy's money, but I don't give a shit. If I need to, I will find something around here to bust you on."

"What the hell is your problem," Donald hissed, his lower lip quivering.

"My problem is arrogant little losers like you, *Donny*. You were an only child, so there is no way you are the world's greatest uncle. But I'm sure it's a clever way to make the ladies—or as you so nicely put it, the hot little chickees—think you're some nice, caring family man. I can't believe you're stupid enough to allow trained investigators into this cesspool. The left eye on the teddy bear…yeah, I know it's a camera. The smoke detector by the door is real. The one above your bed, not so much. It's another camera. And the bookend on the third shelf up. Yeah, the one next to the Kama Sutra—nice touch. The bookend has a camera in it, too. You said practice makes perfect with the video editing. I can just imagine what kind of videos you've been watching in here, practicing your editing with one hand."

"Oh, my God!" Britney's face turned ash-white. "Oh, my God. Oh, my God." She ran down the stairs and out the door.

"Just as I thought," Richardson growled. "I don't give a damn what consenting adults do in private, but if I find out from Britney, or any other hot little chickees, that you were recording them without their permission, I will have cops all over this place and make your life hell. Let's see how the partners in your law firm would respond to that. I don't think they'll care whose coattails you rode in on. And just in case a smug little prick like you thinks you can get rid of the evidence...trust me, we have some of the best tech guys and gadgets around. We will find it. Isn't that right, Mister Patrick?"

He cleared his throat. "Um, yes, that's right. With the DHS grant money, we were able to purchase the all new DTX 3.9 MFR program. MFR stands for magnetic fractal re-imaging. Even hard drives that have been swiped with magnets, or any type of erasure tools, can now be reconstructed. Every little fractal of info is still in there somewhere, like shattered glass. But those shards can all be put back together with this program. Takes a little time, but each piece of a computer's drive can be reconstructed completely. Even better, any device that played a downloaded copy—including a DVD, thumb drive, or external hard drive—can be used to recreate all images and then trace to the original computer and owner. This is the new program developed to snare the child pornographers who would try to wipe their hard drives and cover their tracks. This is why you hear more of them being caught now."

Winston swallowed hard as beads of sweat broke out across his forehead.

Richardson leaned in even closer, looming over the shaking man.

"Let me make myself clear, *Donny the third.* Or should I say, Donny the turd? If it comes down to it, you piece of shit, I will make sure you go away. And I promise, I will also make sure you are surrounded by the very best—the best inmates I could imagine filling your dance card. And trust me, they won't mind that growing bald spot on the back of your head. They'll just grab your ears to guide your mouth." He turned to a smiling Wayne and a wide-eyed Patrick. "Let's go, guys. I think I need to take a shower and wash off any nastiness we may have come in contact with here."

Walking across the room, Richardson could see Donald in the mirror, touching the back of his head.

As they stepped off the front porch, Wayne laughed. "Well, how about that, amigo? I do believe you made that man shit himself right then and there."

"He deserved it." Richardson smiled. "What a prick. Oh, Connor, thanks for the additional info. I haven't stayed in touch with IT as much as I'd like. I had no idea about the new equipment. Sounds pretty impressive."

Patrick returned the smile. "Yup. Sure would be impressive if something like that actually existed."

"Wait, are you telling me you just made all that shit up?" Richardson said.

"Well, he pissed me off with what he did to Brit."

"Hot damn." Wayne laughed as he slapped the intern on the back once again. "Well-played there, Con-man. Magnetic fractal re-imaging. Holy crap, kid. That was good. Remind me to never play poker with you."

As they continued down the walkway, Richardson and Wayne noticed Winston appear a few feet inside a window. Just as they began heading down the driveway, Richardson coughed at Wayne and winked.

"Hang on a second there, guys." Richardson wiped the beads of perspiration off his face. "I am literally sweating my ass off today." He reached into the back of his pants and ran his hand across his dripping backside. "Okay, now we can go." He wiped his hand off on the Porsche's hood and then made a greasy smiley face on the windshield.

CHAPTER 35

He opened his eyes and stared at the stucco ceiling. It was dark, but he knew exactly where everything was in Paul's room. Ambient light from outside the window dimly lit the familiar features of the room.

Something didn't feel right. It hadn't since his visit with Dr. Oh on Friday. The short scouting run from last night seemed off as well. He knew portions of Friday hadn't gone as well as he hoped. Was there something he missed?

Didn't matter. It was time to push those worries aside. He had a schedule to keep. It was a Tuesday night, which meant he needed to rid the world of another monster. He hated himself for doing it, but it needed to be done. It may not be fair, but was it fair for Paul to suffer so much with his pain? There were now just two more hunts to go before he would decide if this should continue.

He stood and slipped off the blue sleep pants Paul wore to bed. After he untied the drawstring, they fell to the floor. Paul hadn't bought new ones since he lost the weight. He stepped over to the dresser and pulled open the bottom drawer. Sitting on top was the dark sweatsuit purchased at Sheila's insistence. Two days ago marked the one year anniversary of the last time Paul had put the running clothes on. Today was the anniversary of when his life fell apart.

He felt bad for Paul. But in all likelihood, the pain would be over soon. He laced up the black running shoes, zipped the sweatshirt, and flipped the hood up over his head and down to his brow. He dropped down the back steps and began running down Mackinaw, toward Louisiana Street.

This would be a short run. Dr. Oczinski was less than two miles away at the small boat harbor. The fifteen-minute run was hardly enough to break a sweat, let alone focus on the details of what was about to happen.

He narrowed his eyes as he turned left on Louisiana, and began heading to where it merged with Ohio Street just before the lift bridge. At this time of night, he didn't need to worry about a ship coming under the lift and halting traffic. Everything around the grain mills at this end of the canal was either abandoned or closed for the night. The warm smell of Cheerios from the General Mills plant indicated there were plenty of people working closer to the lake side of the canals.

He shortened his steps a few inches, leaned forward, and began using his arms more to run up the steeper grade as Ohio Street rose over the train tracks running through to the rail yard. He paused in the tunnel where Ohio ended. Light traffic on Route 5 passed overhead. After gathering his thoughts, he turned down Fuhrmann Boulevard and ran the short distance before arriving at the small boat harbor. He smirked at the formal name—Safe Harbor Marina. It would be anything but safe for Dr. Oczinski tonight.

As he slowed to a walk across the parking lot, he could see Charlie's Boat Yard. That was where Paul and Sheila would often go to grab an ice cream and watch the sun's deepening colors as it dropped into the water. They also enjoyed going there for the occasional Sunday brunch. Paul would joke about how Sheila could eat her weight in French toast and sausage.

He had scouted things last night, and was glad Oczinski lived on his boat most of the summer months. The quick two-mile run was much easier than the grueling nineteen-mile run to East Aurora would have been. The shorter run gave him more time to do what he needed and wanted to do.

Unlike the other kills, he was going to savor this one. Oczinski deserved it. This doctor had decided to work on someone who was perfect—the most beautiful woman Paul had ever imagined. For what? A few more dollars in his bloated bank account? So he could say he improved perfection? It seemed fitting that Oczinski should die exactly one year after Paul's world came crashing down.

As he walked across the parking lot, he noticed the metallic blue Volvo S90 belonging to the doctor. He knew from Oczinski's posts that there was a matching silver one sitting in the parking lot at the Bay Harbor Marina in Erie, Pennsylvania, just ninety miles down the shoreline. Both marinas were owned by the same company. Oczinski had posted how he owned slips at both marinas, and the owners had allowed him to purchase only one salvage policy to cover both locations. The doctor also liked having a personal car waiting for him right there at each location. He would spend the workweek in Buffalo, but then usually spend the weekends in Erie, where he would brag about his time and money spent at the racetrack and casino nearby.

As he passed the doctor's car, he wondered if the esteemed surgeon had some sort of affinity for Scandinavian power. The sporty sedan featured Volvo's T8 twin engine that served as a fuel-efficient hybrid. On the other hand, his Formula 45 yacht was powered by dual diesel-powered Volvo Penta IPS600 engines. Each one cranked out an impressive, yet smooth, 435 horsepower. A full tank of gas would give the doctor nearly two hundred twenty nautical miles, and could easily handle the one-hundred-eighty-mile round trip to Erie without stopping.

Continuing around behind the restaurant, he headed toward the long dock out back. Dr. Oczinski's yacht was tied off on the last finger pier at the far end closest to the break wall. The doctor had posted how he enjoyed being as far as possible from the traffic along Route 5, and enjoyed the convenience of getting in and out of the harbor with minimal obstacles. Tied off with only the outer breaker wall to his starboard, Oczinski also enjoyed the quiet and privacy offered by the three empty slips to the port side.

Looking up from under his hood, he could see the doctor's yacht all the way at the end of the pier. He felt too exposed walking out in the open along this long dock, but he knew it had to be done—and done tonight. Sheila deserved it. Keeping his head down, he started creeping out onto the wooden slats, when he heard a noise. He dropped to a knee. Hoping to blend in, he crouched next to the piling post and pressed his gloved hand against the thick rope wrapped around. He peered into the darkness and looked down the walkway.

Crap. A woman was stumbling off Oczinski's boat, dropping one of her shoes in the process. Who the hell gets off a boat at nearly two in the morning? Her unsteady steps indicated she may have had a few drinks. He hadn't planned on this. As far as he knew, the doctor spent his time alone during the week. Yet here she was. And she was staggering straight toward him.

To his right, tied off to the post, was a Sea Ray Sundeck 200—a sporty boat offering a sufficient escape plan. He had come too far and done too much to be seen now. He had to disappear before she noticed him.

On the right side of the back platform was a small opening leading to the main seating area. Inside was a curved sitting area that could easily hold up to six people. Even with the open design, he should be able to lay along the sitting area and not be seen from the walkway.

He slowly extended his right foot over onto the Sundeck's rear deck. With one palm on the dock, he lowered the other from the piling post and placed it on the boat's rear platform. He gingerly shifted his weight from the left leg on the dock to the right one on the boat. Flattening on his stomach, he slithered through the opening and rolled up on to the seats. Working hard to control his breathing, he could hear her half the conversation as she approached.

"Hey…it's me. Yeah, sorry it's so late, but I needed someone to talk to on my way home. I'm really tired and still a little tipsy, I think. I'm at the small boat harbor. Yeah, him. It just sorta happened. I kinda drunk dialed him a couple hours ago, and he invited me over again. Come on, he's not that bad. You gotta admit, he did a great job on my nose and lips. I like it, and you said yourself it looked nice. Oh, give me a break, it's not like you never hooked up with one of your former men when you wanted to get some." she laughed. "So what if he's not Mr. Right? He does pretty well as Mr. Right Now. And besides, he is good at what he does. There's more than one reason they call him Dr. O, if you know what I mean."

He peered over the back of the boat after she passed by. She was still giggling and laughing at whatever her friend had said. He watched as she slipped on her shoes when she reached the parking lot. He hoped she was able to get home safely. She was walking at an angle, and stumbled a little as she fumbled through her purse. Headlights turned on as she pointed her keys at the car parked behind the blue Volvo. He decided to remain in the back of the Sea Ray for a few more minutes. There were no lights or signs of movement from any of the other boats, but he decided exercising caution would be the best approach at this time.

Aside from the sound of water lapping at fiberglass, the night was still and silent. Slowly, he sat up and peered along the dock. There were no more surprises. No signs of activity. He wanted to move quickly and quietly. He couldn't chance someone popping up out of another cruiser.

Staying low, he hustled along the wooden walkway. The rubber soles of his shoes made little noise as he hurried to the forty-eight-foot boat. The doctor had pulled his yacht straight into the dock. Ever-alert, the dark killer slipped past the front of the boat and turned down the finger pier on the starboard side. He wasn't about to jump up and walk across the front deck. He had done his homework. The main bedroom was right below the deck. He couldn't take the chance of footsteps being heard. Tonight was too important. It had to be completed.

There was minimal lighting as he stepped onto the back of the luxury cruiser, but enough to make out some of the features. He had watched videos of the Formula 45 many times. The boat's designer, John Adams, did a wonderful job narrating the videos and showing all the aspects of the boat. The videos also worked well as a tutorial for someone who wanted to be able to enter quietly without tripping or drawing any attention.

Just ahead of him, off the back platform would be two steps up. After another few feet, there would be another two steps up into the cockpit area, with the adjustable seat, computer monitors, steering wheel, and throttle controls. To the left of the control center would be a narrow door and stairway. Six steps down would take him to the floor of the salon and galley. Even if it was pitch black, he could find his way. Once he went down the stairs, it should be a straight path across the room. There should be no obstacles.

Potentially, a table could be in place just to his right, but if he stayed in the middle, there should be nothing to bump into.

On the other side of the salon, in a straight shot from the stairs, was a short hall to the main bedroom. The room was dominated by a large wall-to-wall bed with a memory foam mattress.

Remembering the young lady he had just seen, he thought this probably wasn't going to be the first of Dr. Oczinski's memories to be soaked into the memory foam. But it would be his last.

He approached the stairway and silently thanked the young woman for leaving it open. He figured the doctor probably wouldn't have locked it anyway, but he wasn't sure how much noise it would have made as it slid open.

He turned sideways before lowering himself on the steps. Toe first, then rolling back to the heel. Things looked dark below, but he couldn't be sure if he was visible. From the videos, he knew you could see the bed from the steps, but that also meant someone lying in the center of the bed could look across and see movement on the stairs.

Ever so slowly, he tiptoed to the bottom of the stairs. Once there, he froze. There was light coming from the bedroom. Was it the television? The changing shades made it seem like it was. He couldn't see anyone lying on the bed. He stayed tight against the wall and tried to let his eyes adjust more.

There was also a sound. It was muffled, and he wasn't sure what it was. Was it static? Sounded like it. But who has static these days? Seems like all video and music sources are digital now. He wondered if anyone under twenty even knew what static sounds like.

He knew. It sounded like this sound. But then again, it didn't.

Damn it. It wasn't static. It was running water. The doctor was awake and was taking a shower. Apparently, he had decided to wash the young woman off himself before going back to sleep. Maybe this wasn't a bad thing, though. He didn't have to worry about being seen from the bed, and he knew where Oczinski was. The doctor had no idea about the stealthy stowaway lying in wait.

A cold smile came across his face. He had surprise on his side.

His eyes were getting better in the darkness. He could now make out a few shapes. From the videos, he knew the galley was to his left, and the eating area was to his right. After the dining area was the short hallway to the bedroom. On the right side of the hallway was the door to the main head. That was where the doctor was lathering up. The door would swing out, blocking the view of the galley. The monster would probably just go straight back to the bedroom and would have no reason to turn toward him.

This could work well.

He walked across the galley and stood at the corner where the dining area narrowed into the hall. With a hundred gallons of water capacity, the doctor could shower for a while.

He waited.

The doctor was singing off-key and butchering the lyrics to "Brandy." Was that the name of the young lady?

He waited.

The water shut off as the doctor cleared his throat.

He waited.

A towel rustled against damp skin.

He waited.

An electric toothbrush buzzed as the doctor continued to hum the classic refrain from Looking Glass.

He waited.

The waiting was almost over. He heard the toilet flush, then the door handle rattle as the panel opened out. Now, just a thin door stood between predator and prey.

As the doctor stepped toward the bedroom, the door closed. Dr. Oczinski stood there wearing nothing more than the towel he was drying his hair with.

Unaware of the man following just one step behind him, the doctor walked into his room and tossed down the towel.

"Damn! What a night," Oczinski said. "It's good to be me."

"Hello, Doctor," a venomous voice spat, as Oczinski's face was buried ear-deep into the memory foam.

The confused doctor struggled in a futile attempt to draw in air against the mattress and the arm around his neck.

Still sprawled over the doctor's naked back, the intruder pulled the doctor's face out of the bedding.

"Oh, no, no, no. You are not going to suffocate tonight. That would be much too peaceful. I have bigger and better things planned for you."

A late-night talk show played quietly on Channel 4. It provided just enough light for him to see the look of terror and disorientation in the plastic surgeon's face. The entire room now smelled of sex, soap, sweat, and fear.

The intruder had his legs wrapped around the struggling doctor's knees, preventing him from being able to stand or turn over. From behind, an arm slid under the doctor's armpit and clamped onto the wrist of the arm around his throat.

"How's that feel, Doc. Oh, yeah, I can feel your Adam's apple bobbing in the nook of my elbow. Don't worry, Doc. Your trachea is nice and safe. Keep on breathing. Like I said, I won't let you suffocate. Is it still good to be you? Hmm? Is it? Let me ask you something. Do you remember Sheila Schon, from about two years ago? Today marked fifty-two Tuesdays since she died. Technically, it's now Wednesday, which means it's the one-year anniversary of when she passed away. Was it good to be you when you injected her with death?"

The doctor knew what was coming next, and was helpless to stop it. He could feel the rock-hard bicep pressuring into his left carotid artery. The assailant had now turned his wrist as he shoved the other forearm's radius against the right carotid. Much like the walls that tapered at the head of the bed, his field of vision narrowed as darkness closed in over him. Without the oxygen-rich blood flowing from the arteries, his brain shut down as the doctor slipped into unconsciousness.

Over two hours later, a solemn killer stepped out of the shower and began putting on the running suit. He thought there would be more satisfaction with this one.

After lacing up his shoes, he headed back to the galley table and pulled out a sheet of paper from the pack. With a sigh, he went back into the bedroom, turned to the right and placed the newest poem in the center of the large mirror on the wall.

Alone and lost in a world of pain.
My everything's gone with nothing to gain.
Growing rage from a blackened soul.
So many more should pay the toll.

—Isiah Gleeson

As he looked at the sheet, he noticed the reflection of the TV. A darkly clad man was edging across a stone wall.

He spun around. Across the bottom, in large letters, it stated, *Video of a Killer?* He listened as the pretty anchor began speaking.

> *"We have breaking news from overnight. Coming up on Wake Up at 4:30, new video has surfaced which may show the killer who has terrified the local medical community. We will hear from the man who shot the video. Stay tuned. That, and your workday forecast, coming up at the bottom of the hour."*

He ran. Jumped out of the boat and hit the wooden planks.

He ran. His shoes slammed against the slats.

He ran. The echo of his footsteps chased him across the parking lot.

He ran. His chest was tight.

He ran. It was hard to breathe.

He ran up Paul's driveway and fumbled with the backdoor key before he crashed into the house.

Things had changed. But the plan still needed to be competed.

The schedule needed to remain the same.

CHAPTER 36

Richardson and Wayne strode past the sergeant's desk area. Tony looked up and nodded back toward the hallway. They continued down the hall and paused as Richardson growled in front of the lieutenant's open door. Finch, holding a phone to his ear, nodded and pointed further down the hall. They kept going past several closed doors, and then knocked on an open entryway.

"Good morning, Alyssa," said Richardson. "I am so sorry about all this. Jon and I were having breakfast at the diner just now when Kerry called me about Winston. That asshole is all over the news."

"He sure is." She sighed. "And every one of the news shows has made sure to add, *No one from the police department has responded to our requests for more information yet*. I swear they think I work here twenty-four-seven. Aside from the generic lines of bullshit, I'm not sure how I'm supposed to comment on something I don't know anything about. Care to clue me in?"

"This guy is a jackass and is looking for media attention to make himself feel better about his pathetic life." Wayne sneered. "I specifically told him we wanted to keep this under wraps for a little while to not tip anyone off."

"Yeah, he did tell him," Richardson said. "The damage is already done, but I'm going to head over and have a little meeting with him anyway."

"Oh, no you are not," said a stern voice from behind them.

"Hey, Bill," said Wayne. "What's going on?"

"You saw me on the phone when you just walked past. It was Mister Winston's law office. They don't want you speaking to, or anywhere near, their employee. He said you threatened him and were hostile."

"What a friggin' pussy," Richardson said. "Sorry, Alyssa. Shouldn't have said that. Look, Bill. This guy is a scumbag. Yes, the video could prove helpful, but it doesn't show much. I didn't really see anything on there to identify who he is. Winston is just a piece of shit who only wants his fifteen minutes of fame. Maybe I was a touch hostile, but I didn't threaten him. I simply told him I was pretty sure of things he was doing, and I just let him know what happens to people who break the law. That's it. If he took it as a threat, that's on him."

"Whatever. Save the bullshit for someone who believes it." Finch scowled Finch. "He might be an asshole, and his office probably knows it. But remember, his firm is well-connected around here. I don't need any crap coming from the mayor's office."

"Look, guys," Joseph said. "I need to get ahead of this. The story is already starting to get national attention, and this supposed video is going to make it even worse. Channels two, four, and seven have all been showing pieces of it since four-thirty this morning.

Captain Reynolds has already told them there will be a brief news conference a little after nine this morning. That means I have about an hour and a half to get my ducks in a row, put on a sweet smile, and do my best to keep this from becoming another shitstorm just because some friggin' pussy wants his fifteen minutes in his pathetic life. Got it?"

"Um, yeah," Richardson said.

"I'm heading up to IT to watch the full video now. I will be back down here in about a half-hour to go over things with you. And let's be clear. When I'm standing there answering the same questions over and over, the two of you will be right there on the stage behind me."

Richardson said, "I don't think—"

"I'm sorry. Did I make that sound like a request? It's not. You will be there. You will not say anything, and you will not answer any questions. You are simply there as a sign of force, and to show we are taking this very seriously." She turned down the hall. "I will see you in thirty."

"Well, I guess that settles that," Finch flashed a hint of a smile. "Good luck with that, boys."

Shortly after 9:00, Alyssa Joseph stepped up to the podium in the briefing room. Two serious-looking detectives followed her. Over his career, Richardson had been in countless situations that would make many men buckle. He had once fought off three men who were armed with chains and knives. He had also stared down the barrel of a shotgun during a domestic dispute. Another time, he had rushed into a burning house and carried out two children before the fire trucks had even arrived. There were few situations that could rattle him. But standing in front of a bunch of cameras and reporters was one of those.

He swallowed hard and glanced over at Wayne before turning and staring straight ahead.

"Good morning." Joseph smiled as a few flashes went off. "First, I would like to acknowledge why we are all here. The safety and well-being of our citizens is of the utmost importance to the Buffalo Police Department. We are taking this investigation, and any subsequent information discovered, very seriously. Behind me are the two lead detectives. To my right, your left, is Detective Rhody Richardson. Next to him, on my left, is Detective Jonathon Wayne. Most of you know them from other high-profile cases we have had over the years. Detectives Richardson and Wayne have been heading up an extensive task force looking into every detail of these horrific incidents. This is just one indication of the level of attention we are placing on this series of crimes. Please know, like you, we only received this video late yesterday. We have not had sufficient time to go through it yet and verify its authenticity."

"The owner has said he will testify to it," said a voice behind the video camera light poles. "He said the time stamp also shows the proper timeline."

Alyssa held her hand up over her eyes as she squinted against the glare. "Is that Alan? Oh, yes, there you are. Well, Alan, of course he would say that. I also heard that he seems to be really motivated to get the reward money, too. I am not saying it's not authentic, but we want to look into it. We haven't had time to investigate yet. As far as the time stamp, I also know that when I buy a new laptop— before I ever let it hook to the Internet—I can set the date and time up myself. I can switch time zones and do all kinds of fun stuff in the settings. You guys, of all people, know how easy it is to manipulate electronic information. I'm not saying this is the case at all. We simply have not had time to analyze and verify everything yet."

After pulling the microphone from the stand, she stepped around the podium. Using her other hand to brush her hair behind her right ear, she looked at them with her disarming smile.

"Can I be candid with you guys for a bit?"

As they nodded, she continued gliding across the stage. Her fluid movements were captivating and mesmerizing. She had a way of showing strength and vulnerability at the same time.

"Let's be honest, we have some of the best investigative journalists in the business right here in Buffalo. I hold you all in high regard. I may not always agree with you, but we both know you are thorough and detail-oriented. When you tell a story, you know it is accurate to the best of your ability. You won't admit it publicly, but I'm betting many of you are extremely disappointed that your morning show producers didn't do a better job vetting this information. It must be frustrating to have someone twist information into something that is more fiction than fact."

Joseph turned, went to the back of the stage, and walked back across with a chair. She then sat down near the end of the stage and again offered her smile.

"Look, you are all trained observers. You notice things. That's what makes you so good at what you do. You've probably seen the video more than I have. I only found out about it when I woke up and saw it on TV just a couple hours ago. Let's try switching roles for a little bit. Seeing as you've watched it so much, would you mind if I asked some questions of you guys to see what you noticed?"

The reporters looked around at each other. They shrugged and then turned their attention back to the attractive information officer.

"All right, then." She smiled. "Dan from the *Buffalo News*. I know you haven't written your copy yet, but when you do, can you tell me for sure the video was shot Friday night?"

"Well, not for sure. We only have the homeowner's word at this time. As you pointed out, he seems really interested in the money. We don't know his motivation, and there is no corroborating information yet."

"That's true. Steve from Channel Two. Can you tell me what color his eyes are, or if he has facial hair?"

"Um, no. The video isn't in color. And besides, he's wearing a hood and we never really see his face."

"Good point." Alyssa smiled. "Luke from Channel Four. Let's make it a simpler, broader type of question. Do you know what race the person in the video is?"

"No, I'm not sure. Like Steve said, we never see his face, and the video mostly just shows his back, and he's wearing a dark hoodie and gloves."

"Good. I noticed that, too. Let's try one more. Charlie from Channel Seven. How'd he get there? Did the alleged assailant walk all the way along the wall, or did he paddle a kayak or canoe right up to the inlet wall?

"You can't really tell. The video starts with him already well on his way along the wall. We can't see if there's a boat below."

"Those are all really good points." She stood again. "Now you see the issue I have with giving you guys any credible information. We are not trying to keep anything from you. As you noticed for yourselves, there just isn't anything worth reporting yet. Trust me, we are working on it and following up every lead possible. And now, thanks to your assignment editors, we have non-stop phone calls coming in from everyone who has ever seen anyone wearing a hoodie. I would hope you will all talk to your producers and think about what you want to put out there. I realize everyone wants to be the first to report things. But I also know how much your journalistic integrity means to each of you. I know how important it is for you to give your viewers, followers, and readers all the facts. Neither you, nor I, want to mislead the public with incomplete information. You know me. When I have something concrete to share with you, I will."

In the break room, Richardson poured coffee and handed a cup to Joseph and one to Wayne.

"Damn, Alyssa. That was smooth the way you buttered them up and left them with nothing. And they were happy with it." He shook his head. "You had them eating right out of your hand."

"Well, that's my job. So I may have buttered them up a little, but it's easy to have them eating out of your hands when you're telling them the truth and they know you are. This should help to minimize the video story for a little while, but you can only keep the wolves at bay for so long. They want results. And so do I. I want the next press conference to be bragging about our success. So get your asses out there and catch this son of a bitch."

CHAPTER 37

JUST A COUPLE HOURS AFTER THE NEWS CONFERence, the two detectives pulled into the parking lot in front of Charlie's Boat Yard restaurant. The CSI team and the coroner were already there.

The overcast skies and cooler temperatures were a welcome respite from the recent heat wave, but the walk to the crime scene was an unwelcome venture into an all too familiar scenario. Like eight times before, a victim lay dead with a number cut into his chest and a poem left at the scene.

Richardson and Wayne stepped around onto the finger pier and shook hands with Jeff McDonald. The forensic investigator mirrored their thoughts with a solemn look, a heavy sigh, and a head-shake.

"Another doctor who works with him came out to check on him when he didn't come in this morning and didn't answer his phone," he said. "Not sure what's going on with this one. A few things are noticeably different, but Dan and I are pretty sure it's the same guy you're looking for. Not a copycat."

"What's different with this one, Jeff?" said Richardson.

"You'll see. For one, the victim is naked this time. Like the other vics, there is no indication of any sexual assault or molestation. In fact, it looks like the perp covered him up with a towel. It was like that when we walked in."

"That kinda goes along with some of our thoughts on his psychological profile," Richardson said. "He might be a twisted psychopath, but he seems to have a sense of modesty and propriety."

"Anything else, Jeff?" Wayne said.

"As a matter of fact, yes." McDonald drew a deep breath. "It's something concerning Doctor Matthews and me. In addition to his signature cuts, he also stabbed the victim in the chest and made a mess of it. Come on in, and I'll show you. Let me clear out a few of our people, though. There's not a whole lot of room around the bed, and it's pretty crowded down there."

The three men headed down the stairs. Standing in the middle of the galley area was Dr. Matthews. The coroner greeted them with a handshake and a grave look.

"I trust Jeff gave you the heads-up on this one," he said. "It is particularly disturbing."

"Yeah, he did." Richardson looked through the door at the bare feet near the end of the bed.

"It's not as if the others weren't disturbing," Matthews said. "It's just that this one seems more...well, it appears to be...let's just go in, and you will see."

"Damn." Richardson looked at the deceased surgeon. "You're right. Definitely a little different. He is certainly covered in a lot more blood than the others were."

"And that is one part of what is so disturbing about this one," the coroner said.

"What do you mean, Dan?" said Wayne.

"Take a look at all the blood around his torso. As you may recall, with all our other victims, the numbers were carved into their skin postmortem."

"Not this one, though," McDonald said. "It appears the number ten was carved out while his heart was still beating. He was basically skinned alive. That's why there is so much blood on him."

"What the hell." Richardson sighed. "Those numbers are at least an inch wide and eight inches tall. Who the hell could do that to someone while they're still alive?"

"And what about the big circle cut into the middle of the zero?" Wayne leaned over the deceased. "Makes it look like he has an archery target carved into him."

"Yes, something else decidedly different," Matthews said. "I will need to examine it more during the autopsy, but it appears a large knife was plunged into him just once. Then it was twisted around and around to create the full circle."

"Shit. What the hell is going on." Richardson grimaced. "Why the change? Why now? Doctor Coleman had a sixty on him. With Doctor Harrison, there was another ten, like this one. Yesterday, we found Doctor Oh with a twenty cut into him. As Connor pointed out, the killer is following the Botox chemical formula. But why is this different? All three of those doctors had a zero in their number, but this is the only one punctuated with a stab to the heart."

"Any thoughts, Rhod?" Wayne said.

"I'm thinking this one is personal. They may have known each other. We need to look even more closely into this doctor. There has to be some sort of personal connection. This is different than the other eight were. Why is this so much more depraved and gruesome? With this one, not only did he want to torture and kill him, but he wanted to cut out, or at least destroy, his heart."

"Speaking of blood," McDonald said. "You were right, Rhody. We were able to recover a small sample of blood on those stones near Doctor Oh's deck, and get some DNA to check against any other samples."

"Like you, Jeff, and I were thinking," said Matthews, "this one was personal as well. The autopsy will show more, but we believe the killer may have slashed the throat and then plunged the knife into the doctor before he bled out. It was probably the last thing the doctor saw. It just screams personal."

"Hey, Jeff, is that our latest poem behind you on the mirror?"

"Yeah, Jon. At least that stayed the same with this one."

The two detectives stepped up and read it.

"Okay, Butch," said Wayne. "Isiah Gleeson. What is he saying to us with one?"

"What the hell, Jon. It's not like I'm Rain Man, or something. They don't always just pop into my head. Sometimes it takes me a little while. Give me a bit."

"I have my guys giving it a go, too," McDonald said. "They haven't come up with anything yet. Let me know if you figure it out."

"Will do. Come on, Duke. Let's head out and let these guys finish processing. Let's see what we can find out about Doctor Oczinski."

In the parking lot, the two detectives faced each other across the hood of the department sedan. The frustration on Richardson's face was punctuated by him slamming his fist on top of the fender.

"Damn it! I want this asshole. All right. Let's focus on what we have right now. We know it's personal. So let's look into the doctor. We'll head over to his office now, then maybe head to East Aurora and see if we can come up with anything at his house or from his neighbors."

"Sounds like a plan," Wayne said. "But let's step on it. I think we should try to give Alyssa an update by the end of the day in case the reporter vultures are still circling around. We should try to see her before she is gone. It seems like this case is…what's with the look? Hey, Rhod? What's going on?"

"Holy shit!" Richardson started running back across the parking lot. "Come on, Jon. I'd kiss you if you weren't so butt-ass ugly."

Two breathless detectives jumped back onto the boat and dropped down the stairs. Richardson pushed into the crowded bedroom and stared at the paper hanging on the mirror. He reached down and pulled his phone out, hit send, and held his hand out.

"Hello."

"Doctor Taylor, this is Rhody. I have you on speaker. Jon and I are with Doctor Matthews, Jeff McDonald, and other members of the CSI team. Even though others are here, this conversation is confidential. We are at another crime scene."

"Oh, no. What happened?"

"It's another doctor. Are you free this afternoon?"

"As a matter of fact, I had a cancellation, so I am free for most of the day. Where are you?"

"We're at the small boat harbor, but that's not where I want you to come. I believe we have enough now for a search warrant. Once we have it, I'd like you to meet us there while we're executing it."

"Sure, Rhody. When and where?"

"I'll let you know when we're heading over. Again, this is strictly confidential in your capacity as a consultant. You already have the address. We will meet you at Paul Schon's house."

CHAPTER 38

Dr. Taylor slowed her Lincoln MKZ Hybrid as she approached Paul's house. The girly-girl in her loved the amenities and luxury offered by the upscale sedan. But the pragmatic tree-hugger in her loved the battery powered alternative which left less of a footprint with greenhouse gases.

The car rolled past several police vehicles until she found an open parking spot.

"Detective Richardson asked me to come," she said, as a uniformed officer blocked her from walking up the driveway.

"She's good, Scott," Richardson yelled from the front porch.

She nodded as she walked past, then looked down the block. Several nosy neighbors had stepped out into their lawns to see what all the fuss was about. Her hardened eyes countered her forced smile as she walked up the steps.

"Hello, detectives. You do realize we may have a serious conflict of interest here."

"Yes, I know," Richardson said. "Kaileen, we are not looking to put you in a bad spot. Quite the contrary. Believe it or not, we want you here to help us understand your client. And if we should come across him, we want someone he trusts. Someone he knows. Someone who is able to talk him down if it turns ugly."

"So he wasn't here when you arrived?"

"No. It looks as if he left in a hurry, though. Several drawers were left pulled out, and the back door was wide open. That's how we let ourselves in. And yes, before you ask, a judge did sign off on a search warrant."

"Do you mind if I ask what made you believe it was Paul?"

"You know, I've had my suspicions for a while. More of a gut feeling than anything concrete. And there is just something familiar about his name, even though Jon and I can't remember what. It keeps sticking with me. But it was the newest poem that put things in place for me. This one was signed Isiah Gleeson."

Richardson held up his phone with a picture of the poem on it. He expanded the photo to show the newest signature.

"Isiah Gleeson? Hmm. You're the anagram expert, not me. Maybe if I had some more time...but nothing is jumping out at me."

"Me neither." Wayne laughed. "Until I helped him see the light."

"How was that?"

"Jon and I were discussing everything we needed to get done. Jon mentioned that he thought we should speak to our public information officer before she is gone for the day. That's when it hit me like a ton of bricks. Who knows how my brain works? Well, maybe you would. Anyway, when he said *she is gone*, I realized those letters were all in Isiah Gleeson. That left only three letters left out from the name—I, L, and A. Once we put them in there, it says, *Sheila is gone*."

"Oh, my God." The doctor shook her head in disbelief. "I know how much he has struggled, but I never dreamed."

"Let me ask you something, Kaileen," said Richardson. "How long did Paul and Sheila date before they were married?"

"Um, I believe it was two years. Yes. Yes, it was. They dated through their entire junior and senior years. Then they got married after they graduated from college."

"That's what I thought. It was one of the things throwing me off. The very first poem said, *Ten years loved and lost.* So it had me thinking it was someone who was married for ten years, but it wasn't. It was about their ten years together. They were married for eight when she died, but he loved her from the start—that was the ten years."

"Excuse me, detectives." Patrick stepped into the doorway.

"Hey, Connor," Wayne said. "What's going on?"

"Jeff sent me out to find you. We found a whole collection of extremely sharp knives. Not dinner or food knives, but the types of knives used for crafts and stuff. I think they're called X-ACTO knives. The owner has quite a few boxes of them."

"That would make sense," Richardson said. "Jon, remember when he was telling us what he does for a living?"

"Oh, yeah, that's right," Wayne said. "He designs and builds models out of wood and plastics. He would need knives like those ones for carving the details."

"Well, Jeff says they would also do a great job at precisely cutting numbers into skin," Patrick said. "The boxes are in his office area, and he said it looks like a few of them are missing."

"Well, Doctor Taylor," said Richardson. "I hate to say it, but it looks like one of your patients is possibly a danger to himself or others."

"I didn't want to mention it, but there's something I think you need to know." She sighed.

"What's going on?"

"I told you I had a cancellation this afternoon. It was Paul. I received an email early this morning. The time stamp said it was about quarter to five. He has never missed an appointment, and his language concerned me a little."

"Why's that, Kaileen?" said Wayne.

"Like I said, he has never missed an appointment. Paul would never break his promise to Sheila. He has always showed up on time. He didn't even say he would reschedule. He also thanked me for all the help I had given him. It was a bit cryptic. It felt more like a goodbye than a cancellation."

"He probably saw the news coverage this morning, with the video. He knew he needed to change things. A panicky person is even more unpredictable. Would you care to join us inside and offer your insight?"

Richardson, Wayne, and Dr. Taylor followed Patrick into the office area. The room was well-organized. Several members of the CSI team were going through and logging items.

"Hey, Rhody and Jon," said McDonald. "Take a look at these." He was standing next to a small shelf along the wall above the desk. "It's not the murder weapon. That would be a larger knife. But I'm betting these are the kind of knives used on the faces and for cutting into the chests. They are precise, like the cuts were. There are a few of them missing from these sets."

"Connor mentioned that," said Richardson. "I know this is the guy. I can feel it. The poem mentioning Sheila cemented it. We're always looking for motive, means, and opportunity. He had the means—anyone can carry a knife, and all these murders were within ten miles of here. He had the opportunity—they were committed at night, using information that can be easily found online. It's his motive that I'm trying to figure out. We know his wife died of an infection. Does he blame doctors for not catching it? But that wouldn't explain the salesman or the nurse. And why plastic surgery docs? It's like this guy just wants to destroy anyone associated with this beauty stuff. It doesn't make sense yet. What set off his hatred for Botox, and these people in particular?"

Everyone looked at each other.

Dr. Taylor said, "Did you find a large envelope in the desk?"

"We just finished cataloging the items on top," McDonald said. "We haven't gone in the desk yet."

"What large envelope, Kaileen?" Wayne said.

"You know I am very conflicted in divulging any information, but it appears you may be correct about him. If he didn't take it with him, there should be a large envelope in his top drawer. It contains a detailed autopsy report about Sheila's death. Last I knew, he had not read it. It was too hard for him. But it may shed some light on what's happening."

McDonald pulled the drawer open with gloved hands. He reached in and handed the large manila envelope to Richardson, who unwound the string from the paper buttons and pulled out the thick report.

"Hasn't read it, my ass." He flipped through. "Take a look by the staple. Every page is creased. It has been opened, and every page has been folded back. And there's more evidence."

"What's up, partner?" Wayne said.

With a sigh, Richardson looked up. "It's kinda sad if you think about it. Look at the ripples on some of these pages. This is where the paper got wet and then dried out. Someone was crying pretty hard when he read this."

"This is awful," Dr. Taylor said. "Rhody, he told me he couldn't bring himself to read it, and I believe him. I don't think he did."

"The evidence shows otherwise, Doc.

"Yes, I agree. But I know Paul, and I don't believe he is capable of this. Remember when I spoke up at the first task force meeting. I mentioned that the killer may not even be aware of what he was doing. We discussed the research by Edelstein and Van der Hart. Van der Hart, in particular, had compelling research showing how a dominant alternate personality could take over and do things to right a perceived wrong. These acts of vengeance would be completely unknown to the main personality. He would have no idea what he had done."

"Fine," Richardson said. "That's your end of things, Doc. You can discuss his issues with him all you want. But first, on my end of things, I need to stop him."

"I just want you to consider it if things come to a showdown and you think you need to draw your gun. Perhaps you can just do what you need to do to bring him down. I don't believe he knows what he's doing."

"Well, I do know what I'm doing. And I'm sorry, Kaileen, but a wounded criminal is even more dangerous to those around him. I have to consider the lives and families of others first. I hope you'll understand. I'm trained to stop a threat, not wound a suspect. I don't give a damn about his unknown vengeance."

CHAPTER 39

A LONE TEAR TRICKLED DOWN DR. TAYLOR'S CHEEK as she walked out of the room. What Richardson said was regrettable, but understandable. She knew he was right. It was part of the job, and he needed to think of the bigger picture. She needed to as well.

She consoled herself with the idea that Paul could still be brought in unharmed. Even with everything that may have happened, she wanted to help him through his pain.

"Excuse me, Doctor Taylor? Do you, um, have a moment?"

"Of course, Connor." She wiped her cheek. "What can I help you with?"

"Can we go over there, away from all the activity?"

"Sure thing."

Richardson had entered Schon's living room, and was seated on the edge of the recliner, thumbing through the report. There was a lot of information, so it was going to take some time to read through it.

He grimaced as he opened it back to the first page of text.

"Hey there, amigo." Wayne grinned. "While you're having fun with that, I'm gonna take a stroll around and speak with the neighbors."

"Good idea."

"I want to see if anyone knows anything pertinent. Maybe someone knows where he likes to go when he disappears. Call me if you need anything. I'll be back in a while."

"Sounds good. I'll let you know."

"Back to reading, then, Mr. Bookworm." Wayne headed out. "You can give me the CliffsNotes, or at least the Reader's Digest version of it when you're done."

Settling back to go through the report, Richardson glanced up and a look of concern came across his face. In the opposite corner, Patrick was speaking with Dr. Taylor. The normally confident young man seemed uncomfortable and bashful. His guilty look was emphasized by a nervous smile.

A few minutes later, the psychiatrist reached into her purse. After flipping her wallet open, she pulled out a business card and handed it to him. She nodded, smiled, and patted his shoulder went back onto the front porch. Patrick slipped the card into his back pocket, and then drifted back into the office area to join the rest of McDonald's crew.

Richardson followed Dr. Taylor out to the porch.

"Hey, Doctor," he whispered.

"Detective."

"Look, Kaileen. I'm sorry if I was a bit harsh in there. We're all a little edgy. Please know that I will always explore all options before I ever pull a trigger."

"I understand, Rhody. And I don't doubt it at all. I know you have to do what you have to do. I trust you will always use good judgement. So far, you've never given me reason to think otherwise."

"Thanks. I couldn't help but notice you speaking with Connor in there. I hope the kid is all right. He has seen some things in the last couple weeks that no one should see, let alone a kid just starting his career. If there's anything I can do to help him deal with all this, please let me know."

Kaileen smiled and nodded. "That is very kind of you. But I don't think you have to worry about him. He seems to have a good head on his shoulders, and is able to separate his personal and professional lives. He's doing just fine."

"Really? That's good. He looked a little nervous and unsure of himself when I saw the two of you in there."

"He was nervous." She laughed. "He was asking me for a favor and wasn't sure how to approach me. Am I that scary?"

"Nope, not at all. What's going on?"

"Well, he knew I was a lawyer, and he wanted to know if I know of anyone who was looking to hire a law clerk. He said he has a friend who might be looking for a new job."

"I think I know who she is. We met her yesterday at the crime scene. They were undergrads together at UB."

"Yes, that's what he said. It just so happens that I may have the perfect opportunity for her. I was having lunch on Monday with a friend of mine who's a federal judge. She said her clerk is going out on maternity leave, and my friend doubts she'll be coming back. She asked me to keep my eyes open for a good candidate. I gave Connor my card and told him to have his friend call me. Should work out well all the way around."

"Very nice. Would you be available tomorrow morning around nine, in the squad room? I'd like to read through this report a few times tonight, and I'm sure I'll have a shitload of questions for you. I'd like to get a few of us together to discuss what Jeff's team found. I'll stop and grab some coffee and donuts on the way in."

"Sounds good."

"Well, it's about damn time," Wayne said, as Richardson entered the conference room.

He slid boxes of donuts into the middle of the table and placed two large coffee containers at the edge. After flipping an empty cup off the top of the stack, he held it under the spigot.

"Who else needs some?"

Everyone grabbed their share of sugar and caffeine.

Richardson said, "Jon and I were going through the autopsy report last night. We had to do further research on some things noted but not really explained in there. There is a lot of information, and we found some of the reasons why Schon may have done some of the things he's done. Care to get it started there, Sundance?"

"No problemo there, amigo," Wayne said. "As you all know, Sheila Schon died one year ago. But our story starts more than two years before that. Halfway around the world, in India, there was a medical supply company along the Damodar River. Now, the Damodar is known as one of the most polluted rivers in the world. In addition to the normal nastiness flowing through, there was one big-ass flood upriver which flowed down and ravaged the area. Tons of dead animals, dead people, and factory sludge was washed downstream. The medical supply company had a warehouse right along the river. They shipped most stuff by boat to head downriver to the ocean freighters. A whole bunch of skids with medical supplies and equipment, like needles, were flooded under all that germ-infested water. This soup of the dead created some seriously mutated germs—the kind of shit antibiotics couldn't do anything with. It was all supposed to be destroyed, but pirates got hold of it, labeled it as sterile, and put it back out on the open market."

Richardson said, "The tainted equipment somehow made its way to the US, where a couple legit companies bought it, thinking they were getting a bargain. About two years ago, using the lot numbers, they discovered what happened. Most all of the products were accounted for and recalled, but salesmen had also distributed some of the products as samples for doctors to try out. Some of those products were the needles used for Botox injections, among other things. One of the supply companies, Draxson Industries, services med suppliers across the Northeast. One of those companies is Pharmer-Grown, where the salesman Sean Hill worked. As it turned out, among the doctors who may have received and used the samples was none other than Doctor Harvey Oczinski. We also learned a few things from Mrs. Schon. Before her death, she disclosed more information to her doctors and nurses. She told them she had contacted several doctors before she became one of Oczinski's patients about two years ago. Although it is not known for certain yet, it appears the infection that killed Mrs. Schon was from those tainted needles."

"Well, that explains why antibiotics didn't work on her," McDonald said. "And it also explains the personal nature of Oczinski's murder."

"Yes, it does," Wayne said. "We had the means and opportunity. This now gives us the motive."

"Any thoughts on the other victims?" said Captain Reynolds. "I can understand the motive for Hill and Oczinski. One supplied the needles, and the other used them. But it seems he is acting out against anyone and everyone who is in the business."

"Yes." Richardson nodded. "We were about to get to that. We weren't sure until Jeff's team came across something yesterday. They found the missing pieces that tie all nine of the victims to Schon."

"What did they find?" Finch said.

"Schon is a very organized, detail-oriented man," said Richardson. "Lucky for us, his organizational skills helped pull it all together."

"Sure did," Wayne said. "Jeff's team located where he had saved every receipt, credit card statement, canceled check, phone record, utility bill, and everything else. He must have saved over ten years of crap. All organized by date."

"Those records are how we tied all the victims together," Richardson said. "Captain already mentioned the direct tie from Schon to Hill and Oczinski. Now the first two victims were at the office next to where Sheila worked. She had a friendly relationship with some of the workers there. Schon would have to assume she would reach out to them for treatment. Taking a look at the credit card statements, we found several charges to AllNewU in Orchard Park. Mrs. Schon went there before the two of them started going together. Again, Schon would probably assume she had asked them about the treatment. This ties him to Hallock, the nurse."

"That gives us a direct connection to five of the victims right there," Wayne said. "But we still needed to find a connection to Harrison, Nigel, Oh, and Nadeer."

"When Jeff's team was going through the call history on the saved paper phone records," Richardson said, "they noticed the history associated with Sheila's cell. It had some phone numbers highlighted."

"It turns out," Wayne said, "those highlighted numbers belonged to Harrison, Nigel, Oh and Nadeer. Nadeer wasn't her dentist, so it seems logical that she may have called him to ask about his side Botox business."

"If any one of those doctors had treated Sheila," said Richardson, "she wouldn't have come in contact with the tainted needles. In Schon's grief-addled brain, that would have made them just as guilty in her death. He seems bent on destroying anyone who had anything to do with it. And as Doctor Taylor noted, he doesn't seem as inclined to stop."

"I'm telling you, Kaileen," Wayne said, "I don't envy you trying to crawl around inside that man's twisted brain. Schon is one jumbled-up mess."

"Holy shit!" Richardson looked up from his notes. "This has been about anagrams from the very beginning."

Everyone looked around at each other with puzzled expressions.

Wayne said, "Um...yeah, Rhod. You were the one who first picked up on that, remember? I was the one who got knocked in the head. Are you having some sort of sympathetic amnesia?"

"No, smart-ass." Richardson smiled. "I'm saying I think the anagrams go back further than I thought. Connor, what was the chemical formula for the Botox?"

"Um, C6760—"

"No, I don't need the numbers. Just the chemical stuff."

"Oh, all right. Carbon, Hydrogen, Nitrogen—"

"No, sorry. I meant just the letters for the formula."

"That would be C, H, N, O, and S."

"That's what I thought." Richardson smiled. "Duke, once again, you said something that made me realize what I was missing."

"Well, it is true that I am a bit of a god." Wayne smirked. "I do try to use my powers for good, though. What did I do this time?"

"You just told Kaileen you thought Schon was a jumbled-up mess."

"Yeah. He is."

Richardson grabbed a marker, walked up to the white board and began writing the letters across the top.

"Check it out. Like Connor said, the letters for the chemicals are C, H, N, O, and S. Now take those same letters, and as Jon said, *jumble* them up. S, C, H, O, and N. It spells Schon! The formula was an anagram for his own name. It isn't the Botox he's angry about. He's trying to destroy himself."

CHAPTER 40

It was another Friday evening with his bride's arms wrapped around his waist. Richardson revved the motorcycle as he passed the apex of a tight curve. Squeezing the clutch, he tapped the shifter with his heel while the big bike roared up through the gears. Kerry held on tight and laughed when their helmets banged together as she tried to kiss his neck.

Paul Schon had disappeared. There was no sign of him, and aside from the brief email to Dr. Taylor, he hadn't communicated with anyone who knew him. Was he just laying low for the time being? Had he skipped town?

Richardson, Wayne, and Dr. Taylor didn't believe so. They didn't think it was in him. Richardson felt Schon was too obsessive about the process. The first few poems spoke of ten victims, and there had been nine so far. At a minimum, Richardson was sure Schon would go for one more.

Riding with his wife relaxed him and helped to clear his mind. They had eaten earlier, and were now enjoying some V-twin time before heading back home. The vibration from the motorcycle had him reaching down to check his phone. He had the volume up, but he kept reaching just in case.

Richardson and Wayne had decided to not take the girls out for karaoke. If the pattern continued, there would be another victim that night. Although they hoped for the best, the two detectives wanted to make sure they were clear-headed both that night and the next day.

With his wife wrapped to him, Richardson kept riding. A sliver of burnt orange caressed the purple horizon as he pulled into their driveway. It was getting late, and he wanted to settle in with Kerry for the night.

Dr. Taylor was also concerned there would be another victim, and she believed it would be in the next few hours. She told the team that she'd tried to call Paul for the last couple days. Wednesday had been the one-year anniversary of Sheila's death. She told them of his issues with Tuesdays and Fridays. His actions seemed driven by these. She wondered how she hadn't put it all together before this.

With a mountain of evidence all pointing to her patient, Kaileen had to acknowledge her fears. Now that he'd disappeared, she believed Paul may have permanently slipped into an alternate personality. Perhaps the explosive, hostile person she'd witnessed in her office had now taken complete control—not just while Paul slept.

She poured through her notes. The rapid eye movements, the nightmares, the anger, the personality changes, the fluttering left hand with his wedding band. How had she missed it?

They were now faced with the one-year anniversary of Sheila's burial. The anniversary of the last time Paul said he'd kissed her face. If it was going to happen, she knew this would be the night someone else could die. Like the other team members, she knew why and when, but she had no idea on who or where.

It was getting late. She wanted to get through a few more of the 128 unread emails on her laptop. She skimmed through, but there didn't appear to be another email from Paul. Many of them were unwanted solicitations, but she still wanted to buzz through some of the work-related ones before she turned in.

Wayne slammed his fists into the heavy bag in his basement. His hands were wrapped under the gloves. Sweat splattered off his oily arms with each punch.

He and Richardson had struggled with a stressful and frustrating day. The clock was ticking. Each lead had turned into a dead end. Nothing seemed to be jumping out at them. Like his best friend, Wayne was sure Schon was still around. Schon wasn't planning something. Whatever he was going to do had already been planned. Now it was going to be all about the execution.

Wayne grimaced at the thought of the double meaning of the word. Doing something and ending something were the two sides of execution.

He could hear his wife walking across the living room floor above him. She was being so patient and understanding. She waited while he punched his frustrations into the canvas cover. His arms felt heavier than the bag he had been beating for the last couple hours.

Sitting on his weight bench, he unwrapped his hands, toweled off, and walked upstairs. It was time to hit the shower and finally spend some time with his wife.

•.•.

It was nearly 10:30. Richardson and Kerry were wrapped around one another. Kerry's light, even breaths were evidence that she had, once again, slipped off to sleep after enjoying her husband. He tenderly kissed the top of her head, laying on his chest.

While he rubbed her bare back, a satisfied smile came across his face. No matter how shitty the outside world was, he had his petite piece of heaven right there in his arms.

The phone blared. Richardson had forgotten to turn the ringer down before he and Kerry collapsed in a tangled embrace on the bed. He jumped as the piercing sound ripped through the silence of the room. Again, Kerry was jerked along as he sat up and reached for his pants on the floor.

"Oh, my God," Kerry said, with unfocused eyes. "What's going on?"

He pulled his pants onto the bed, yanked the phone off his belt, and pressed the dot on the screen.

"Hello?"

"Rhody, this is Kaileen."

"Um, yeah, Doc." He cleared his throat. "What do you need?"

"I was going through my email, and I read about an event we're having, and I think I know what might be happening."

"Whoa, hold on. Take a breath, Kaileen. Slow down a little. You are speaking way too fast. What event is going on, and what do you think is happening?"

"Sorry, Rhody. Please give my apologies to Kerry for calling so late. I hope I didn't wake you."

"Don't worry about it. Is this about Schon? What's up?"

"Yes. I mean, I think so. Over the years, I've been on a bunch of committees at UB, so I'm still on a lot of the email lists. Early tomorrow afternoon, the med school, law school, and the communications department are all holding a joint seminar about handling public relations nightmares and how to minimize damages both monetarily and with your reputation."

"All right. But what do you think this has to do with our case?"

"The featured presenter is Frederick Sandholtz. Doctor Frederick Sandholtz. He led his company out of a PR crisis a couple years ago, and now they are stronger and more successful than ever. He is the CEO of Draxson Industries."

"Holy shit!" Richardson stood. "That has to be it. That's where the needles came from. Schon would know that. Sandholtz is the S-name—the last one in the formula. He has to be the target."

"I had heard he was the speaker, but I didn't know anything about him. I just saw his bio on the flier in my email, and I realized the significance."

"Well, now we know who. We just need to figure out where."

"I think I know that, too. UB likes to make a great impression on out-of-town guests. They have a corporate account at Salvatore's Garden Place Hotel."

"Beautiful place. Kerry and I spent our anniversary there a couple times."

"It is very nice. With the conference tomorrow, I'm sure Doctor Sandholtz is staying there tonight. But there is another reason I'm sure it'll be at that hotel."

"What's that?"

"Paul and Sheila spent their wedding night there. I believe he would think it's fitting to end this rampage in the same place he started his marriage with her. They had stayed in the Emperor Suites. The University usually puts their guests in the Emperor. I'm on my way now."

"You have to be right. I'm on the way, too. Should only take about fifteen minutes. I'll call Jon."

CHAPTER 41

Dr. Sandholtz walked around the massive Emperor Suite. He was a successful CEO, and accustomed to the best. But he had to admit this was impressive, even by his standards. Not just the size of the room, but the way everything was laid out. From the partial privacy wall near the outstanding king-size bed, to the separate living and eating areas, the room screamed elegance and comfort. He wished all of his travel arrangements included places like this.

As he scrolled through the pay-per-view movie selections, he heard a light rapping at the door. He stood from the couch and moved across the room.

"Yes?"

"Hello. Doctor Sandholtz?" said a voice from the hallway. "This is room service with a bottle of wine for you."

"I'm sorry. I didn't order anything."

"No, sir. It is compliments of the University. They wanted to welcome you to Buffalo. My apologies for the delay. You should have received it when you checked in."

Sandholtz placed his palms against the door as he put his eye to the peephole. In the hallway stood a man dressed in a tailored tuxedo. At his side was a small cart on wheels. The cart held a large marbled container filled with ice. A bottle of wine was nestled into the cubes. Next to the ice container, a small cutting board contained an assortment of meats and cheeses in bright-colored packaging.

Sandholtz pushed the handle down and opened the door. "Well, thank you very much. Looks wonderful. And I was just thinking I could go for a little snack. Please come on in."

"Very well, sir. Where would you like it?"

"Just leave it there by the kitchen area. Perfect. Hang on a moment. Let me get you a little something for your efforts."

Sandholtz walked around the large privacy wall and into the bedroom. He continued around the bed, to the nightstand, and reached in the drawer for his wallet. As he started to stand back up, an arm wrapped around his throat and an oily rag was shoved into his shocked face.

"Hello, Doctor," snarled the man behind him. "Do you like my tuxedo? This is a special occasion. You should be honored. It hasn't been worn since the day Paul and Sheila Schon got married."

Richardson rushed across the lobby. Dr. Taylor was standing there looking exasperated.

"Rhody, I've been trying to call his room. There's no answer."

"What room is he in?"

"I don't know." She pointed to the employee behind the desk. "He says they're not allowed to give out guest information. He can only call the room."

Richardson started toward the man with the fearful eyes, and glanced back as he heard Wayne running across the room.

"Look, son. We have an emergency situation here. Here is my badge, and it goes nicely with the gun. This is official police business. We need Doctor Sandholtz room number. Now!"

"Um, I-I'm going to have to call my m-manager at home," the young man said.

"Listen here, Junior," Wayne growled. "We don't have time for any bullshit. This is a matter of life and death. Now tell us which room, and program a key card for it. Otherwise, this big guy and I are going to kick in every goddamn door until we find him. Got it?"

"Uh, o-o-okay." The man swiped a white card along the computer. "One floor up. Take those stairs over there. Go to the end of the hall. It's the last room on the left."

"Thanks, kid." Richardson grabbed the card.

He and Wayne ran to the stairwell. Taking three steps at time, they headed to the second-floor doorway.

Richardson held a finger to his lips as he and Wayne slowed. They crept toward the last room. Wayne pressed his ear against the door. He could hear a muffled voice.

"Someone's in there," he whispered, "but I can't hear what they're saying. How do you want to handle this?"

Dr. Taylor was hurrying down the hall. Richardson motioned for her to be quiet. She slowed as they stepped toward her.

Richardson whispered, "We have to do this quickly. If we can avoid it, I don't want to just burst in and spook him into doing something. Let's see if we can get him away from the doctor. Kaileen, can you knock and say you're with housekeeping? Tell him you have towels or something. Maybe we can get him to come to the door."

She knocked lightly on the door. "Hello. Housekeeping. I have the extra towels you requested."

Nothing.

She waited a few seconds and knocked again. "Housekeeping. I have your towels."

"Um, thank you," a voice called out. "I'm busy right now. Just leave them by the door. I'll get them in a few minutes."

"Okay." Dr. Taylor turned and whispered to Richardson and Wayne, "Oh, my God. It's him. That was Paul's voice."

"Shit," Richardson pulled out his gun and looked at Wayne. "All right, Duke. Take the card. Try to be as quiet as you can. Push the door open, and I'll go in first."

"And I'll be right behind you, amigo," Wayne whispered, and nodded.

He dipped the card into the lock. A light chime rang out as a small green light flashed. He swung the door swung open. The 9mm Glock led the way as Richardson stepped in.

"Freeze!"

Behind the partition wall, Richardson could clearly see the large bed. Sandholtz was laying sideways across it. Richardson could see the cuts around the eyes and mouth on the left side of the doctor's face. As Sandholtz turned toward the noise, Richardson could see the matching cuts along the right side. Several cinch straps held the arms and legs of Sandholtz tightly in place.

Richardson's gaze locked on Schon. He was kneeling over the doctor. His naked body straddled the doctor's torso. In Schon's left hand was an X-ACTO knife. Blood dripped off the sharp point. He dropped the small knife and grabbed a larger hunting knife alongside the doctor. A beam of light danced across the ceiling as the blade reflected the recessed lighting from above.

"Drop the knife!" Richardson said.

Wayne came around behind him, scurried across the room, and stopped at the far edge of the partition wall, with his gun also pointing at Schon.

"No. This needs to happen," Schon hissed, his eyes narrowed. "They all need to pay."

"Paul, please stop," Dr. Taylor pleaded, from behind Richardson. "You know Sheila wouldn't want this."

He glared across the room at her with ice-cold eyes.

"Sorry, Doc. Paul isn't here right now. But if you'll leave a message at the sound of the tone, we will get right back to you."

"It's over, Schon!" said Richardson. "Drop the knife right now, or I will drop you."

"No. It must be completed. She deserves to be avenged, and Paul deserves his revenge on these monsters."

"Paul, it was a tragic accident," Taylor cried. "It wasn't their fault. It happened. And yes, it was horrible. It should have never happened. But it all happened because Sheila loved you. She was trying to be even more beautiful for you."

The icy eyes warmed and misted over. A tear rolled down his cheek, as his posture slumped.

"But she was already beautiful," he whispered. "She didn't need anything. She was perfect."

His posture became rigid. Eyes hardened again.

"No! She died. They don't deserve to live."

Schon brought his left hand up high over his head. Reflected light bounced above the headboard. Then the knife arced down at the doctor's chest.

Blam!

The bullet whistled across the room. It slammed in between the phalanges of Schon's middle and ring fingers. There was a nearly imperceptible clink when lead bounced off gold. As the bullet continued on its path, it ripped apart the connection between the third and fourth metacarpals. Crushing the hamate and capitate bones, it continued to tear through the hand before bouncing of the lunate bone and exiting at his wrist.

The knife flipped through the air before falling into the mattress. Schon screamed as he fell off to the far side of Sandholtz.

"My ring! My ring. Is it all right? Oh, my God. I can't feel my ring. My ring! Where is my ring?"

Schon curled into a fetal position. He wrapped his right hand around the torn-apart left.

"Oh, there it is," he said, breathlessly, as he glided his fingers over the bloody, viscous metal. "There it is. My ring. It's still there. My ring. I still have my ring. It's still here. My ring! I have my ring."

Richardson walked up with the Glock pointed at Schon. He reached down to flip the knife off the edge of the bed, and kicked it across the room. He pulled Schon off the bed and clamped handcuffs on the muttering man. Kaileen emerged from the bathroom with a small towel and wrapped it around Paul's gushing left hand.

Wayne was on the phone calling it in. An officer-involved shooting. No officers down, but they needed two ambulances.

Richardson pulled the tape from the doctor's mouth.

"You're safe now," He and Wayne began removing the straps. "Ambulance is on the way."

The doctor looked at Kaileen with pleading eyes.

"My phone. It's on the dresser. Please call my wife. Tell her I love her."

"Of course, Doctor. I'll call her right now."

"Hey, Rhody," Wayne said. "Check it out. Here's the poem he was going to feature for us tonight."

Leaving Sandholtz with Dr. Taylor, Richardson walked across the room. Wayne handed the sheet of paper he had pulled from the black backpack sitting on the dresser.

What was lost cannot be undone.
More lives lost for the cost of one.
Lost in loneliness, anger, and fear.
My life is lost without her here.

—Austin Wade Plot

Richardson read the poem with a solemn face. He looked over at Schon. Kaileen had wrapped his hand with a towel that was soaking through. With his hands cuffed behind his back, Paul continued stroking his left through the damp terry cloth. He was still rambling about his wedding band.

"Not yet, you asshole." Richardson looked at Schon and tossed the paper back onto the dresser.

"What? You gotta be shittin' me," Wayne said. "Did you figure that one out already?"

"What can I say. Sometimes they jump out at me. Sometimes they don't."

"Well, Butch...care to share with the rest of the class?"

"Austin Wade Plot—*Paul wants to die.*"

"Damn, you're good. So he wants to die, huh? Why the hell didn't he just do it himself."

"Because he couldn't." Dr. Taylor looked sadly at her muttering patient lying on the floor.

Richardson and Wayne stepped aside as paramedics and other police officers poured into the room.

"What do you mean, Kaileen?" Wayne said.

"He made a promise to Sheila, and he would never break a promise to her. She made him promise he would go on living after she was gone."

"So he thought cop-assisted suicide would be some sort of loophole?"

"I don't know, Jon. I'm not sure how he was thinking yet. We need to realize this wasn't Paul. It was someone else who took over when his family life was torn apart. It wasn't really him."

"Whatever," Richardson growled. "I can think of at least nine other families who don't give a shit."

CHAPTER 42

A WEEK LATER, MEMBERS OF THE TASK FORCE MET again. They gathered together around the large table in the conference room.

Alyssa Joseph had been featured in many national news stories. Much to their dismay, so had Richardson and Wayne. They were more than happy to divert any attention back to her.

Good-natured teasing went back and forth across the table. Now that the pressure of hunting for a serial killer was off, the room was much more relaxed.

Wayne walked in with an armload of donuts, and another arm filled with coffee.

"Hey, hey, hey! Goodies are on me. My treat."

"Holy crap,!" Richardson said. "Since when do you treat? Did the *Buffalo News* have a coupon?"

"Bite me, smart-ass." Wayne smiled. "And yes. Buy one dozen, get the second half-price."

The room burst out in laughter as they all grabbed from the boxes.

Richardson looked around the room and smiled. This was what he needed. The camaraderie, the closeness, the happiness.

Patrick said, "Rhody, can I ask you a question?"

"You just did."

"Huh? Ugh. Funny. You got me with that again."

"What's up?"

"When you disabled Schon, how did you know it was his left hand that would undo everything for him? Doctor Taylor was saying that as soon as you shifted his focus to his wedding ring, everything changed for him. That was impressive."

"Well, Con-man, that is something you pick up on with experience. It's all about understanding the psychosis, and the driven behaviors behind them. With careful observations, you see and learn what motivates others. How does he respond to certain questions? What stimuli affects him the most? It's all about understanding their focus. Astutely noting what they are obsessed with can help you in finding their kryptonite."

"Oh, my god." Wayne laughed. "I think I'm gonna barf. Con, please tell me you don't believe any of his bullshit."

The entire room started laughing again, including Richardson. Patrick's face turned deep red, and he bit into a donut with a tight grin on his face.

"Well, I would like to thank both of you for a job well-done," Dr. Taylor said. "Actually, a great job to everyone in this room. Rhody, I would like to also thank you for disarming him the way you did. And I must admit, I'm impressed with your marksmanship. Hitting his hand like you did worked perfectly. After our earlier conversation, I was worried it would turn out much worse."

"Well, I'd like to say I was aiming for his ring, but I think I've spread enough bullshit for today." Richardson winked at Patrick.

"I'm glad it turned out like it did. But as I told you...we are trained to stop a threat, not to wound a suspect."

"Then what happened?" Joseph said.

"I guess sometimes it is better to be lucky than good. When I shot, I was aiming for his heart. He just happened to swing the knife down across his chest as I pulled the trigger."

They all turned to look as someone knocked on the open doorframe.

An officer leaned in. "Hey, Rhody. Captain Reynolds says he needs to see you in his office, now."

"Ooooooooohhhhh," Wayne said. "The honeymoon's over. Please report to the principal's office. What did you do this time, Mister Richardson?"

•.•.

"Hey, you wanted to see me, Captain?"

"Yes. Thanks for coming up. Rhody, we would like to speak with you about something. A pretty big opportunity. I'd like you to meet the deputy director of Homeland Security."

The tall man stood and shook Richardson's hand.

"We've heard a lot of good things about you, Detective Richardson. It's nice to finally meet you."

"Thank you."

"And if you look behind you," Captain Reynolds said, "I believe you already know the lieutenant governor."

"Oh, yes. Rhody and I go back quite a while." She smiled as she shook his hand. "Good to see you again. I knew Detective Richardson back when I was a congresswoman here in Buffalo a few years back. So Rhody, are you still as politically correct as ever?"

"Yes, sir."

The captain cleared his throat and looked around uncomfortably.

"And funny as always, I see," said the lieutenant governor. "Let me tell you gentlemen about the first time we met. We were dealing with some serious threats against elected officials. Rhody was investigating letters sent to my office. I asked him if he knew what these people were thinking of. What makes them tick. Without missing a beat, he looked me straight in the eye and said he has no idea why anyone would ever hurt a politician. They would only replace them with another politician, so nobody wins."

The deputy director snorted a laugh. Captain Reynolds looked down nervously and smiled at his shoes.

"But Deputy Director," said the lieutenant governor, "if you are looking for an investigator, there is no one more tenacious and thorough. He gets results. And as I mentioned to you on the way here, you never have to worry about a yes-man reporting the company line to you. He will speak his mind, whether you want to hear it or not."

"Excuse me," Richardson said. "Reporting to you?"

"Occasionally, yes," said the deputy director. "Let me ask you... do you have any immediate plans? If you do, it's fine. But I'm just wondering for our own timeline."

"Um...nothing really planned. With the captain's permission, I'd like to take a week or so off, now that we've arrested Schon."

"Granted," the captain smiled. "You and Jon both should take some time and decompress."

"Thank you, Captain. I'd like to take Kerry down to Bristol again for the NASCAR race next weekend. It's our favorite race of the year. It would be nice to just drive down and do a lot of sightseeing along the way."

"Now that sounds like my kind of vacation," said the deputy director. "When you return, we would like your help with a special task force. You would be in charge. This is being done in conjunction with Homeland Security, several governor's offices, the Buffalo Police Department, and other national law enforcement agencies."

"What does that mean? What is it all about?"

"You see, Rhody," said the lieutenant governor. "All that good press you've been getting turned a lot of heads. I remember how much you hate the spotlight, but you should be flattered. It made a lot of people aware of your successes."

"I am flattered. But I'm happy staying here in Buffalo. I have no intention of leaving."

"That's the beauty of this task force," said the deputy director. "You are, and still will be, a detective here in Buffalo. However, when something pops up, we may need you to travel in a moment's notice to other areas or states to investigate serious crimes. You will have jurisdiction anywhere you're sent, and will work with local law enforcement teams. With so much focus on international and domestic terrorists, our national agencies are stretched thin when it comes to the local criminals wreaking havoc in our country. We'll let the agencies that use letters for their names focus on the terrorist types. We are looking for someone with your skills to work alongside other law enforcement to catch the regular domestic scum."

"It sounds great, but this is something I would have to discuss with Kerry first."

"Of course," said the deputy director. "Here's my card. Call me when you've decided, and we'll go over your compensation and all the other details."

"Will do, sir."

"Any initial thoughts about this opportunity," said the lieutenant governor.

"I need to discuss it with Kerry first. But when she and I get back from Bristol, I'm thinking I may have to keep a suitcase packed, and be ready to go in a moment's notice."

ACKNOWLEDGEMENTS

To my wife, Kerry: My life changed the very first day I met you. It can't be easy being married to me, but I'm glad you are. Thank you for bringing your entire family into my life. Thank you for being there through all the ups and downs - for sitting with me through all the low-budget movies and thousands of bad jokes. PS: I love you.

To Jon, Alyssa, Kaileen, and Connor: Being your dad has brought me more love, happiness, and pride than I could have ever imagined. Each of you are so different – and so perfect – in your own way. You have all grown into such incredible individuals. Everything about you makes me so proud of you.

This is dedicated to the memory of my father, Richard O'Brien, and my grandfather, Rhody O'Brien. They are two of the biggest influences in my life.

To my publisher, Cayelle Publishing: Thank you for taking a chance on a debut author. I am so grateful for the opportunity. Since the first contact, it has been a pleasure to work with you.

CayellePublishing.com

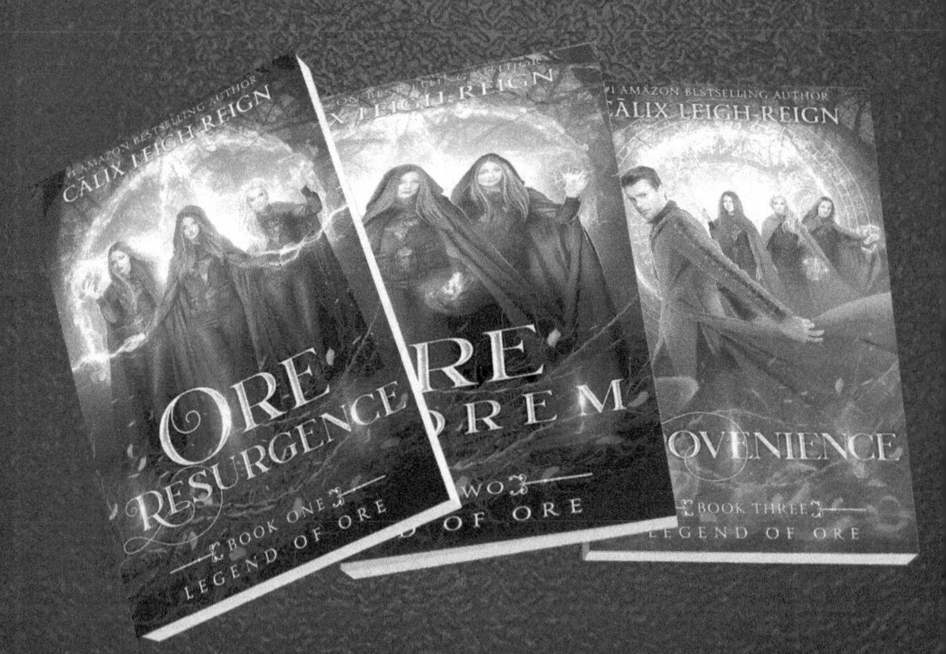
#1 AMAZON BESTSELLING AUTHOR
CĀLIX LEIGH-REIGN
ORE
RESURGENCE
BOOK ONE
LEGEND OF ORE
#1 AMAZON BESTSELLING AUTHOR
CĀLIX LEIGH-REIGN
BOOK THREE
LEGEND OF ORE

CayéllePublishing.com